THE TESTAMENT

THE TESTAMENT

S. LEE GLICK

atmosphere press

To my wife and children, to my many friends,
and to my father, Floyd Leroy

True devils with no ear, they howl in tune, with nothing but the devil.

—Alfred, Lord Tennyson, "Sea Dreams," 1890

INTRODUCTION

This book is a "what if" retelling of my family's history. The idea for it came to me as I was reading my great-grandfather's ledger. Then I asked, what if? Inspiration is all around us: in photos, music, storytelling, shared memories, the dark sky and the bright sunny day. We encounter new ideas and can find inspiration every day, in almost every moment. I am a writer because I love writing. Another reason I write is because I had a life-changing stroke on May 29, 2016. Please teach the signs of a stroke to your wife, husband, partner, children. When a stroke attacks you, your mind may not be able to understand and react to what is happening to you, just as I was not able to react when it happened to me. So please, if you find yourself or a loved one in a similar situation, overreact! Call 911—it is, after all, just money. I can't tell you how many times I wish I had done that.

Below are the warning signs of a stroke. They were given to me by my current doctor, and, with some variation, can be found on the internet:

- You may have a numbness or weakness in your face, arm, or leg.
- You may have sudden confusion or trouble speaking or understanding.
- You may have sudden trouble seeing in one or both eyes.

When I had my stroke, I experienced sudden trouble walking, dizziness, loss of balance and coordination, and I fell twice. Lord only knows why I did not feel the need to dial 911 at that point. I was in trouble, serious trouble! Dammit. As I replay that evening's miscues in my head yet again, I remember that ten minutes before the stroke I was driving on a state highway. Oh well, count your blessings!

You may be having a stroke if you experience a sudden severe headache, with no known cause. So please, overreact. Every minute counts! Now you have at least learned that much. I suffered from extreme dizziness. I even fell, but what was happening to me did not register! I was in terrible trouble. Since then, there has been many a time when I wished that I could have reacted, some way, any way. But alas, that is life.

When I told my general practice doctor what my book was about, he told me a story about how he and a friend almost answered an ad for work in the construction field. The name of the construction company was Gacy. It later became known that the founder of the company, John Wayne Gacy, was a serial killer. "You never really know what your neighbors are up to on the other side of the fence," my doctor commented. He strongly encouraged me to write the book that was in my head.

This book is dedicated to you, the reader. You are why

I and other writers write. I have really enjoyed reading various writers myself, both male and female. A book may take you away to worlds of wonder, fear, excitement. Please, teach your children to enjoy reading. Your child may very well be the next Stephen King!

My own modest library of books has finally topped five hundred. There are such good authors out there, and I am determined to keep writing and reading, to continue to get better and better at the craft. When I first started writing, my head was filled with good intentions and not much sense and talent. This, my second book, should be a more enjoyable read. I hired writing coaches and found a new publisher. Please read on, and I hope you enjoy my work. Thank you for choosing this book and sharing your precious time with me. Happy reading!

A big thank you to Doctor Weintraub: "You never do know what goes on on the other side of the fence." And, as Alex says, "What is normal for the spider is chaos to the fly." Of course, a big thank you to my two supportive and loving children. And thank you to my father, Floyd, who supported me his entire life. I got it done!

PART ONE: SIMON

CHAPTER ONE

It is early autumn. I am a fiction writer and a teacher in a one-horse, sleepy Wisconsin town. I had high hopes for this place, none of which had anything to do with the title of wet nurse or teacher. Maybe teacher at a university, but definitely not at a tiny high school with corn fields in its yard. My dream was to be the next great novelist and to join the fat cats on the speaking circuit. I flipped my silver coin. Heads, work on a horse ranch and get laid by snooty, uppity women who get off on being the boss. Tails, get a job teaching. And tails it was.

I wish the town's name were Hollow. That has a nice tone to it, doesn't it?

My name is Simon Luchk. I am just shy of thirty-nine. My hope is to be teaching in a larger community in the not-so-distant future, possibly Madison or Eau Claire, or to hit the big one as far as writing goes. My writing career began with a blast. My book Home Security System got good reviews and sold enough copies to make the bestseller list. For some time, anyway. I even gave books out as gifts. But that was three years ago and there hasn't been much since, so I teach. I don't like moments of indecision in my life. I flip my coin in times like those. Boom: it's done.

The town is home to two thousand residents and has more bars than churches. That's Wisconsin, eh? Most of the town's businesses are on Main Street: bars and thrift stores, a small grocer and a quaint hardware/feed store. The town's name is Ruby. Named after the old gem mine five miles north of town. Ten years it's been now since the once-vibrant mine shut down. And let's face it, the name Ruby hasn't worked so well. So just think how the town would have progressed if it were named Fracking. This is the type of town you can't find on any map, and if you're passing through, do not blink or you will miss it.

But Ruby does offer a classic four-lane bowling alley, three bars, a garage, and a grocer, and it's still hanging on to its high school. This is where I teach literature. The school was built in the fifties. A blond-brick two-story structure. I also teach English and coach the boys' varsity basketball team. In addition to driver's education, and of course track, and so much more. The boys, they are good this year, possibly a class-six contender. Gene Walter is the best player on the basketball team. He is our point guard. Five-foot-nine, 185 pounds, and I also have him and the rest of the team in my literature class. Not bad kids, just a little pushy and mouthy. They are told, over and over, that they are gods on the hardwood, so they start buying into it. That belief transcends into their off-the-court antics. They don't know what it's like. You go to college, you do everything right, and your wife drives a four-year-old

Range Rover that her daddy bought her for shits and giggles—later he will also buy a house for your wedding gift, which is a nice gesture and you'll both be very grateful, but you are never allowed to forget what side the bread is buttered on—while you work your ass off and drive a damn Pontiac. It's an auto they don't even manufacture any longer.

But let me not get carried away. Back to Gene Walter. Tonight I get the pleasure of speaking with young Mr. Walter about his behavior in English lit class. It is now 6:30 p.m. The school closed hours ago. It's after school, after practice, and well past my cold sandwich and chips. My head is splitting and I... need a drink. This event is interfering with my drinking time. Three Excedrin in my mouth to crunch on, this should help. I add a mint to the crunching—it dilutes the bitter taste. I am still hungover from last night's drinking binge. The bottle is just one of the many bad habits I have picked up while living at 7445 Purgatory Lane.

Mr. Walter joins me. His head is down. He is avoiding eye contact. As he enters my room, he flips his coal-black hair out of his eyes. I begin. "Gene, I understand the love you have for the written word. It is obvious, and your desktop shows it. It is all right here on your desk. Let's see." I read the scribbles: "'Mr. Luchk sucks donkeys.' Well, yes, 'Robin has a nice ass.' I could go on and on, Mr. Walter." He begins to loosen up. He is shaking his head up and down. He knows he is being led into a trap, and his smartass smile fades just a bit.

"Yes, please come to your desk," I continue. "It is covered with the history of Mike Emmett's and your antics from this year thus far. You two have covered this desk completely. If I weren't so upset, I would think your life's work, written here on this desk, is absolutely brilliant." Even though I am upset, there is a small smile behind my stern glare. "Janitor Glenn said he would 'burn in hell' before he cleaned that desk. That's a quote, son. So, it's on you and your friend Mike to do it." The old wooden desk is covered stem to stern with adolescent drawings of boys' and girls' anatomy, plus notes from one day with responses from the next, and so on.

"Mr. Luchk, you expect me to clean this desk?" Gene asks.

I lean forward for effect. "You wrote it, you clean it. Here is your ink eraser." I hand him a new eraser. He stares at me. "Mr. Luchk, you're kidding, right? I got a date tonight. You have seen me and Mike doing this for two months, and now you want it cleaned?" The boy is making a point. "Tonight?" he repeats. "Mike is cleaning tomorrow night," I tell him. "It aint fair, teach," says our star point guard, and then his hands are on my chest and he shoves me. My mild OCD kicks in at his touch, but what follows is my absolute worst fear.

What should have been a simple teacher-student interaction is taken a few levels too far when Gene physically pushes me in my chest. I am not much larger than him, and my balance goes. Falling backward, I trip over my own feet and land ass first on the aged tile floor. I am stunned and angry, but for the moment my temper is still in check. The boy straightens up and stands fully erect over my sprawled legs. In a moment of defiance, he spits. Hawk pew. "Screw you, Luchk!" His spit, it lands on my chest. One final act of defiance: he turns and flips me off.

The next few moments seem to move in slow motion.

My rage allows me to move at ninja speed. I am unable to stop myself from what I am about to do. I bolt to my knees and grab Gene from behind by his belt and I pull him down in front of me. Then I roll him onto his back. In a moment of extreme rage, I grab him by his throat with my right hand. I feel my fingers closing around his windpipe. Our eyes lock just as my temper explodes. I can feel my entire teaching career passing right through my hand. I still have a lock on Gene's throat, and as I begin to pull him off the floor and toward me, I hear the boy wheezing and gasping for air. He is reaching desperately for my throat. Then suddenly the night janitor, Glenn, marches into the classroom, alerted by the noise that something is amiss. My face is flushed and twisted with hot anger. The janitor gives me a chastising glare. He then charges me to get the student away from me. I immediately know what the outcome of this will be—my dismissal. They always wanted me gone, the dirty little bastards. An outsider who would not allow laziness and slacking, pushing the little shits to be all they could be.

The drive home that evening takes forever, on purpose. I drive down every side road possible. My mind keeps replaying the last hour or so at the school. I will be dismissed at the first bell tomorrow. And when the news reaches Faith's mother, it will only solidify her belief that her daughter deserves better. Soon I fear she will be able to pursue someone better. Her father has been holding the house we live in over my head since day one. Actually, Faith herself has held the house over my head like a chopping block. Ready to come down with deadly force. Without this paltry teaching post, how are Faith and I to survive? My writing is so spotty and inconsistent, it's similar to a girl who is turning into a woman—not steady at all. My mind races back to Gene, that dirty little shit. He and his teammates, they've been plotting and planning, waiting for the moment to push me over the edge. I will get the little bastards. I will.

I sink further and further into self-pity and self-loathing. I can imagine Faith bellering to her father about my loss of temper and job. Oh, I can hear it perfectly. "Simon lost his temper and choked a kid. No, it wasn't the kid's fault at all." I want to teach Faith a lesson in loyalty. My fingers hold a crushing grip on the steering wheel. I am white-knuckled for no reason but shame.

I stop at a bar and grill on the opposite side of town. I've already stopped at every bar near the school. My forehead is in a constant twist of agony. As I enter, no one raises their eyes to me. Just as well. But I hear their whispers and feel their eyes upon my back. Good news and all that. I drink one, two, four beers. Maybe more. Possibly the looks and whispers are all in my head.

I drive to the next town, way out of my way. My plan comes to me in a song from the jukebox. I hear the voice singing "fire away" many times. I decide to leave at 2 a.m., when the bar closes and am pushed out the door. I will make those school pussies fire me. I won't just go away. They will have to confront me. Yes, that's it. In my drunkenness, I plan.

I move through the late-night shadows like a specter. I stumble through the alley back to my car, then drive to the school parking lot, where I sit and wait. The hours drag by. I wake up suddenly because someone is pounding on my window. It's 6 a.m. and the sun is bursting through the eastern sky, telling me to get up. I look up to see Mr.

Trusdale glaring in at me. Behind him, young Gene Walter enters the parking lot, followed by many other students. Gene drives a sporty job, a Honda Del Sol. His window is down. His music is loud. I want to bash in the little bastard's face, but instead I just flip my coin. What will it tell me? I shall spare him. I place the coin into my right pocket and enjoy the sunrise. Probably my last as a teacher. With a bitter smile on my face, I take a long sip of rum, and I watch as Gene places his arm around his sweet little girlfriend. I think to myself, paybacks are a bitch, sonny!

At 7:50 the pompous Principal Trusdale calls me to his office. Glenn is already there, seated to his right. I reek of booze and I still feel sloppy drunk from last night. I am directly in the center. As expected, based on just Glenn's word, I am fired. I explode into theatrics. "Are you kidding me! That little shit pushed me, then spat on me! On this shirt! Right... uuh... right here!" I point at a spot on my shirt. "And where is he? He cannot even face me!" I stand and scream at Principal Trusdale. "Luchk, sit down," he tells me. "Control yourself!" Funny, my jury stands but I sit.

"What are my wife and I to do?" I go on. "We moved here from southern Illinois, just two years ago!" But it's all in vain. Shortly, Trusdale has me escorted outside with four of the maintenance staff, plus a sheriff's deputy. I voice my indignation: "Gene Walter would not even show up!" He did not even bother to show up! The bastards are firing me without my accuser setting foot in the principal's office to face me. It all hinges just on Glenn's word. A simple custodian. Glenn was in the school as I packed my belongings. However, he gave me a wide berth, like a person who has the plague.

I drive north. No paycheck, no job. What shall happen to me? Yes, a rhetorical question. My internal monologue comes on strong.

My loss of temper and loss of control, it just cannot happen. Not when I'm working with youth. My temper had been in check for so long, for ten years at least. Since my heavy-partying days. I beat an ass-grabbing jerk the last time, close to death. I knocked his right eye from his socket. Damn, I was so pissed then. Most of his teeth fell out. Busted two knuckles as well. I had, well... I had too much liquor in me and was pissed off at Faith, but I defended her honor. Faith, who was feeding my jealousy monster, to get my attention. So I went ballistic on a jerk named Bobbie. Police and Tasers got involved...

I shake my head and focus on today's happenings. That damn kid, that little piece of shit! He touched me and spat on me, made me see red. Damn him! When I pull into my driveway, the time is close to 8 p.m. I keep a fifth of rum in the auto just for such times. Faith is already storming out from the house, barking at me like a terrier. Her arms are flailing in the air and she's yelling about the time and me not calling. When she is close enough to me to read my face, she slows her roll a bit. "Simon? Simon, what is wrong? The school called. What did you do? What the fuck happened?"

I cannot look at Faith. I get out and walk to our bar, reach into my well-stocked beer fridge. The first beer is gone in three minutes or less. "Simon, you haven't told me." Faith is on me again. "What's wrong? Damn it, Simon!" I hang my head and begin. "That kid that I've been telling you about, Gene, he lost his temper and spat on me." I shake my head and lower it in shame, as a dog who has just peed on the carpet does. "Well…" Long pause. "I lost my temper."

"No, Simon, you didn't hit him?"

"No." There's a longer pause and a small smile on my face.

"What, Simon? What did you do to him?"

CHAPTER TWO

"I began choking him."

"You fucking what?!" Faith chucks a full beer bottle at my head. "My God, Simon, you stupid son of a bitch." I let the bottle hit me on the left side of my head, hoping it may slow her anger. You know, guy logic.

"Simon, Christ on a stick! Do you, DO YOU EVER THINK BEFORE YOU DO DUMB SHIT?! That's it, I am going to my mother's house. You'll see me when you see me." She storms off.

I know there's no use trying to stop her, so I just watch her get into her car and tear out of the driveway and up the blacktop. With Faith at her parents' place, I think I will take the five-hour trek to my father's empty cabin on the big lake. The house had been willed to me, but we had not felt like moving that far north. Before the drive, I will take my medicine like a man. I spend the next several hours sipping rum with a Fireball chaser. I stagger into my auto. My head is heavy. Perhaps a short nap before I go.

When I wake up, I notice a smell in my auto, a smell I find disagreeable. It smells like the inside of a purse with many-days-old food in it. I look under some clothes on the floor. What's this? Spit up from last night, yum, between the seats. Ooh, what's this? Nice. I had forgotten that I had helped myself to my dead cousin Joey's clown mask. Taken from his room. My anger surges and I decide that Chicklets the clown will appear soon. Nah, later. Now is not the time. Uncle Johannes had found the mask in a thrift/antiques store and paid quite a lot for it. The mask carried a script. Joey had first seen the mask when he was ten, and he became infatuated with it, even though the mask was quite frightening. Joey never knew what was actually written on it. He said he always felt like a comic book hero or villain when he wore it. He was Super Joey. He claimed he could run faster and jump higher when he was wearing the clown mask.

But anyway, back to today's business. Time's a-wasting, I gotta get on the road north. It's Route 126. I turn onto the two-lane road. There's no traffic. I daydream a bit about what I wished I had done to Gene. I dream he has pain and confusion pasted on his face. I hurl my right hand at his head. He reacts quickly as my fist lands against his teeth. He spits blood and bits of teeth. I release a scream in vengeance and anger. Gene's basketball season is all but done. Ha ha ha!

I find myself screaming as I drive. I need to focus. The road rolls between ever-growing hills and tree-lined fields. I am close to a national forest. Just the medicine I need to calm my brain. I'm still thinking about trying to defend myself while Gene Walter did not even show up! He did not feel strong enough to come, to face the accused! And so the bastards fired me, even without Gene stepping foot into the principal's office to face me. Just Gene's and Glenn's words against mine. Against all that I have done! And now here I am, with no paycheck, no job. I keep driving north. What shall happen to me? A question with answers yet to come.

CHAPTER THREE

Johannes Luchk wishes he were a character in one of his own novels. He would be able to rewrite his ending, his impending death. He would stay forever in his thirties, forever young and vital. In reality, Johannes Luchk is in ill health. Now that his chronic obstructive pulmonary disease (COPD) has advanced, breathing is a chore.

Johannes is in his attorney's office, glancing out of the window into the early autumn. The maple and birch trees are showing off their splendid colors. Attorney Dewey's office is located at the southernmost tip of Illinois.

For Johannes, there have been too many years of rum and pipe tobacco. Poor health choices stirred into the cocktail of long hours spent in front of his typewriter: rich food and heavy smoking, with too little sleep. Johannes preached to me once, "There are few things you can enjoy in life. Food and drink are but two of those. The other is a woman's touch." Now his lungs are afflicted with emphysema, as were his wife's. It has taken years away from Johannes. Now he would trade all his pleasures for a few more precious hours of life.

Johannes has summoned his dearest friend, Captain James William Petty, to speak with him one last time. "James, you and I, we had great adventures, did we not?" Johannes is interrupted by a coughing fit. He raises a finger to make a statement.

The captain looks at Johannes with sad eyes. He knows this is the final time they shall speak to one another. "That we did, dear Johannes," he says.

Johannes continues. "Remember when we sailed out of Whitefish Bay? That fast-rolling fog that nearly sealed our fate, so many years ago. James, I feared that I would never see land again. I thought we were forever lost in the fog."

"What a grand adventure it was," James agrees.

"Yes, James, that tale allowed me to break into the novel-writing industry. Lost in the Fog: a chilling tale of survival of the unknown."

"There is nothing quite so compelling as a good ghost story! People just love them."

Johannes has a warm, broad smile on his face. Dewey has started a fire in the fireplace to warm his friends. Johannes reminisces about the days gone by with his friends Dewey and the good captain. "Friends," Johannes asks, "who, if any, of my offspring shall carry on my legacy, my good name? I should hope for them to have dear friends such as you two. Friends to be with through thick and thin their entire lives. Why, you can't wish for more."

Johannes now contemplates his life. He sits in a comfortable European high-back reading chair in the company of his oldest friends. Attorney William Dewey's office is large and lavish in décor. Framed photos of Dewey with southern Illinois congressmen and senators are on the walls. A photo from some years back shows the three men—William, Johannes, and James—aboard the captain's fishing vessel, The Emmalee Rose, and an oncoming storm reaching across Superior with its dark tendrils, touching sky to lake. The photos capture the high points of the attorney's life and career. Now Johannes makes one last effort to make his voice heard. He and Dewey have come together to refine Johannes's will. Johannes speaks: "William, my last entry into my will shall be: To my nephew—he fancies himself the next great American writer—I leave to you my last novel. With that, I have done what was needed to ensure the wellbeing of my family. I felt that I had to create a better life for my children and of course for myself. You may discover a side of me that would tarnish our good family name. I will rely on your discretion and family honor to make the proper choices. Simon, think not ill of me, my brother's son. Finish my book in your words and write on, dear nephew. Write on. Now, dear Simon, the road has been paved, go to it and push the wheel hard, my nephew."

***

Many months have passed since my final visit to my uncle. Now our family has gathered around an oblong oak table at the office of my uncle's attorney, William Dewey. I look across the table toward my cousins: Edmond, Vivian, Nancy, and Danial. Their father—my uncle Johannes—has passed away just recently. Edmond and

Vivian, the twins, they have always had it, whatever you want "it" to be. Not a hair out of place. They pose on the other side of the table. The faces of movie stars, as if ready for a photo. Sculptured foreheads and necks, not a trace of aging on their faces. Nancy and Danial are both lovely people, but not of the same caliber, polish, or quality of their brother and sister. Danial is a hulking man, built more for battle than diplomacy. I would and have stood side by side with Danial as the bars have cleared out. All of my cousins have a look of wonder and curiosity as to why I am there. After all, I am but a nephew to Johannes, not a son. I hold the same question.

Back to it: one hundred; one hundred and one. There, I am done with that tile. During times of stress, such as being stared at by my cousins, I will use my psycho-therapist's recommendation to calm and to occupy myself with counting. My cousins are probably speculating internally as to my fascination with the pale ceiling tile. We are not a close-knit family. We have bickered terribly about finances and wealth. There has been much jealously over the years, with back stabbing and arguing in all forms and manners. Truly, when it comes to money, the family is at its worst.

I continue to amuse myself by counting the holes in the ceiling tiles. This is one of the tricks I was taught to keep myself calm and on track. I sit patiently as the attorney, Dewey, reads my uncle's rather lengthy will. Dewey has a voice that does not match his body. He is a tall, good-looking man with a solid head of gray hair. He and my uncle look very similar in their old photos. Dewey's voice is a rather low-pitched, growly monotone more suitable to a preacher. And now, with the beneficiaries and donations, the attorney enters the fifth hour of the reading. Dewey is on his fifth scotch, I believe. The time has come, finally, to find out why I'm here. With a sly nod aimed at me, Dewey makes it known that he is about to announce the final item from Johannes's lengthy will. Dewey reads, "To my nephew, Mr. Simon L. Luchk—" I can feel my cousins' stares burning through my skin. That's me! Dewey continues, "I leave to you, Simon, all the rights to my published works." There is a great stir across the table. "In addition, I leave you my final manuscript, yet to be completed and published. It is the final novel in the very popular Doctor Schultz murder series: Doctor Schultz: The Island. It is for you to finish." A climax to the Schultz series! There are already a ton of ideas stirring in my head. But Dewey continues: "This is with the understanding that you, Simon, will complete my final book within twelve months from this day, period. This period should allow you enough time to complete this task. The publisher and I have a strict timetable to bring the manuscript to print. There has been extensive advertising and an aggressive pre-sale program. If the manuscript is not completed, the publisher will enforce a substantial monetary penalty. Simon, I doubt that you have the financial means to pay this penalty. May this aid you in your writing endeavor. The novel will be the finale of the Schultz series. The doctor has built a rather good following, and the pre-sales are into the thousands. Good luck, Simon, and write on! Your uncle. J. L. Luchk."

Dewey glances at us all with a drained yet whimsical grin. He then stands and announces, with a slight slur, "That's it, folks. I invite you all to join me at the Fox and Hound for cocktails. Johannes would have loved to join us, but he can't. Those of you who can, join me. I look forward to it. For those of you who will not be able to join us, you may then meet me at the estate tomorrow promptly at noon. I have a fishing date to keep. Tomorrow I will be able to hand over the keys and paperwork to you. I will see you then, if not at the Fox and Hound." With that, Dewey leaves his post of the last five hours.

I stand there almost in a shocked state. Money... has been so very hard to come by. I chose the safe and respectful life as a high school literature teacher. I have just lost the teaching job through no fault of my own. We are now in dire financial straits. My college loans were substantial, taking a large chunk out of my check. And now I don't even have that paycheck. Looking back, I did enjoy teaching when the students were paying attention and got what I was talking about. Teaching high school students can be rewarding, but it does bring its challenges, like the students' peacocking and back-talking.

The rights to my uncle's books are worth a small or large fortune. The royalties from his latest book alone would mean I could pursue writing as a full-time venture. I would be able to buy a more reliable auto. Something with less than 250,000 on the odometer. Twelve months seems an ample amount of time to finish my uncle's novel. I get back to my car and just stand next to it for a moment, stroking my chin. A little "what if" enters my mind. What if I freeze? What if I don't finish the novel? I need a drink. My hands begin to shake. I spot a bench and sit down to calm my breathing. I run through the worst-case scenarios. But, if I succeed, I will prove to my wife and her family that I am not a screw-up. My wife and I may be able to have some nicer meals, with some meat included. That would be better than beans and rice for dinner. So I lost my temper with that little bastard. It is only a matter of time before my teaching license is pulled. Just imagine the penalty if I were to truly enjoy the power of Chicklets the clown's mask. What terrible business it would be. The lore of nightmares.

If I somehow were to teach again, I would still have to eat shit from the students over and over. All I did was correct that student. I did it to put some discipline back in my class. If I showed him, I would be showing all of them. Gene is their leader, and I put him in his place. But no. You touch one of the precious darlings and you're out the door. I'm a teacher who is forced to clean horse stalls at night, just to put bread on the table. It happens over and over.

My wife, Faith, runs a moving and storage company with her brothers. She can do all the work from home on her computer. She also loves to write—children's books. And she has some charities she is involved in.

But speaking of books, I have the opportunity to finish one of my uncle's books, and it does weigh heavy on me. This gift gives me a happy/sad feeling. Uncle was a good man to me. He stepped up when my father passed away. I will miss him greatly. He was the last of my father's family that I felt close to. My uncle was an author and has a massive fan base. He is well known. As they say, fly or die, baby. Sink or swim. He has been regarded with the same respect as the likes of Fitzgerald, and modern writers such as Kim Suhr, Mark Edwards, and Jim Brakken. There are also the two K's: King and Koontz. If my writing takes off, Faith and her family will quit badgering me for being a failure.

***

The attorney and my cousins show up at the country club. The building is a beautiful three-story log estate with a blond pine stain. Indian totems adorn both sides of the entry doors. The building was constructed in the mid-forties with my family's tobacco money. My family has always been pro-smoking. The land and building were donated and built with the idea of giving the wealthier residents in the surrounding area a place to frequent without all the riffraff standing around with their long faces and hands out. My grandfather owned the only bank in the county. His need for an exclusive location to escape to was essential.

Today, the midday bar crowd is thin, and we have a choice of all the tables. We gather at a large oak slab table near the stone fireplace. The log chairs are well kept and clean, covered with light oak stain and green upholstery. We seat ourselves, just ten feet beyond the bar. The large windows are framed into eight smaller square sections. Lead-framed, they called it at the time. As I look again at all my cousins, I notice how cheap my clothes look compared to theirs. I have no doubt that my fortunes will change, but they haven't just yet.

"Ladies and sirs, many years ago your grandfather Jedediah built this very building, this country club," Dewey tells us. "Ezra and Johannes were both my friends and were both my clients. Over the years we had many wonderful conversations and shared one another's lives, happiness, and sorrows. Please stand and join me in a toast to my two friends, your fathers."

Dewey is the first to stand. He is a tall, slender man, six-foot-three if not taller, with aging skin. His eyes are set back, and his features are similar to President Lincoln's. We hold our drinks up high. "To Ezra and Johannes," Dewey continues, "you have left us all many wonderful things, the best being your friendship and guidance. Thank you for being part of our lives. Prost." After our glasses clink, we gather in a circle. We are a family where bickering is the go-to mode, but for the moment all bitterness is abated.

Edmond and I stand to toast each other and our fathers Yes, our fathers were indeed part of the team who built this country club. "Simon," Edmond says, "join me, raise your glass in a toast to our fathers."

"I spent many hours with each of your fathers," Dewey proclaims. "They were good men and dear friends. We had many stimulating conversations and high times together. Simon, I was shocked to hear of Ezra's passing. His hard, laborious life seemed to keep him young and in excellent health."

"Yes, Mr. Dewey," I respond, "he had a fulfilling, rich life. He did die suddenly at the logging site in the Northwoods. One mistake by a rookie logger is all it took. No second chances when felling a two-ton tree. My father greatly loved the outdoors in all seasons, even building log homes in the dead of winter."

"Simon, I never heard him complain, not once. His construction company demanded much of his time, but it is what he loved."

"Mr. Dewey, did my father mention to you his part-time sheriffing?"

"He did! He enjoyed busting heads, as he called it. Ezra

did have a love of rum. As do you, it appears. But, Simon, I remember he showed up for work early every day and prepared, and lord help the man who didn't!"

Danial stands now. He gives his brother and sisters a stern look. I witness a tear sliding down Dan's right cheek. "Would you all join me in a toast to our fathers?" he asks. We all stand. "To my father, Johannes, and my uncle Ezra, may you live through our lives. Prost!" We clink our glasses again. I want to buy the next round, and I decide to include the four old souls at the bar. They stand and raise a glass with us. What the heck, I'm filled with joy at my good fortune! Cheers, everyone!

The late autumn weather brings with it a small snowstorm. Here, in southern Illinois, this early in the season it's a wet, heavy snow. It is a beautiful area of Illinois, with hills and sharp ledges. It's more inviting without the snow though. Just four inches this early in the season can create travel issues. The wind whips the remaining leaves, stirs them into a frenzy before they are covered by the snow till the spring thaw. The country club has a massive stone fireplace that even in modern day still burns only wood. The smell from the wood fire is heavenly. Add to it the crackling and the occasional pop, and it all creates such a warm feeling. At 4 p.m. the staff switches. The new bartenders and barmaids are all dressed in white shirts and black ties and slacks for the evening crowd.

CHAPTER FOUR

"Cousins, tell me about your father, I haven't seen him much the past two years," I ask.

"Simon, as you no doubt noticed today," Edmond begins, "my father had a small empire to keep track of. It grew from one small plot to what it is today. His property stretches from here, in southern Illinois, to just past your cabin in Bayview."

"Actually, that cabin, as you refer to it, is my house now, my home," I say. "Edmond, I remember our fathers joking that if you looked to either side of the road, one or the other owned the land you saw."

"Simon, how do you like living up north?" Edmond asks.

"I like it just fine. It suits me. The change of seasons is so strong. It is brutal in winter but I love it. Just this week I started planning on moving full time to Bayview. Anyway, Edmond, are you taking over the reins?"

Nancy, normally quiet and reserved, barks out, "My

dear brother thought that he was!"

"However," Dan explains, "that is why Father split up the properties and the business, so neither of us would have complete control." Dan turns to Edmond and continues, "Father spent more time with you and Vivian. It was obvious you two were his chosen ones! A payback for staying by his side those years."

Edmond leans back in his chair, his arms crossed on his chest and a smirk on his face. "Dan, you and Nancy don't need to be so sad. In the end, we were treated equally well," Edmond boasts. "Come now, Nancy, get over it. You and Dan, you chose your life in the big city, far from here. We were here, with Father, till the end! Why would he reward you for leaving the family?" Edmond turns to me next. "It was falling apart, Simon. That was when Mother and Joey had both fallen ill, and Joey was starting to get really weird then. Simon, I didn't know if you knew all this."

Danial stands. He is an imposingly large figure. He is so upset that his neck and face are now crimson. He points and leans toward Edmond. Edmond is a slim-built man who looks like a movie star, and on whom I don't think a fist has ever landed. He also stands and points a finger back at Dan, the big bear. I am hoping I have a great seat for this show. I have for many a year wanted to take a swing at Edmond. Based on Dan's facial color, I would guess that Edmond has just poked the bear. The two are now staring intently at each other.

"I had to help Mom daily when she couldn't walk, little brother," Edmond says through clenched teeth. "I had to do everything for her. Dad was always busy or drunk." Dan's voice and finger are now shaking. "I'll knock that smirk off of your face," he barks. But Edmond seems determined to continue testing the water. He goes on, "I was there with Joey as he wailed day and night, till he finally hung himself. Where were you? You wouldn't answer your damn phone, Danial! And I had Father's business to run, since you proved incapable again. Father wanted you to run his business, but you turned out to be useless, over and over again."

I can sense years of pent-up feelings are about to explode, for the midafternoon bar crowd's entertainment. "Little brother, you hid. You helped me with nothing!" Edmond continues.

"Not here, guys!" I tell them. "This isn't the place." I stand and put one hand on each of the boys' shoulders in an attempt to calm them.

"Simon, you are standing between two sneaky, back-stabbing, money-grabbing SOBs," Nancy says to me. "Watch your back, cousin, or there will be a knife in it."

Dan is now focusing his gaze on me. He puts his large right hand upon my left shoulder. "You shut the hell up, cousin, and stay back and out of this!"

"Tell us how you really feel, Dan," I say. "I am right here, come get some!"

As I mentioned, he is a big dude, Dan. He doesn't take my joke lightly. I am thrown back by a thunderous fist, straight onto the floor. I feel every bone in my body crack as Dan lands upon me. Once I'm down, Dan doesn't allow me to get to my feet. I roll to my knees. "Come on, you big German, come get some! You big pussy."

The big bear and I roll about, knocking over chairs and spilling drinks. Edmond and Nancy, who started this, are now having a laugh at my expense. The four old-timers yell for Dan to finish me and for me to carry on and get him. Damn, it's a good brawl. Really gets your blood stirring. One of the old-timers has decided he wants to get more familiar with us. The tall, weathered gentleman approaches our group. Dan and I stop fighting, to see what he wants. His deep-set eyes and high protruding cheekbones make his expression hard to read. He stands directly in front of me. Weighing one hundred pounds less than Dan, I must be the least dangerous-looking guy in our group. I expect as much. "Son, I heard the talk at the table. Will the Luchk mansion be torn down? My name's Frank Johnson. I lived here my whole life. I knew your old man and uncle. I knew your family. Over the years, there ain't been nothing good that happened at that house. There's been too much sadness, from the builders to the workers to your family."

"Sir, I am Simon. I am sorry you feel that way."

While Frank stands in front of me, his eyes open wide, as if something he had long pondered suddenly comes to him. It is one of those aha! moments. He leans in closer, raises a finger, and asks, "Simon, is it?"

"Yes, sir, I am Ezra's son. Simon."

"Aren't you a writer, like Danial and Johannes?" Frank asks. "Those books your uncle wrote, there was a lot of truth in them books." His eyes stay focused on me, then he relaxes. The subject switches to more pleasantries.

"Young Luchk, I worked for your father, logging." We exchange small talk about my father for a moment or two. At some point I notice that my cousins and Dewey have all left without bothering to say goodbye.

"Frank," I say, "it was a pleasure speaking to you and sharing a memory or two, but I must be on my way to my uncle's estate. I will consider passing on your concern to my cousins when I see them."

I get back to my car and drive off. The brief snow has all melted by now, and the maples and birch trees, with their autumn leaves of orange and red, are like a blanket along the forty-rod-long driveway. They hang a canopy of color above the fresh blacktop. Just next to the tall maples, the bright yellow cornstalks chatter and rasp back and forth, ready for harvest. I have a full view of Uncle Johannes's house, or mansion, rather, and I decide to take a few minutes and drive by my uncle's estate and down memory lane, aka 101 Briar Wood Lane. I park about a quarter of a mile from the Herman Munster–type house. I get out of the car and lean against the hood. A bright ray of sun is cast upon my face, and yet I cannot shake this feeling of dread that's filling my mind. I need to call Faith.

"Faith, I am to meet the attorney at my uncle's house tomorrow. I have such vivid memories of that house. It is an immense house with eight bedrooms, three floors, an attic, plus a full basement. I wish you were here with me. Faith, do you feel that a house can be evil, from the time it was built? There is evil living in its construction, from its foundation through its beams and glass. Do you feel that a structure may be pure evil from its creation?"

"Oh God, Simon, you're scaring me. Are you starting to believe the books you write? No offense, hon."

"Faith, my cousin Joey hung himself in the attic. As kids we would dare each other just to go up there. It was horrifying. I remember there was this narrow black door, with a shiny black doorknob, that allowed you up there. As children we would dare each other to see who could stay in the attic the longest. Once, I was to stay in the attic for half an hour. When I opened the black door and looked up there, I saw my cousin swinging back and forth by his neck from the rafters. He had just hung himself. He was still swinging back and forth. His face was gray, turning to green. Then his eyes opened and he looked directly at me. His mouth opened, and these gurgling noises came out. He raised his arm as if to reach for me. And I ran, I ran so hard. I didn't stop till I ran into my uncle's arms. He told me that there was nothing in that attic that could harm me. That I needed to get tougher. No one would believe me. My cousin Vivian did, but she was cruel. I feel she was the one who drove Joey to hang himself. From that day on, I was terrified of that house. And I still remember that black door with its shiny black doorknob. It would squeak and rasp as it opened, announcing to all that the attic was to have a visitor."

CHAPTER FIVE

The roof of the house has many peaks and valleys. It's an extremely large Victorian on steroids, and the outline is similar to the Addams Family's mansion. Gomez and Morticia would love my uncle's house.

The sun is high in the sky on this late September day. There is a crisp bite of autumn in the air as I drive up toward the mansion, which sits high upon a hill, within its thousand-acre plot. It overlooks the nearby community and fields. From the top of the hill, the treetops make for a beautiful cascade of color. The occasional steeple juts past the treetops to accent this Rockwellian view of the home of a well-known author. Evening approaches. My uncle's three-story home will soon be casting its shadow down the hill, as the sun begins to lose its grip upon the day.

My cousins have arrived before me. I'm late again. There are many automobiles parked in the half circle leading to the brick-and-stone steps in front of the heavy red-stained wooden doors with their large iron lion-head knockers. They were forged by special request of my uncle. An Audi, a BMW, and Edmond's vintage Mercedes. They're all sparkling and shiny like a new-car lot. The autos surround a large fountain with three winged cherubs spraying water into a trough from their plaster smiles. The grass is manicured to a pristine two-inch height, with nary a leaf on the lawn. My wife's new black-and-gray 2001 Range Rover looks as though it truly belongs with my cousins' cars. This is the first new and nice vehicle Faith and I have owned. The oldest auto in the circle, but it is in tip-top shape with a shine so bright you could lose a coin in it.

I pull over to the side, away from the others. I'm close to the white wooden fence. From here I have a splendid view of the estate, plus an express exit if Edmond decides to continue the fracas from yesterday. I look back at the mansion. Lightning rods are jutting up from the roof toward the heavens, awaiting a lightning storm to activate Frankenstein's monster. I always felt the roofline is the perfect conduit to speak to and draw toward it the dead. The fright monster that lurks inside wakes up as my imagination takes off.

I stand on the lawn near the cherubs with their creepy little smiles. They glare at me as they guard the house, this mansion born of wood, glass, and cement. Also born of evil. Frank was right yesterday, nothing good has ever come out of this house. I focus on the gentle sound of the water and let it lull my tired brain and calm my fears. It's soothing my nerves.

After my mother's passing, my father sent my older sister to live with my uncle's family here in this house.

Father felt that a lady's touch, from Johannes's wife, Claire, would help round my sister. I believe that's what it was called: makeup, hair, clothing, and other things a young woman needs guidance in. But my sister never could get beyond her terror of my uncle's attic. She spent most of our family's money on therapy and institutions to deal with her night terrors and visions. The good it did. Thousands and thousands spent trying to calm her head. Finally, my sister French-kissed my double-barrel 16-gauge. She may have been led to believe that the firing pin had been removed from my Parker VHE ten years back. She darn near ruined the gun! I spent days if not weeks cleaning the shotgun. That is when I first realized that there are times when it's just about the money, period. With her, I always felt that sooner or later it would be the gun, or a train, or a lake bottom, or the rope. The list goes on and on. Father and I carried a substantial life insurance policy on her. My father and I had a bet on how my sister would die. I won. It was just good business sense, really. Father invested his money wisely back into his business. With his portion of the insurance, he purchased four fishing charter boats: two on Lake Michigan, two on Superior. All booked except for four weeks of the season. The boats made money like a printing press. That Chicago and Minneapolis money poured in. That is when I realized that money taken is sweeter than money earned. Being a business partner to myself was a solid way to cut my life short. My dear sister's was the first life to be taken, but not the last. Next was dear Joey, by rope.

Vivian comes out to meet me. She waves her hand while she squeals in her Eastern European accent as I finally make my way toward the front door. I think back.

As a teenager, I would admire her shape from afar. She had long slender legs and a thin waist that flattered her long legs all the way from earth to heaven. Plus Marcia Brady's fair skin and hair. If this analogy is before your time, Google it. But my fancy for her never exceeded a glance, or two or three. We are cousins, for God's sake, and here, up north, cousins are off limits. I hadn't seen Vivian for years, and now I've seen her twice in as many days. She is still a beauty. Long blond hair, a model's face and neckline, a bottom you could bounce a quarter off and get change from it. She was born beautiful. Then, as time went, she was sent to the finest schools and universities, as were her siblings. A top education. Her effort and money have only enhanced her good looks. Arrogance and confidence round off the package. Her beauty should never be taken as anything other than money and proper work on her part. And no one should believe that there is weakness, any weakness, hidden within her beauty whatsoever. She is well educated and as ruthless as any storybook villain. I have long felt that cousin Joey couldn't bear the strain of having the so-called perfect brother and sister. Joey had to live within their shadow day in and day out. She and her twin brother are business-savvy too. It is money they love first and foremost. Family isn't in the top three of their priorities. Neither of them ever got married. They are married to their work, however. They are both majority holders in several corporations, some of which are listed on the NYSE. Crossing either of them would be a fatal mistake. They employ the best muscle money can buy. That is how I have always felt about them.

Vivian is close to me now, in a pantsuit and jacket. Her wardrobe is that of someone running for office. We meet with a polite hug.

"Simon, so good to see you again. Edmond informed me that you are interested in the property off of Route 12?"

"That's right, Vivian. I am going to do a walkthrough this afternoon. The property is not being rented out, is it? Faith's brother is interested. If you wouldn't mind selling it out of the family?"

"Not at all, Simon. Money is, after all, money. Here is the access code to enter the house. And no, there's no one living there right now. Just lock it when you leave."

"I will, Vivian." I open my jacket to expose my shoulder holster. "That's right, doll," I say dryly with a wide grin on my face.

"Why, Simon?" Vivian looks aghast at the sight of my revolver protruding from its holster. "Still playing the detective, I see."

"Vivian, you know what a careful soul I am," I say as I pat my revolver. "Have you become squeamish in your older years?" She doesn't answer, so I cut to the chase. "I will take the manuscripts and be on my way. It is always a pleasure, Vivian, though I'm sorry to see you under these circumstances."

My cousins have always been beautiful people. They have always had that air of believing themselves better than the other side of the family. Or that may have been just my perception. Possibly jealousy. My father worked with his hands, often two jobs, just to offer a better life to us. Their father, my uncle, made a well-above-average living as an author and a bit of an adventurer. Yes, it is jealousy. But until I put in the time and the effort to produce a novel, I should hold my opinion to myself.

"Simon, what time do you think you'll be by the

property off 12?"

"It depends greatly on traffic. Plus I intend to stop at Danial's on my way." Danial lives in a lakefront property in the south-central part of the state. It is not exactly a drive-by, but close enough. My visit coincides with the local festival, the Wo-Zha-Wa Days, which has turned into a huge event for the community.

CHAPTER SIX

I exit the interstate and enter Highway 12. Only thirty minutes later I am standing on Danial's front lawn. He has a lovely dark-brick ranch set back from the road, with many mature trees upon his lot. Dan is a divorcé. He loves his life after the divorce. He's been writing books for teens like a mad hatter. You would think he has a team of ghostwriters working for him.

I charge at Danial as if we were children. The skirmish from yesterday is completely forgotten. It is so nice to have a reprieve from the peering eyes and loaded questions of my other cousins. Dan is not like them. He is not pretentious, and his ego is small. That is not a common trait today.

"Dan, my man, what's up?" Dan picks me up with a massive bear hug.

"Simon, I'm glad you decided to stop by. The festival is this weekend. Do you have a stack of your books in the trunk?"

"Yes, I do. Every author carries a stack, your father taught me that. But why?"

He takes me to his porch, which has a mountain of his most recent books.

"Wow! That's a lot of books, Dan."

"Cousin, I have us set up for a book signing at a booth. The response should be off the wall. My father's name is huge down here, so we should do well."

"Dan, that's great! When do we do it?"

"Tomorrow, from eleven till two. We're just going to sell books at the booth."

"Danial, on a more serious note, I have been here ten minutes and my hand is empty. Come on, my hand is empty!"

Danial laughs. "Simon, I know just the spot. The Sand Bar. Let's head there."

Fifteen minutes later we are sitting in an almost packed bar.

"Hi, Mr. Luchk," the barman greets Dan. "What will it be today?" Dan orders us each a festival drink—something called the Wolf Bite. It's an orangish drink, very tasty, a bit like an Old Fashioned. It's served in a glow-in-the-dark wolf-shaped sixteen-ounce cup. From where we are at the bar, we can see the autumn sun shining bright through the window.

"Dan, I feel like a pro: the sun is full out and we are on drink two," I say. I am drinking, oh yeah. I post a photo on Facebook of Danial and me, plus a post alerting the world as to the time and location of the book signing tomorrow. The young waitress brings our next drinks and asks for our autographs. We take a quick photo of the three of us cheek to cheek. It's a nice feeling. Six hours later, Dan calls us a cab.

The next day comes too soon, especially as I am sleeping on a tattered couch on the porch. I don't dare to speculate how many women have been bedded on this very couch.

I wake to a warm breeze. It will be a glorious day. A perfect autumn Saturday. The booths at the festival are located in a huge blacktop parking lot just behind the bar district. Danial and I wind our way through the endless tables of vendors. Our destination is deep into this flee market heaven. The breeze is light, and the sun is beating down on us like a pissed-off cop with a club.

We arrive at our booth. There's a sign for "Claire's Antiques," except the Claire who meets us doesn't look like a Claire—she looks more like a Maude. She has wild dark hair with some gray filtered through, and a gravel edge to her voice. Claire introduces herself as "the owner, been that for ten years now." She is wearing cats'-eye rims with coke-bottle lenses. I stand in front of her. Her eyes narrow as she takes me in. I reach out my right hand. "Claire, I am Simon Luchk." She continues to hold onto my hand as if she wanted to read the lines. Moments later my hand is released. I go over the details of money with Claire. Dan gives me that "cat and canary" look. She reaches to her right, where there is a stack of my Home Security System novel, along with Danial's many books in a box on the blacktop.

By 11 a.m. the crowd swells to possibly 100,000. The festival will peak at 250,000 before the day's end. The small community is home to a mere two thousand residents, so this is a big local event. I notice Claire has a stream of chew juice forming at the right corner of her mouth. Claire uses the back of her wrist to redirect the juice. She moves to her left and spits toward an antique-looking bronze spittoon just beyond the table. I had thought it was an antique for sale. Her aim is flawless. I offer to move the box of books, which looks as if it weighs more than Claire. She won't have it. Her knees shake, she lets out a loud "ooftah," and the books slowly rise to the table. Claire must have five hundred books for sale, mostly graphic novels and comics.

Dan and I are perched and ready to answer readers' questions, such as where do you get ideas, and how about the language? It is an unusually warm day, or is it that I am hungover, or both? It is September after all, and we are in southern Wisconsin. We both have the wonderful stale day-after fragrance coming from our pores. Much too much to drink last night.

One by one the book fans stop by. The stacks on our table slowly sell off. Sometime in the afternoon, a tall man, dressed well, stoops down in front of me. He has a warm smile. He continues to smile at me as he claims to be an old friend of my father. He is in his mid-forties and possesses a handshake like a vice. Danial seems to know him. Dan reaches over the table and introduces him to me. "Simon, this is a friend of our fathers'."

"Plus a fan," the man says.

"Patrick Krist, he is one of our local doctors," Dan continues, "and so much more."

Krist bows to Danial and me. "Yes, just a humble doctor. May I purchase one of each of your books? And do you have a moment to sign them, please?" While I sign, Danial speaks to Doctor Krist off to the side. Krist blurts out, "Dan, are you to finish your father's last novel?"

Before Danial can answer, the doctor continues. "Danial, would you and Simon have time to visit tonight?"

Danial looks at me with a "read my mind" look, however, I am unable to. "Doctor, Danial and I have nothing planned," I start, and then we both say, "Yes, that would be fine" at the same time.

"The Showboat at seven? The festival offers many fun stops," Krist says. I give Dan a quick glance—is that all right? The three of us are in agreement. "Seven it is, Doctor," Dan says.

He and I continue signing books, answering questions, and taking selfies with fans. It would be nice to finish the hot day with some well-earned beverages under a shaded outdoor venue. Though soon no shade is needed, as the sun starts to lower and the temperature declines.

"A perfect evening, eh, Dan?" I say.

"Yes, it is, cousin." Dan leans close to me and starts whispering in my ear. "Simon, I cannot put my finger on it, but I have always felt uneasy speaking to Krist, so watch yourself tonight. Didn't you see me give you that look?"

"What look?" I ask.

Danial opens his eyes wide. "This look."

"Oh, that look!"

"Yeah, the international look for 'What the hell!'"

I should know that look. I slap the table. "God bless you, Dan, what a day, what a day!"

"Regardless, Simon. Watch what you say around him. He seems sneaky. Dad never told me, but I think that one of the characters in my father's novels is based on Krist."

"Wow, very cool. Does Krist know?"

"I am not at all sure."

By now the sun is sliding down over the small tourist

town, creating shade and a reddish sky for all the festivalgoers to enjoy. The sidewalks are elbow-to-elbow, hip-to-butt, swaying like zombies. Back and forth, back and forth. A duck's waddle. They are invited to come back and join in the evening's festivities. There's a real carnival feeling in the air. Street magicians, musicians, and beer tents adorn the side streets. Nothing like a carnival to empty mom and dad's pockets.

At precisely seven, the good doctor arrives at the Showboat Saloon. A smiling barmaid named Marie begins the process of bringing our drinks. We've ordered the festival drink, the Wolf Bite, which seems to be very popular in the local bars. After a day in the heat, the icy drink tastes so good. I can't help myself and I immediately ask Krist if he was the inspiration for a character in my uncle's novels.

"Yes, Simon, I suppose I was. Your uncle and I had an agreement."

"Father wanted Simon to finish the novel," Dan blurts out. I see the doctor's expression tense up as he glances sternly at me. The friendliness has left his face. Brrrt, brrrt. My phone is ringing, and I walk away from Dan and the doctor to take the call. It's Vivian.

"Hi, Vivian. Listen, Faith and I really don't need or want another property at the moment, but I will stop by the house off Route 12, like I said. Faith's brother, Matt, he may be interested. You never can tell with him." Faith's brother. He has always fancied moving farther north. Chicago money and all that. "Yes, Vivian," I continue, "I understand that the area is growing rapidly. It will be tomorrow or maybe even the next day before I can get there. No, Faith can't meet me this time. But maybe she and I can drive back in a few days, so she can look at the property too."

***

Later that night, after a couple of drinks with Dan and Doctor Krist, I drive back to the country club and check into the inn. I want to spend some time reviewing my uncle's unfinished manuscript. In my room, I kick my feet up, open a new bottle of rum, and dive in. I spend many hours that evening enjoying my uncle's writing. I need to get intimate with his unfinished novel.

My room is cozy. It has a small fireplace, a solid oak desk, and a high wingback reading chair. On the wall is a painting of the local land, the way it was before the modern city was built. Horse-drawn wagons, a steam locomotive, dirt roads, wooden sidewalks. There are many such paintings along the hallways of the inn. There are also several rooms with my surname on them. I am treated well here, even after our antics yesterday in their lounge.

In the box of my uncle's papers is Joey's clown mask. Did I toss the mask into the box myself? I don't remember. Joey used to call himself Chicklets the clown. There were days he wore the mask from morning to night. And below the mask, I discover my uncle's journal. Wow. Did Dewey add the journal to all the manuscript papers? If so, to what end? I flip through it. The entry that grabs my attention is dated some fifteen years earlier.

My dear Claire has just passed. Twenty minutes were spent to try to revive her, till she bled inside and the doctors were unable to save my love. It's 1:35 a.m. She is gone.

Next entry:

Three days have passed and my dear friend Pastor Steve has been in touch to invite me to a grief counseling meeting. I have never felt the need for such crap or ever felt so weak as to consider it. That is why God has made rum and other fine brown liquor. I donate to the church, so I am sure that this is his way of repayment.

Two days later:

I have just returned from a grief counseling meeting. We gathered into a spacious room in the hospital basement, with gray walls and large potted indoor plants guarding each side of the door. Not including Pastor Steve, there were sixteen of us in attendance. As we introduced ourselves, it seemed to be the time to explain what had brought us there. So all the meeting goers, we all shared our losses with each other. There were variations: from old age to the tragic, the whimsical, the horrific. No details were spared. As I write this, I have learned that, for humans who have suffered a loss, there is a common thread in their grieving. There is a weakness that the grief allows to come forth. A sickness, as it were. You who are reading this, take notice of my writing. Do not allow your sad emotions to consume your thoughts. It is a dark, difficult time that I write about. Stay strong. It is in times of great need that people are at their weakest. In such times, I feel that people would be considered sheep for the shearing.

The date of the next entry is more than a year later:

My belief that the grieving process weakens people tremendously has proven to be true. I hired five men and a lovely woman named Tess, all of them actors. Together, we have been able to easily persuade landowners (sheep) who are grieving to sell their most cherished land. The Boylands come to mind. Mandy Boyland is a young widow, about thirtyish, whose husband, Joe, drove his truck off the edge of a gravel pit. It was a two-hundred-foot drop, and fifty feet of icy gravel water waited for him below. When dear Joe's truck was recovered, they found many beer cans and two empty bottles of cheap whiskey on the floor. Entangled in the clutter were also two women's pairs of underpants. I can only assume that they did not belong to Mandy Boyland. My daughter Vivian never could keep all her belongings on her. Mandy, a dark-haired beauty whom Joe had grown tired of, was consumed with anger, and soon despair. But she was much tougher than we first thought. My dear son Edmond was to spearhead this project. This particular play has been performed many a time, it's just the names and faces that change. My son Edmond is a rather dashing young man, with many features that mirror that of the actor Paul Newman, and he is adorned with a full head of dark hair, black as the night. He became intimate friends with Mandy Boyland. They began their affair soon after Edmond paid his condolences for her loss. There was a spark between them almost at once. Edmond wasted no time in the manipulation of her emotions. Soon they were an item. Edmond was an excellent student. He followed my direction to the letter. He paid Mandy the attention she had starved for. Before two months had passed, Edmond was allowed into her bed and her home, plus he was given access to all her inherited wealth and her family's farm business. Through good business sense and an inheritance, Mandy owned over two thousand acres of prime land just west of Lake Michigan. Edmond worked as a surgeon to bleed Mandy's dead husband's accounts dry. He also exercised great discipline in order to have his name listed as being in charge of the farm and the estate. This was all done with the idea of helping to relieve the grieving widow of her burden, of course. And the pattern played out over and over again, just the players were different.

A more recent entry:

Over the past four decades me and my children have, through similar methods, been able to relieve some fifty sheep from their land, till my family's wealth swelled to the tens of millions. Not bad for a humble writer. Another excellent example is Mr. and Mrs. Watts, a lovely couple in their forties. John Watts's mother and father had passed away. Two months after their funeral, he was persuaded to sell the family's estate of five hundred acres of farmland, plus the house and other buildings, for the low price of $600,000. The cooperation sold just one year later for one million dollars. All for the sake of avoiding pain, anguish, and memories. And, of course, for convenience. The names change, as do the numbers, but alas, that's just good business. As I feel my health slipping, I am left to ruminate on how fond I am of my children, especially Edmond and Vivian. My Nancy, she's willing to be the practical one, with her head in the books and working toward becoming a pharmacist. And finally, big lovable Danial, the children's author. Well, enough said. Both are strong-willed, plus they are ruthless as sharks once the prize has been announced. Now I search for answers to the unanswerable question. What's in the wooden box? What happens in the box? Is that all there is? Does my family who went before me stand and greet me?

My eyes light up as I catch my father's name.

Last night my dear brother Ezra broke it to me that he would no longer play the cat-and-mouse game that has made us both so wealthy. Ezra is now a sheriff and seems to dislike the business of sheep shearing. Yes, he feels that is a higher calling, I assume.

CHAPTER SEVEN

I have written this journal in the hopes of telling my story to whomever ends up reading it. Not for the purpose of cleansing my soul, but as a vehicle to pass on my knowledge.

I am baffled and sad at this new knowledge I've come across in my uncle's journal. I want to hurry home to show this to Faith. Yet I still must stop by the house off Route 12.

The drive the next day takes me longer than expected, and it is already dusk by the time I pull up to the empty house off Route 12. I stand outside the Rover and take in the cool autumn air. Then I twist and stretch a bit, and take several photos of the exterior of the building. I call Faith. "Yeah, hi, Faith, I am at the house off route 12. It's a Cape Cod design. The exterior and roof look to be in good condition. It's a two-story house with four bedrooms and two bathrooms, around two hundred acres. I'll take a look inside and send you and Matt some pictures. Tomorrow, if it's worth it, we can come down again. Okay, see you in about three hours."

I enter the access code and I hear the bolt slide. That should do it. The door swings inward toward a small farmhouse community washroom. I am met with a whiff of stale mildew smell, as if the house has been empty for a while. A large mirror faces me. I see someone move and I'm startled for a second. Then I smile. I am reminded of an old black-and-white detective movie where the detective is being stalked and he is hiding out in an empty farmhouse. Wow, knock that off. It isn't helping. Seems I am a bit nervy today.

The sun is setting fast, casting long shadows all through the house. I enter the kitchen. On the dining table are three empty pizza boxes. Various snack wrappers, empty soda cans, and empty beer bottles are strewn all over the kitchen counter, on the table, and on the floor. What the! Is this a party house? My head swivels around. This is not what I expected at all. I bump the table, and the bottles fall and roll about. There is more movement in front of me. I grab a bottle and throw it in that direction. It's another mirror, which I've knocked off the wall. The mirror lands with a thud, then breaks into a million pieces with a hard, heavy crack. One more bottle rolls toward me. I marvel at my reactions as I grab it just before it rolls off the table. Ha ha! I laugh at how good my reflexes are. Then I realize the bottle is ice-cold, full, and still capped. The light bulb in my head finally turns on. I stand in silence, my eyes affixed to the full bottle. Damn. I am not alone in the house. There is someone else here with me!

I see something coming at my head from the corner of my eye. I hear and feel a strong, loud thud, followed by a sharp pain on the side of my neck, and then the sound of wood cracking. My ears are ringing loudly. I reach for the kitchen table. I grasp at it for a moment, but my hand glides past the tabletop. My legs are getting soft and I waver, then I feel pain in my ribs and fall to the floor. There is a sting in my neck as I roll to my side. A fuzzy warmth comes over me just as a kick lands on me, then another, and yet another. The warm feeling washes over me. It takes my body and I feel it lift up and away. Then I see a pair of black boots moving closer to me. There are men talking. No way can I understand the words. One boot kicks my ribs, then another stomps upon the left side of my head—boom!—as the right side of my head smashes into the floor. My head. Everything fades to black. I have the feeling I am being dragged by my feet. I am pulled downward, thud, thud, my head bouncing from stair to stair. Then the bottom. I lose consciousness.

I come to in a dark, damp corner. My head is pounding, along with the left side of my neck. I roll onto my right side. I can't see anything, and I cannot fully wake myself up. There are two voices somewhere nearby. Wherever I am, it is black, cold, and hard. There are small windows, with very little light coming through. I am lying on something that feels like rocks. I flounder on the floor for a bit. I think the rocks are charcoal. I don't know. I can't get my head to clear. A taste of tin is in my mouth, and there is a crust around my mouth and beard. I slowly start to stir and carefully touch my face. It seems that blood from my mouth and ear has clotted all around my earlobe. I try to stand, but my legs will not hold me. There is still the strong taste of tin. I shake my head, trying clear my eyes and my head. There are too many cobwebs in my brain from the beating I took. I slowly scoot on my bottom till I feel a wall to lean up against, then I am out again. Hours pass. I stir, woken by what sounds like sleet falling against a small basement window high above me. I spit. The tin taste is still strong. I try to move around on my hands and knees. Finally, I hear a door slam and some light shines down to me. I notice that my revolver and my cheap phone are gone. There are two sets of footsteps moving about upstairs. One person sounds heavier than the other. Are they here to help me, or finish me? I wail out a loud "Hey up there! Who shoved me down here?" I hear someone walking down the steps toward where I am. No surprise.

It's Faith. She's here with the realtor. When many hours passed and I didn't come home, Faith must've become concerned and called the realtor to come and find me, and find me they do, in a corner of the basement. Faith bends over me and gives me the armpit lift. With aid from the realtor, I am upright. Within fifteen minutes an ambulance arrives to whisk me away to the local emergency room. Faith keeps looking down at me with concern. I am so glad she is here with me. Seeing her so worried about me makes me know she has forgiven me for losing my job. That argument is behind us. I am so glad that Faith is back.

Soon we are at the emergency room. My hospital bed is stiff, but so much softer than a basement floor, and warm, so warm. The hospital can warm up the blankets if you request it. I do. My small room smells like Faith, a very soft and light perfume, which is very comforting. I drift off.

The ever-present background hospital noise seems to be growing louder. I fight to block it out, but there seems to be more and more traffic, building to a fever pitch of noise. It is rousing me, whether I want to wake up or not. All I want to do is stay curled up safe in this bed. My neck is very tender, and whether I move it left or right, chin up or chin down, it's extremely painful. Faith mentions that there is a welt at the base of my neck. Possibly a bite? I am awake now. The panic monster in my head is alert. My OCD begins to go into overdrive. I wonder who was in this bed before me. Did they die? What about the person before them? My internal panic man is running hard, and my mind begins to ask unanswerable questions. A funny thing about hospitals and nursing homes is that they smell a lot like death. Death that has come. Death that will come. Like a chariot riding up from the gates of hell to take its victims. You can mask it with sanitizer and cleaner all you want, but all the polish on the floors won't take it away; it's still there and always will be.

I have grown familiar with its smell. My grandfather was a heavy smoker and drinker, and my mother was too. They both spent their final days in various hospitals and homes. That smell makes my stomach tighten into a knot. It activates memories, and it stirs up a great fear—the fear of growing old. Or worse, not. Those memories are easier to suppress than to face.

Faith is looking at me, concerned. She gives me a comforting warm smile, followed by a warm kiss. "You look better with all that blood off of you," she says. Then she changes the subject. "Congratulations on your uncle's book! That should help us a lot, right?"

I spring upright. "Yeah, babe, it may be just the thing to get my writing off the ground. I was and am pretty amped up by the chance."

"Great. Now I just want to get you out of here and get you home, Simon. The house has been lonely the past few days."

"You know this, but I will tell you again," I tell Faith. I slide up on my elbows. Just then a soft-spoken nurse comes in. She gives us a concerned look as we prepare for a good money spat. The nurse brings in the food cart. I am starving. Food, coffee, yes! I am enjoying that first cup of coffee so much, I am almost chugging the hot black liquid.

Soon I am visited by a Sheriff Crane. I repeat what I have just told Faith, plus a little more.

"Mrs. Luchk," the sheriff asks Faith, "have you had a chance to tell him..." He trails off with a nod toward me.

"Tell me what?"

Presently we are joined by a Detective Lammer. She has a very matter-of-fact look on her face, plus the personality to go with it. She pauses for a moment. Her face scrunches and her eyes narrow. Her pantsuit doesn't do her justice. So cute, but very little chitchat. That's what's missing in the world today, chitchat.

The nurse intervenes. "Okay, what's your name, and what day is it?" she asks me. "Detective Lammer is here to ask you some questions." The nurse tells the detective not just yet, as she needs the doctor's approval first. Doctor Lee comes in and gives me a quick look while Lammer and Crane wait outside. The doctor shakes his head. As he leaves, he tells Lammer she may come in.

I get the first question right: I know my name. The second question is more of a challenge. The date and time? I have no idea how long I was unconscious in that basement. The questioning goes south fast. What did I see? What did I hear and smell? How did I enter the house?

Why was I armed? I answer as best as I can, but Lammer seems unconvinced.

I have a solid welt on the right side of my head. The good news is, there's no skull fracture. The nurse says I will be out in a day or two.

On my second day in the hospital, Detective Lammer comes to visit again, with a few more concerns. She mentions that as she examined the house, she noticed a fire had recently been set in the basement's woodstove.

Lammer says there was trash, notebooks, and papers strewn all about the basement. "I retrieved all of the papers," she says. "It's all evidence." She beams as she speaks.

The panic begins to run in my head. Damn. I didn't take the box of my uncle's papers into the house, did I? I am not sure. My thoughts are all running together. Did I keep my uncle's papers safe in the Rover?

"Mr. Luchk," Lammer continues, "quite a few papers had been set ablaze in the stove in the basement. Much has turned into ashes. The charred leftovers looked to be spreadsheets and ledgers." As she tells me this, I sit upright. Damn! I put my head in my hand, as all the terrible possibilities are dancing in my brain. A feeling of panic and dread now rushes over me. Did I leave the manuscript in my Rover safe and sound? Or did I have the manuscript in my satchel, where anyone would have had access? I can't remember!

Lammer goes on. "Maybe a few articles of furniture were broken apart to burn. Mr. Luchk, there also was a used syringe in the corner of the kitchen. It's possible that the person or persons who jumped you were nothing more than squatters whom you may have surprised. It is also possible that you were and are their target. You claim that your cousins knew you would be at that house? The fingerprints pulled from the house are yours and those of your cousins. There were five other sets. However, so far we've only been able to match one of them to someone we have on file. We'll keep trying."

CHAPTER EIGHT

Faith arrives at the hospital for a visit. Her voice is quiet and her face is turned down. She says, "I got a call from Edmond today. He knows that the timing is poor but he asked have you made a decision on the house? He really wants you to take the house."

"Tell him no! Hell no! You tell him that!"

Faith sees my face is turning crimson and she backs away from me. I flail my arms in anger and I slap the bed for effect. "You tell him, hell no!" I shout. "I am writing the book! I always thought he was a heartless prick. He just confirmed that!"

"Simon, settle down," the nurse calls from three rooms away. She must have heard me yell. After a few seconds, she walks in with a concerned look upon her face.

"Mrs. Luchk, you'll have to keep a tight rein on this guy," she tells Faith. "Try to keep him from getting too excited. He has been through a big trauma. He will be released tomorrow, as long as he doesn't blow a gasket here tonight. I will get you all his restrictions." I take Faith's hand in mine. "Faith, that whomp to my head wasn't all that was happening in that house. You said you found me in the basement." I glance into Faith's eyes. "I didn't go into the basement. You know that welt on my neck? Here, feel it. I would say a wasp sting, maybe a bite from a spider." My hair is still matted down from all the blood. "Nurse, what's the chance of a shower?" I ask.

"Hon, that won't happen," the nurse says with the matter-of-fact tone of a barmaid. "Maybe a tub, that might be possible."

"Why not a shower?" I scoot to the edge of the bed. My bare feet touch the floor. The second I try to stand, I know why. My legs wobble about. Nurse Betty looks directly at me as she holds me up by my upper arms.

"You may not feel it, Mr. Luchk, but your balance for standing upright in the shower? Well, it's not good."

I reach up to my hair and feel a bandage meant to keep me away from picking at the stitches on my head. Most of the dried blood has been removed, but my hair is filthy with it from the whack I received. Plus the side of my face and my shoulder are covered in carpet rash, blood, dirt, and charcoal.

Step by step, Nurse Betty explains the process of my relaxing visit to the tub.

Shortly, a team of nursing assistants charge into my room like stormtroopers. I am quickly ushered onto a hard, cold, plastic shower chair, buck-naked, covered with only a thin sheet. I am then removed from my bed by a Hoyer lift. If you are ever accused of getting too big for your britches, this small act is extremely humbling, as your ass is exposed for too many to see. The lift is a safety measure for the workers. It is a small version of a car engine hoist. In just moments, I am at the far side of the facility, in a shower room with a very liberal-sized tub. Moments later, my plastic chair backs in, docking with a loud clunk. I am not a bashful person, but being stripped to the bum in front of three strange women would be difficult even on my best day. Yes, it's a humbling feeling. The room is a bit cold; however, the tub is soon full of warm, sudsy water, and the nursing assistants help me get into the bath. The aches and pains don't totally leave, but with the help of drugs and the warm water, the pain subsides. Bless the CNAs for doing their job. Their kindness is much appreciated.

The bath seems cut way too short. I am escorted back to my room with the same sense of efficiency and urgency. The team is off to their next patient in need of a bath.

Doctor Lee, Nurse Betty, and Faith have all been waiting in my room for me. Betty closes the door. "Mr. Luchk, your blood showed more than a trace of heroin in it," Doctor Lee starts. "How long have you been a user, and is there anything else we should know?"

I sit up in the bed and reply "Bullshit!" with a slightly insulted tone. "No, not ever."

Faith interjects, "That's not entirely true, Simon. When we met, you were using."

"Well, Doctor, in my youth I used. You know, prescription painkillers after my auto accident. Then I turned to heroin when I couldn't get the scripts any longer."

"Mr. Luchk, it is possible that your previous drug use saved your life. If you hadn't built up a tolerance, the amount that was in your system might have killed you!

And now, Detective Lammer would like to see you." Nurse Betty opens the door. Detective Lammer stands there glaring at me, ready to pounce, like a lioness on meat.

"Mr. Luchk. I spoke to your wife while you were having your bath. Have you been honest with us about your drug use? I know that you were injected with heroin at that house. At least we can assume that's what happened. With that in mind, who may want to harm you? The house yielded many fingerprints. I told you that we're trying to match them to our database, and hopefully we'll come back with some names."

I glance at Faith absently as I rub my sore neck and then turn my body toward Lammer. "Gosh, I wouldn't know who would want to harm me." Faith stands and holds my left hand. I explain once again who owns the house and that I thought it was empty. Questions arise about my cousins.

"The trash that was in the kitchen area, was that present when you entered?"

"Yes, Detective, it was."

"And you entered despite what you saw? That did not strike you as odd?"

"Yes, it did, but the small entry room was clean. It was only when I entered deeper into the house that I saw all the bottles and everything else."

"How is your relationship with your cousin who owns the house?"

"A little strained, more so now. Two of my cousins made me an offer for my uncle's book. They said that it holds sentimental and monetary value to them. I understand that it has value to them, however, the book may very well be a great turning point for my rather lackluster writing career, so I'm not giving it up."

***

Meanwhile, in a motel room not far away, the phone rings.

"This is Max. What happened? Well, I'll tell you what happened. I shot him up just like we talked about. I don't know why! He is still in the hospital with his wife at his side. When he gets released, that's when I will get him. Both of them. Yeah, I know. Huff and puff all you want. They're as good as dead. There is a storm brewing. Good as dead!"

The man called Max leans back in his seat and takes a sip from his whiskey bottle. At noon the next day, Max parks in the hospital lot. He's watching and waiting for Simon to be released.

***

My neck is super sore. I wonder if it's because of the heroin? It's so stiff, it's killer to turn my head.

Lammer continues questioning me. She keeps asking the same things, maybe hoping to catch me in a lie. "Mr. Luchk, the house appears to have someone living in it. Did you expect that?"

"Detective Lammer, no! I was not expecting someone to be in the house. It was supposed to be empty."

"How did you get into the house?"

"I was given the door access code by my cousin Vivian."

"These cousins of yours, you get along with them?"

S. LEE GLICK

"We aren't close, but, trying to off one another? No."

"Do you and your wife enjoy recreational drugs? There was a lot of heroin in your system."

"In my troubled past." I let out a chuckle. "But Faith knows that I have been clean for over three years. Faith has never used drugs."

Doctor Lee comes back with Sheriff Crane. Doctor Lee repeats what he already told me earlier, I guess for the benefit of Crane and Lammer. "Mr. Luchk, the fact that you used to take drugs may have saved your life. You had more than a trace of heroin in your system. If you hadn't built a tolerance for the drug, you likely would have overdosed."

Sheriff Crane stands like a sentinel at the edge of my bed, glaring down at me. "Can you think of anyone who wants to harm you?" he asks.

"No, not at all, Sheriff. I am just a writer. I, or we—we keep to ourselves and all that."

"Mr. Luchk, you do carry a Taurus 380 revolver, do you not?"

"Yes, you know I do. I told you that already. A lot of good it did me. Sherriff, what does that have to do with me getting whacked on the head?"

"Your revolver was found on the property. One round had been fired out of it. The body of a man named Albert Spane was found in the backyard, with a hole in the middle of his chest."

The sheriff says this with an animated face and even slaps his chest. "Shot right in his solar plexus. You can consider it a lucky shot, or not, Luchk, however you want to look at it. With that small of a caliber, you had to make it a perfect shot. You stepped into a mess, Luchk."

I sit up with a swirling knot in my stomach. A numb, sick feeling is washing over me.

I am lost for words, but Crane continues talking. "Luchk, we know that Spane was a transient worker who was employed at the Silvis farm five miles south of the property. He hasn't been to work for two weeks. Also, Spane's wife kicked him out of the house around the same time. Two weeks ago. It is possible that he was staying at your cousin's property till he got his feet under him. Warm, empty house. Why not."

CHAPTER NINE

While I am still in the hospital, Faith brings the box with my uncle's manuscript. The box had been found in my car, but the detective seems uninterested it. Lucky for me. At the first opportunity I go back to sifting through my uncle's papers. I dig through the box until I find the journal. It is a small leather-bound book buried among all the printed papers with my uncle's manuscript and notes. Did my uncle deliberately pack his journal tight among his papers, with intention for me to find it and read it? Or did Dewey slip it in for some reason? All good questions. The book is only six inches by three inches. My uncle's personal journey is held between dark leather covers with a brittle binding. Beneath the journal, there is also my cousin Joey's favorite possession: the clown mask. It's just a clown mask, but to Joey it was so much more. The mask would transport him to a world where he could do anything and everything. Joey called himself Chicklets the clown. He'd put the mask on, hands on his hips, his chest puffed out, and he'd let out a malevolent laugh.

I hold the mask up to my eyes, and suddenly Joey's voice rings in my ears. The smell of his perspiration is wafting into my face and making my eyes water.

***

"Max? It's Lucy. I am in the building. Give me an hour."

***

Faith is getting ready to leave for the night. "I will see you in the morning, Simon. I don't see any nurses at the station. Who's with you tonight?"

"Betty, I think."

"Oh, there is a nurse at the station now. Maybe I will go say hi." Faith stands.

***

Lucy is just getting to the nurses' station. She is so glad that Max called. She needs the money and she loves making money. Almost as much as she loves killing. She also loves her work name: the Angel of Death. Lucy puffs out her chest every time she thinks about that name. She may even do a few jobs for free.

Nurse Betty marches up to Lucy. Betty is wagging her finger at the young nurse. "Where have you been? You're late. You know I cannot leave till you're here, and I have been here too long." Lucy backs half a step from the older nurse.

Faith gives Simon a kiss goodnight. She sees the nurses' conflict and wants nothing to do with it. "Betty looks like she will fight the new nurse, so I am just gonna go."

Betty continues to point and wag her finger at the young nurse. "Young lady, I will report you to HR. When they call me about my hours, I will report you!"

Lucy's purpose is to get Simon alone tonight and to kill him. Lucy may just kill Nurse Betty for the fun of it. She cannot let Betty get in her way. Lucy backs toward the women's restroom. She is thinking quickly. "Betty, I gotta go! That's why I was late." Lucy turns and darts into the lady's room. Betty softens a bit, believing that Lucy is not well. Betty slowly steps toward the lady's room and gently knocks on the door. "Lucy, are you okay?" She repeats her question.

Inside, Lucy now pulls a small four-inch knife from her right waist pocket, smiling to herself. The knife is barely noticeable till it strikes. In Lucy's left pocket is a syringe with five cc's of heroin. A delicious cocktail, though the loud, brash nurse doesn't deserve the rush. This will be the last time this loudmouth bitch pisses anyone off, Lucy thinks.

Betty enters the washroom to find Lucy kneeling down, facing away from the door. Betty touches Lucy's back with a comforting hand. Lucy turns quickly and drives the knife high into Betty's ribs. Betty slowly lowers herself to the floor and leans against a large trash can. Lucy kneels in front of Betty and puts her left hand over Betty's scornful mouth and presses down, to cover any noise Betty might make. Lucy's right hand grabs and twists the small knife between Betty's ribs. Lucy maintains eye contact. This is the part of the job she enjoys most. Watching the eyes of her victims as their life slips away. She finds the rush better than sex.

The fight has left Betty. Thirty seconds later, she dies on the cold, damp lavatory floor on the third floor of the Right Way Hospital.

Lucy is only five-foot-three, but at 112 pounds she is much stronger than her size might suggest. She rolls the towel cart into the restroom. She picks up the expired nurse, shoves her body into the towel cart, then covers her with used towels.

It's now 6 p.m. Lucy delivers Simon's evening meal. Poisoning him would be easier and faster, but what fun would that be? He seems a bit suspicious about the new nurse he doesn't recognize, but he doesn't say anything.

2 a.m. The hospital is as quiet as a church. Simon is in a deep sleep, dreaming of floating in a large bath. He is relaxed and peaceful, but then he feels his wife climb on top of him and aggressively snuggle him until he sinks below the water.

Simon wakes with a gasp of air. His mouth is covered. He thrashes violently till his fist connects with a jaw. He is allowed to get up. The person he has hit yells and, as if rehearsed, accuses Simon of being a violent patient. The on-call doctor charges into the room. The doctor administers a sedative to calm Simon. It's an oral tablet. Simon slips the tablet under his tongue, but when he is left alone, he spits it out. He forces himself to stay alert for the rest of the night. Finally at 10 a.m. the following day Faith comes to the hospital, to take Simon home.

There is lots of paperwork to fill out, so it's about noon when Faith and Simon exit the hospital. They are greeted by a bright sky and a cold slap of air to the face. They walk arm in arm to the still-warm Rover.

Sitting unnoticed three spaces south of the Rover is the thug named Max.

CHAPTER TEN

Brrrt. Brrrt.

Damn phone! "Yah, this is Max. I am watching him now. What do ya want, Billy? Yes, I understand you want him gone. I SAID, I am watching him now! Billy, don't think you can scare me."

Billy replies with a snake-like lisp. "I know that's a pause for effect. I intimidate you, Max. Otherwise you wouldn't be watching him, would you? Maximilian, I have killed more in a week than you have your whole life. You would be home with your wife if I didn't scare you. You wouldn't be doing this for me. You owe me enough money that I could take it out of your wife's pretty fluff. She is pretty, Max. I could make all of it back in two months, plus interest, of solid back-bending pleasure! Oh, she is hot, Max. She might even enjoy it. Max, I could have it recorded for your watching pleasure. What do you say?"

Max is trying to stay calm. "Don't forget, Billy. I am the person you called to clean up the mess you got into."

Billy cuts Max off mid-tirade. "Max, you're failing me! I know where your family and their families live. So get going and get this done, or the next time you speak to your wife, you will hear her screams of pleasure. Or maybe her screams of agony, if I sell her and your children into the sex industry. There is always a need in that industry." Billy's voice fades off to a whisper. "Do you like the thought of that? If that doesn't move you, then how about your ten-year-old daughter? Would you like to hear her scream 'Dad, Dad!' Ha ha ha!"

"You don't have the brass in your belly to do the dirty work. That's why you hired me," Max hisses.

"Max, do you think that you are the only muscle I employ? You are the least of my muscle. I hold the markers on many, many individuals."

Max is defeated. His once-strong shoulders now slump in fatigue and despair brought on by the terrible mess he has gotten himself into. Max is a down-on-his-luck fishing-dock worker. He needs a paycheck—a large one— in a bad way. The rough stuff doesn't bother him at all. He had broken both of his hands while beating a man to death. He is used to the toll of violence on the body. Max had killed another guy in a fight up north. Up north they don't ask many questions, especially when the crime is on tribal land and you're white. The tribal police handle it. A lot falls through the cracks. That's where people go to get lost. It's always been that way. It always will be.

Max wasn't born a piece of trash. It just happened. He got into fights and ended up hurting some men. He lost his job and spent some time in jail. Then, after jail, no place would hire him. The spiral began to unravel in full force. Max was short of money. He thought he could gamble his way out of debt, so he gambled at tribal casinos. He learned that this doesn't work well. Max thought that if he could just hit the big one, his snarly stripper wife would possibly keep him around. The rest of the story unfolded in a predictable way. Max began owing a little, then more, and more. Finally, he ended up owing big money to the sharks that walk. To the sharks, someone who owes is called a marker. Max owes money to the biggest shark in the Northwoods: Billy. Billy now pulls the strings that Max is attached to. The people who owe Billy money call him Chief. He is Billy Redcliff, the Chief. No one knows if Billy is truly a chief. Probably not, but it has a nice intimidating ring to it. He runs all the money on the tribal land. He also runs the casinos.

So now it's Max against Simon. As far as Max is concerned, Simon is just a means to an end. Max's debt will be paid in full if he can off Simon. As soon as this job is done, Max will move on to the next one. Too bad for Max, Simon has grown accustomed to living...

Billy is still talking into the phone. "Are you still here, Maxie?" Billy speaks with a moist slur. "Your job was to kill him! A damn pussy writer! You couldn't even get that done!"

"Billy, I gave him enough heroin to knock out a horse. I won't make that mistake again."

"You better not. Your debt is paid by the job. So you still owe me for this one! Get it done, or!"

"Or what?" Max is defiant now.

"Or what? Don't cross that line, Max," Billy exclaims, puffing his broad chest out. As if Max could see him.

CHAPTER ELEVEN

Faith comes to the hospital at 10 a.m. It takes some time to fill out the discharge forms and all that, but around noon we can finally leave. As we exit the hospital we are greeted by brisk, fresh air from the north. I put my arm around Faith's shoulder, to show my affection and to keep warm as we walk through the parking lot. It is great to feel the breeze on my face and to be rid of the hospital's wretched, antiseptic fragrance and the horrific sounds that always come in the night.

"Simon, do you think that someone was trying to kill you?"

I have a brief moment of cockiness. "He or she did a poor job of it, don't you think?"

"All right, smart guy."

I turn and look directly into Faith's eyes. "Faith, I wish I knew for sure. I am glad my head is so hard! Here is what I think. I think someone likes staying rent-free at my cousins' house. Neither Vivian nor her siblings go that far north very often. With no proper caretaker to check on the house, this may have been going on for a long time. That's what I think."

"I won't complain about your hard head ever again," Faith says.

We get to the car. "Faith, do you mind driving? I still feel under the weather from that whack to the head."

"Of course not. And let's stop at the store to pick up some things. We have very little food at the house."

The drive takes a few hours. As we pull into the supermarket lot, I glance at my Timex. Only 5:15 and the sky is already darkening. There is only a thin layer of light just above the western horizon. This time of year, the days are rather short up here.

Faith and I make a quick stop to pick up gourmet deli chicken for dinner. I am so looking forward to food that is not broth or Jell-O! We stop at the wine and beer section next. Faith wants to pick up a bottle of wine. I am more of a wheat beer guy myself, but it's getting chilly out, so a dark stout sounds nice.

Faith leans close to my ear and whispers to me. "That guy came into the shop after us. He keeps looking at us. His chin and beady eyes remind me of a rat. And he is constantly texting."

"Faith, none of that's a crime."

"He does remind me of a man I saw at the hospital. That rat-faced guy. Yeah, that's it. His features remind me of a rat-faced man from a children's book."

I turn to look whom she's talking about. "That guy in the corner with the pointy chin?" He has some minor stubble, a mustache that won't come in, and close-set beady eyes. "Faith, he does look like a rat!" Poor guy.

"Yeah, that's him," Faith says.

"Okay, I will go to the checkout. You keep browsing and keep an eye on him."

I place my items on the checkout belt. I am greeted by a rosy-cheeked dark-haired woman who is in a chatty mood. I look past the cheery cashier so I can maintain a view of Rat Face. "Wow, that chicken looks good!" She glances at her Mickey watch. "I get off in an hour and I am starving." She scans my beer and asks, "Have you tried the Alaskan winter ale? It's so good!" Her eyes almost roll inside her head. She then segues gracefully into "May I see your ID?"

"I have not tried that beer," I say politely as I desperately try to keep Rat Face within view. He scurries toward the exit, giving me a quick glance over his shoulder. He then disappears from my sight, to the right of the door.

***

Max, aka Rat Face, answers his phone. "Yah, I see 'em. I texted you earlier that they was in the store close to me. Billy, don't you trust me? Yah, easy plucking. They don't look suspicious at all. Billy, you should see them! It will be fun."

"That's what you say, Max, but you have been late to deliver. I am sitting with your wife, Max. She has such a pretty face."

"Billy, BILLY! Don't you touch her!"

"It seems I finally have your attention!"

Max is now in a massive panic. He thinks, she isn't much, but she is all I have got. Would life be better or worse if I lost her?

"Billy, I will get this done. You have my word. On my wife's life, I swear."

"Yes, I know you will," Billy says matter-of-factly.

Max can hear his wife making squeaking noises in a panic.

"Dear Max," Billy continues, "I will send you the address of their home. Get there before they do and take care of this business."

"If I don't get 'em now, I'll take care of it tonight."

"You take them out now. I want it done now."

***

Faith joins me at the checkout and holds my arm for comfort. "I don't know where Rat Face went," she says.

"You're enjoying this, aren't you, Daphne?" That's just my way of trying to lighten the mood. I rib Faith. "Get it? Get it?" I can't help but smile. As the rosy-cheeked cashier is bagging our purchases, I glance idly at the stacks of pet food by the floor-to-ceiling windows at the front. I turn to take in a 360-degree view and I realize that there are very few customers in here with us. We almost have the whole store to ourselves.

"Where did he go, Freddie?" Faith asks.

"At least I get to be Freddie and not the Shagster!" I lean a bit to my right and crane my neck to gain a better view of the parking lot. I speak in a low voice to Faith. "There's a truck pulling out of the lot." A well-kept mid-eighties quarter-ton Ford with a white side and brown trim exits the parking lot onto Highway 13 and turns north. "He must have been in that truck."

Faith takes my hand and gives it a squeeze. "Sorry, Simon, I am just really paranoid after your attack." I give her hand a gentle squeeze back. "Me too, hon." I pull her in for a hug. "Thanks for bringing my shoulder holster and my new 380. I know your dislike for handguns. But it makes me feel more secure."

A sharp, cold wind is blowing from the lake, stirring the piles of yellow leaves around the light poles in the parking lot. Winter suddenly seems much closer than it did just a couple of days ago. It's as if the wind is taking revenge on us for an unknown deed, smacking us in the face and turning our skin beet-red. I flip up my coat collar as we scamper to our Range Rover. Faith slips into the driver's seat. As I'm about to open the passenger-side door, I see Faith's eyes dart past me. Her mouth opens as if to say something. I hear a click-click-click behind me. I turn, too late. Rat Face is just inches from me. He shoves me into the Rover. Two things are working in my favor. The first is, I am wearing a heavy wool coat. And also, Rat Face is too close to me. He jams a Taser against my coat and fires it, but the barbs don't get a chance to spread out and make good contact with my skin. I feel the juice hit me, but only a few muscles are affected. I tense as I stare into Rat Face's eyes. His eyes are glazed over.

Once, years ago, my cousin Danial and I were removed forcibly from an altercation in a local bar and grill, the Rusty Pelican. Dan and I were tased in that situation. Dan had reacted to the Taser with a new level of rage. I know what is coming now and how long its effects will be. But it still hurts. Rat Face must have a cheap civilian model that gives only ten seconds of shock. My legs still give out, like a marionette whose stings are cut. I pull Rat Face down on top of me. I smell pepperoni, beer, and stale cigarettes on his breath—a stomach-turning cocktail. He feels heavy, two hundred-plus. He is trying his best to place all his weight onto me. We roll around a bit. I get the use of my legs back shortly. While on the bottom, I pull him close. Rat Face is desperate to get space between me and him. He probably wants to pummel me or drive a knife into me. Either way, space is what he needs. That is also just what I want, space.

He pushes up from me and is then able to hold me down with his left hand and forearm. He now has enough space to strike me with his right fist. I turn my head, deflecting the blow to the left side of my face. It still hurts as my head is hammered into the cold blacktop, even though his fist only grazed me. I struggle to place my left forearm on the back of his neck, and to get my right forearm under his throat. That's it, Rat Face is exactly where I want him. I squeeze my arms together with all my might. As I'm squeezing his throat, I hear Faith screaming and hitting the horn in panic. A few seconds later I feel a terrible pain in my left arm. Faith is whacking my arm and Rat Face with a club that was in the Rover. She is still screaming, and two workers from the store run out to catch the action, as they must have heard the ruckus in the lot.

Rat Face gets up and runs. Faith gets in the car and tries to run him down. That's my girl! I lie on the cold, wet parking lot and watch the Range Rover leaving me. Faith's window is down and she screams at the group of bystanders to call the police. Faith tries to cut Rat Face off from his truck, but he gets to it and starts rummaging in the truck bed for something to chuck at her. He finds what looks to be a brick. It sails toward Faith's lowered window. I cannot tell if she's hit or not, but it looks like she has decided against pursuing him further, and she returns to get me off the pavement. Luckily this time it's mostly my pride that's hurt, and maybe my jaw and my shoulder. Faith is bending down directly over my head, looking at me upside down. "Are you okay?" she asks now, just like she did a few days ago. I feel a ball of fury welling up inside me. Faith has a red spot on her left cheekbone where the brick must have grazed her. She is a tough bird and insists that all she got was a scrape. With the effects of the Taser finally worn off, I bolt up off the ground. Almost airborne. "No, I am not okay, dammit!" I yell. "This is bullshit! Bullshit, Faith. What the hell is going on?!" Then I realize that I am taking my anger out on her. I lower my head and my voice.

"Jesus on a stick, Simon. Have you pissed off someone?"

Back in the Rover, the subject stays on what or whom I might have pissed off.

CHAPTER TWELVE

We finally make it home. What a sweet word, home. On the way back we have picked up Willie, our bull terrier, from the boarding farm. Faith takes Willie by his lead and ventures to inspect the outbuildings. The first winter storm is coming in, and we need to ensure all buildings are properly closed up. I want to help, but Faith insists she is an independent, strong woman and she struts off into the blackness, out of my view. She is armed with the same bat that she used to bash my arm. Bat and lantern in one hand, leash in the other. Off she goes. The autumn air has turned frigid since the sunset.

***

The temperature is now in the teens. Faith enters the dimly lit thirty-by-sixty-five-foot shed made into a dark, damp garage and horse stall. The wind whistles and shadows jump from hiding spot to hiding spot. Rats and mice skitter across the dirt floor. Bangs and creaks fill the darkness, with specters waiting to come to life in Faith's imagination. Faith pushes on, with the lantern held at arm's length. Her arms are full, as she's now holding the bat in both hands, as well as Willie's lead. Willie is constantly jerking and tugging, agitated by the sounds coming from the shed. He's making 115-pound Faith rock to and fro. She shivers and she cannot rid herself of the memory of Rat Face ramming Simon into the Rover's window. She can still see the desperation and anger in his eyes. The wind is increasing and feels like a breath on the back of Faith's neck. The panic monster is pulling at her nerves. She thinks every sound is a specter come to attack her.

***

Twenty minutes pass, and Faith and Willie still haven't made an appearance back at the house. I am getting concerned. I slip on my wood-cutting coat and take my pistol from its holster: a 1911 Rock Island Armory 45-caliber. No frills, just firepower. I go out and follow the faint lantern light toward the shed, through the black-velvet night air. The darkness is ominous.

I hear a high-pitched squeal, followed by every unladylike word in Faith's book. I run to the shed as fast as I can. When I get there, I find Faith on the ground, looking embarrassed and angry and glaring at Willie.

"Dammit, Simon! I stepped on one of your damn boards with nails in it!"

Turns out Willie, seeing or hearing something Faith couldn't, tugged with all his might and pulled her off balance, and she stepped onto a board with nails protruding from it. The nails were out just far enough to go through the sole of her boot and pierce her foot. Good thing she fell on the bales of straw we use as bedding for our horses.

I get to be the hero for once. I reach down and help her to her feet. She is tender and doesn't put her full weight on both feet. Before we get going, I find the board with the nails sticking out and Faith's blood on them. I wonder why the hell that's even here, as I keep the floor pretty well picked up. Willie stares up at me with a look of disgust over my upkeep of the garage. He soon abandons that and flashes me the smile his breed displays when looking for approval of their kill. There is a mouse tail hanging from Willie's mouth.

The straw next to him seems to be moving too, and Willie jumps on it to tackle yet another opponent: a rat. The sound of bones being crushed in Willie's powerful jaws makes Faith cringe. She cannot bear to watch Willie enjoy his killing game, so, gingerly, she ventures further into the long shed. A doorway just ahead is partially open: by wind or something else? Faith inches closer to the cement doorway and slams it shut. Soon we have closed and locked all the doorways and gates. The two horses are all tucked in after fresh straw and oats have been laid out for a treat. The wind is now screaming, wanting to be allowed into the house and the shed. It carries the voices of the lives that Lake Superior has claimed.

I aid in getting Faith out of the shed, and we follow the wooden walkway back to the house. It's partially lit, like in a park—a product of my vision. It's snowing now, so the three of us shuffle through the drifting snow. We enter the house in darkness. I urge Willie to go in first, and he and I diligently check every room, door, and window throughout the house. The panic monster has taken up residence in our brains, but all seems good and tight.

I help Faith to the side of the tub, so I can dress her foot. There are three puncture wounds, which have bled into her boot. I clean her foot with peroxide and alcohol, then apply salve and bandages. Good as new.

We can hear the wind battering down from the north, demanding attention and respect. It's reminding us who is the boss. With the outbuildings locked up tight, I return to the business of lighting our wood-burning stove. "All is clear," I jokingly call out at 8 p.m., then again at 8:30 and at 9. I finally decide to wear my holster. Our nerves are shot, and it helps me feel safer. I've called Sheriff Crane, and I expect he will be over soon to ask us about our grocery store adventure.

Shortly after 9 p.m. Sheriff Crane is standing at our door. He is a large man, six-foot-two or taller, 220 pounds or heavier. With the wind whipping a haze of snow and the yard light shining behind the sheriff, I am reminded of the cover image of John Carpenter's movie The Thing.

"Drop your holster and firearm, Luchk," the sheriff orders. I have to place my firearm on the table next to the front door before he will enter. "I don't appreciate you coming to the door packing."

"Yes, sir. Come in."

Once he is inside, he says, "I haven't had much for trouble with your family in the past. Can you tell me what the hell you have gotten yourselves into?

The questions were much the same as in my earlier encounters with the sheriff and Detective Lammer, except for a few more direct questions. "Luchk, what story are you working on?"

"Sheriff, I am finishing a book that my late uncle passed on to me through his will."

"And is there anyone you've pissed off lately?"

"My cousins seemed a bit distraught about me being asked to finish their father's novel, Doctor Schultz: The Island. But I have a hard time believing that our family would harm each other. I really

don't see why they would do that. It's my uncle's business and he kept himself to himself." Faith and I then give what we feel is a good description of Rat Face.

"Luchk, the folks at the grocery store say they have seen that man before. They think he is a local. Say, Luchk, you and the missus aren't having issues, are you?"

"No. Money is a bit tight, but who has enough these days? That's all."

"Hmm. All right, you think about it and if you have any ideas, call me."

After Sheriff Crane leaves, I hoist my holster and firearm under my left arm. I feel safer and more manly for sure, yet part of me is quite anxious at the thought of possibly taking another person's life. I am sure an assailant will see and use my hesitation against me. Faith and I move about the house as a pair, plus one—Willie is strong at fifty-five pounds, and he has a no-nonsense look and bark. The night settles around the house.

CHAPTER THIRTEEN

The wind is slamming against my home. I can feel the house give and resist as the early winter storm screams to come inside. The not yet completely frozen Lake Superior searches for another victim. The snow that was lying safely on the ground, autumn snow that is with us till late spring, has been picked up and has taken on a life of its own. It swirls and spins itself into a deep white fog. A fog like the one on Whitefish Bay all those years ago, which Captain James William Petty thought was singing to him, calling him to enter her soft bosom. The white beauty draws you toward her, inside her. And you are never to return, forever lost in the fog.

I pull up to the house, letting the Rover warm up a bit. A week has passed since my hospital release. Faith has come down with a fever of 104, plus a nasty hacking cough. She protests that she doesn't want a doctor, but I am concerned. She has been really weak and has even had difficulty walking the past couple of days. She has also begun to spit blood when she coughs. Only now has she finally allowed me to drive her to urgent care. A fever unchecked may turn a person into a vegetable for the rest of their life. I am very worried. I need to get Faith to a doctor as soon as possible.

I set the shifter into all-wheel drive and switch on all the running lights. I haven't yet put on the tire chains. Regardless, the Rover is a stable beast, with an eight-cylinder fuel-injected heart that keeps her rolling. I've pulled up as close as I can to the front door to pick Faith up. I reach out to support her by taking her right arm. She pushes me away initially, but she quickly loses her balance. She can barely stand up, let alone walk. I pick her up as if she's a sack of potatoes, and into the Rover we go. Only now she notices that the snow is as tall as the running board of the Range Rover. Her eyes are sunken and lifeless, and there's a haunting glaze over her whole face. A layer of sweat covers her forehead. The negative-twenty-degree temperature threatens to freeze the sweat straight to her face. I wipe her forehead and cheeks with a soft towel. My love looks miserable, just like someone in a commercial for flu medicine. She no longer argues and is not complaining as I dote on her.

With each roll of the tires we hear the snow crunching underneath. This is the language of bitter cold. The drifts are mounting but they are manageable for my Range Rover. As long as the tires touch the earth, the Rover will keep moving. What is normally a short fifteen-minute drive has now tripled in time. We're now miles from home and miles from the doctors still. Go forward or go home? At this point, both options are dangerous and will take a long time. But I have to get help for Faith. The Rover is pushing snow with its front bumper. We are moving ever so slowly, but still moving.

At long last I pull into the hospital's vacant parking lot. The hospital is deserted. The storm has put people off seeking help. Faith is wrapped in a heavy green wool blanket and her favorite warm toboggan cap. When she is finally examined, her temperature has escalated past 104.5. The doctor admits her into the ER. I have done my job. I have gotten the bull-headed Irish woman where she needs to be, even if she wishes not to be here. Faith is where she needs to be. She needs care now. We have been married for four years, but we were an item for five years before our wedding. Since we met, my days have been filled with wonderful adventures, which revolve around Faith and only Faith. We were finally starting to settle into our life together, and now this.

When I turn, I see her, and I smell her perfume wafting by me. Is it just my imagination? Or could the fragrance be coming off the dark-haired nurse who just left the waiting area? I don't let myself think that this could be the end. This is just a speed bump. It's a speed bump like the ones many other people live through. We have been blessed with many good fortunes. This sort of thing is a common occurrence; it is the type of thing that just happens, all the time. It just hasn't happened to us, until now.

While at the hospital, I spend my time politely chitchatting with the strangers who are all sitting patiently in the small waiting area—all except two very young boys for whom standing still or sitting is well beyond their age. Paintings and expanded photos of local scenery decorate the light gray walls, with engraved nameplates announcing to all who donated each artwork.

The nurse comes to tell me that Faith is now in a private room.

I follow the nurse. The doctor is waiting to talk to me in the vacant hallway. The doctor is a woman, Doctor Starr. She is small in stature, five-foot-six tops, with thick pop-bottle glasses and a no-shit look on her face. She looks weatherworn. I would speculate that the hospital has had many call-offs today. Her long dark hair is pulled away into a conservative bun, mostly just to be out of her eyes, it seems. She wears no jewelry or makeup. That is a shame. A small amount of effort on her part would make a dramatic difference in her appearance. But this is not a priority, I am sure.

"Doctor, how is she, my wife?"

"Your wife is in room 314, just around the corner. She is resting at the moment. Mr. Luchk, I am concerned your wife's temperature is quite high. What we have done thus far has not lowered the fever. The fever has been brought on by an infection that started with the nasty puncture wounds on her right foot, which have been untreated until now. We are considering an ice bath. She also has that scrape on her cheek, but that is not a concern. The wound on her foot is the concern. The cut is infected, and the infection has moved into her glands. We must find what may have infected her. There is no debris by the wound to give us a clue. Whatever it may be, it is spreading very quickly through her body now, through her glands. The wound is quite inflamed. How long has she had it?"

I tell Doctor Starr about Faith stepping on the board with the nails a few nights ago. I'm shocked to hear that injury is what's made Faith so ill. After I cleaned and bandaged her foot that night, Faith never complained about pain in her foot again, so I had assumed those wounds were healing up fine and there was nothing to worry about. I explain all this to Doctor Starr in a panic.

"Mr. Luchk, do you think you can find the board she stepped on? It would be of great help." A nurse with raven black hair passes by. Her nametag reads "Lucy." She is stunning. Her uniform seems to be a naughty Halloween costume. She also looks familiar, but then again, I had a lot of nurses who attended to me when I was here after my encounter at my cousins' house.

The doctor's eyes are piercing. There is a long, uncomfortable pause. "Yes, Doctor. I will leave right away. I will bring what I find." After Faith stepped on the board, I tossed it out of the way, but where? I can feel the young doctor's judgment on me. Doctor Starr has a glare that seems to see into your soul. She should consider being an attorney. I get ready to go back and begin my search for the plank Faith stepped on.

"I hope you find it, Mr. Luchk. The good news is that thus far, your baby is fine. It doesn't appear that the infection has had any effect on the baby."

I bend slightly to look directly into the doctor's eyes. "Baby? BABY? What baby? I..."

I had no idea. A baby! We haven't been intimate for what seems forever. I question whether the baby would even be mine. Faith has been spending a lot of time in Chicago with her family lately...

My complete explosion of surprise and the perplexed look upon my face must have caught the doctor off guard.

The news of a baby is a kick in the crotch. Our life is in turmoil as it is, what with me losing my job and someone apparently trying to kill me. Things between Faith and me have been a bit strained, to say the least. And a baby complicates everything. I have been so obsessed with my own life that I haven't paid much attention to Faith lately. No wonder she's been trying to spend as much time away from me as possible. With my attitude, who could blame her.

"A baby? A baby! Are you sure?" I ask.

CHAPTER FOURTEEN

"Yes, I am sure, Mr. Luchk," Doctor Starr says. "I take it you weren't aware that your wife is pregnant. She is just a month or so along, so she may not have known herself."

"No, Faith had not mentioned that she may be pregnant. She had been unable to get pregnant when we were trying."

"Would you like to see her?" Doctor Starr leads me to Faith's room. I stand just at the head of her hospital bed and watch her chest rise and lower rhythmically while she rests peacefully. I gaze at her face and ponder how this quick sickness has changed our lives. It's taken a huge toll on her. Her eyes are sunken, her hair is damp with sweat from the fever, there is a rasp as she breathes.

Doctor Starr leaves us alone, and I slide a chair next to Faith's bed. I take her right hand in both of mine and start talking to her. "Faith, I wish you were able to hear me. I have been preparing to start on my uncle's novel. In his papers, I found Uncle Johannes's journal. I am not sure I was meant to read his journal." I realize I am clutching her hand and I loosen my grip a bit. I fear I will hurt her. Her face has a tense expression; I wish it would lighten up. Faith would know what to do. Her moral compass has always pointed true north. I continue to speak to my silent audience. "There are several examples of my uncle, my cousins, and even my father jilting and coercing people out of their homes and land. I am not sure they did any lawbreaking, but it was certainly unethical behavior." I lean back in the chair and take in a deep breath, then let it out. "Shit, Faith, what do I do? Do I try to right these wrongs? Aaagh, hell!" I sigh.

Two hours later I am at my home on the lake. I go behind the shed, well back into the woods, where our fire pit is, and I shovel all the snow out of it. Then I carry out the box of papers and my log chair. In the privacy of three hundred acres of trees, I sit by the fire pit, armed with matches, gasoline, and beer. I start a blaze. I glance to the sky. I have made my choice. I toss page after page into the roaring fire, and I watch them burn with the knowledge that I am no better than my cousins. I always have and still do hold my father in the highest regard. I will take this knowledge with me to the grave.

***

Faith's room is warm and small, with a view of the local park. It is filled with the most modern and safest playground equipment, but it's all covered with hip-deep snow. It's waiting for the winter to give it back to the children. There are very few tracks into the snow, just as I would expect. When I look out Faith's third-floor window, it's as if Norman Rockwell has painted the trees and the rooftops of the small town.

Faith's hair is matted down, and her eyes are sunken and have black circles underneath. I put lip balm on her cracked and dry lips. She quietly smacks her lips, then I give her a gentle kiss and her hand a gentle squeeze. She squeezes back, with a faint smile to her lips. I give her another gentle kiss on her lips. Cherry lip balm. I set the teddy bear I bought at the gift shop, one holding yellow carnations and red roses, on the bedside table. The nurse is all business. She has long coal-black hair, dark chocolate eyes. She has sharp cheekbones, and I would guess she is a local Native American, from either the Red Cliff tribal lands or one of the Chippewa tribes. The nurse is keeping her head down as she works, and there's very little chitchat or eye contact. As I am leaving Faith's room, the nurse is preparing to add a syringe full of medication into her IV.

I drive north, thinking about the local landscape. Both tribal reservation lands have small houses and a general store with many authentic souvenirs. There's also a gas station located centrally along the scenic lakeshore drive. Plunked amongst the tall pines is a massive casino, which, just like the ones in Vegas, has been built with the money of losers. The casino offers a wonderful view of the great Gitchi Gummee. The lakeside town is now a big tourist destination during the summer months, though the once-thriving logging industry has faded. At its peak, a major pinery offered hundreds of jobs. That was back when the land value was based on the board feet that could be harvested, not the acreage. The small lake town might as well be a ghost town during the winter months. The frigid winter temperatures, combined with the unabated winds, make the town a place only the heartiest people will venture to. Only the absolute stoutest can live in this harsh environment. The frozen lake surface allows the temperatures to be in the negative degree range for months at a time. The pinery camp brought with it hotels, restaurants, houses, bars, and banks, making the place more lively year-round. One of those houses was my father's home. Now mine, via his will. A rugged, solid structure, it was built in the 1940s out of pine timber harvested by the pinery from our ten-acre plot. Father owned a major share of the camp. My father and his team built everything with their own hands. The massive heavy pines were centuries old. The home was built at the end of the logging boom. At the time of construction, the lake property was not sought after. The old town is all but gone now, and there's a new, streamlined town standing in its place. Bigger cities are eating up the small ones. Just as in nature, it's the survival of the fittest.

I am home at last. My home is just fifteen miles from town, along the lakeshore road lined by trees. It carries a beauty that never ceases to fill me with wonder, as it's always changing. It often amazes me that the flatlanders still come up north. It's a five- or six-hour-long haul, and for what? A piece of what used to be. Dear Lord, at times I miss my father so. The tourists now come to the small Lake Superior town to hear logging and boat stories, tall tales from long ago. They sit by the warm fireside and peer out the windows at the tall pines. The tourists stare at the locals, as if we are part of the rugged scenery. It's happened to me when I've been with our family friend Captain Jim Petty. Many times the tourists will be brazen enough to ask if we are local. Only then do I don my storytelling face. The captain and I, we have both spent many a night at the Pelican without spending a dime. I would lean over my drink and utter my favorite line: "Buy me a drink and I'll tell you a story; buy me another drink and I'll tell you more." The flatlanders, they are fearful about making eye contact. Ha! They shiver as they stare out at the rugged winter weather, speculating why a sane person would live in such a hostile land. We are here because we don't like people. We tolerate the tourists from the big cities because they bring their money by the bucketloads. They're all hoping to regain what they have lost, a past that eludes them. I tell my stories and they introduce me to a drink, then to each other. It's similar to feeding a video game. Just put quarters through the slot. Ha! All for the tourists' entertainment.

Father loved this land. As do I.

I stand on my second floor, peering out at the wind-blown snow. The storm is on day three now. I reach for my snifter, add a few ice cubes, and freshen up my drink with four fingers of rum. My head feels heavy. I'll close my eyes just for a minute, to reenergize. My mind won't shut off. I think about Faith and our life together. Recently it has been a bit of a farce. We've just been going through the motions, with no passion and barely any love. When Faith is released from the hospital, we should consider a separation, or figure out a way to reset our relationship. We'll have to see how we feel. Or maybe a trip to the Stanley out west; it's one of my bucket list items. Room 217.

The chirp of my phone wakes me from a dream that I had discovered my family were crooks and swindlers. It is the hospital. I need to go back there quickly. There is a problem— Faith seems to have had a hemorrhage. That is all they will say, nothing more.

My head is groggy. I need to wake up. I slap cold water upon my face, over and over. If a doctor has good news, they usually tell you. I throw the towel back into the sink, as if I were upset at the sink. But bad news—never. They won't tell you until you're face to face. Damn doctors and insurance salesmen! They only give you enough information to excite you and enlist your imagination.

I charge into the long dark shed in search of the board Faith stepped on. I am on my hands and knees sifting through the straw where Faith had stepped just a few nights before. I find the three-foot-long two-by-four scrap with three long nails driven through the board. It's similar to a punji stick, meant for damage. There's a red stain still on it. I pick it up and run through the knee-deep snow to the large doors that protect the Rover from the elements. I'd just two hours before opened those doors to tuck the Rover in for its short nap. I charge upstairs to my office. I wish I had a chance to finally read what my uncle has written of his novel so far. But how silly to think that I may be given time. I quickly organize the manuscript and place it carefully into my satchel, snapping the fold over. If time allows, I will read it.

PART TWO:
JOHANNES'S NOVEL

CHAPTER FIFTEEN
DOCTOR SCHULTZ: THE ISLAND
BY JOHANNES L. LUCHK

Doctor Patrick Schultz is the resident psychiatrist at the Right Way Hospital. Every week, in a room at the basement of the hospital, he leads a grief counseling session for a group of his grief-stricken patients. There are usually between twelve and sixteen people who attend the meetings. They come together each week for support and a sympathetic ear.

Doctor Schultz is a good-looking man, always dressed professionally. Armani, Rolex, Tom Ford—the doctor has style. Through cracks in his caring façade, you can sometimes sense that he feels he is godlike. He always enters with a quick glance at his watch and a warm smile upon his face. The room lights up at his presence.

The room has peaceful gray walls and a gray carpet. On the walls are strategically placed photos of rowing teams and a great photo of a sunrise over a massive mountainside. All complete with inspirational quotes. The room still has an air of antiseptic to it. It's quite spacious and can fit up to fifty people if need be.

The group doesn't mingle much. Everyone is carrying their own burden of pain, of loss and the grief that follows. Nurse Susan and Pastor Steve are usually present at the meetings. Longtime member Bill Clark is, almost as a rule, the only really chatty participant. He has been fighting an uphill battle with guilt and grief after losing his two children to the lake on his property. In the end it is more than he can bear, and he slips from reality. His wife will later recall that in Bill's final days, he is very solemn and completely withdrawn. Bill has a visit from the doctor, and then he goes on a killing spree.

Bill's wife, Barb, would later wonder how come the doctor didn't notice Bill's odd behavior, which in the end costs Bill his life. She shall never have an answer. During Bill's killing spree, he took the life of Congressman Evers. The congressman had been popular among the voters. He had also been a staunch opponent to an infrastructure proposal that would link the southern part of Wisconsin to the northeast part of the state, connecting the upper peninsula with a four-lane highway, to be called Interstate 43. This new interstate would change the fortunes of the neighboring landowners close to Lake Michigan. The land is considered high priced, and is now out of reach for working-class people. This highway project would dramatically increase the land wealth of a fortunate few landowners.

Over the past three decades, the small landowners have all but vanished, and this prime land is now owned by just a handful of people. Doctor Schultz owns a few thousand acres in the area. Schultz likes to say that land is the only commodity that is not produced any longer.

But back to Bill, who took a knife to a gunfight on that Saturday night. You can imagine how that ended.

There is a bit more chatter in the counseling group at the next meeting. The doctor makes an announcement about Bill's death. Everyone has already heard about it, read it, watched it. All make a face of wonder, even though they all know the gory details. Doctor Schultz then asks if anyone has any questions or stories about Bill that they feel they could share. Bill's wife stands toward the back of the room, sobbing. Some group members go to put a comforting hand on her shoulder and offer a kind word. In between sobs, her face turns to stone and she just stares blankly at nothing. She is holding onto the back of the chair in front of her for balance. Her salt-and-pepper hair hangs down into her eyes. She has a round, pleasant face. She has kept much of her muscle from the rigorous farm life. Barb sobs and she mutters to herself, "Bill just couldn't get past the loss of the twins. He tried, but just couldn't."

With that, Barb goes down on her knees and takes out her Ruger 380 revolver. Bill had always barked at her to get a real gun. Her hands are shaking, but she manages to put the pistol to her left temple. The tears are now flowing down her face.

Doctor Schultz charges at Barb. "Barb, for God's sake, no!" Schultz pauses just for a moment, hesitant to get in front of the gun, as the only person he really cares about is himself. The man seated to Barb's right looks directly into her tear-filled eyes. He has seen people die, but none so close as this. For a moment, he can feel her pain, even read her thoughts, as if she has become a transmitter from beyond. He understands her anguish, her complete loss now that Bill is also gone.

A second later, her shoulders square off quickly, and she now takes aim at him. His name is Henry Williams, and he is running to become a member of the Wisconsin congress. She is filled with pity and rage. Bill had been rambling about the world going to shit, and Henry here is a major part of it. Barb feels that doing something to stop that would be the best she could do for Bill. Her plan is now to put a bullet into Henry.

Suddenly Henry lunges forward and places his hand over the revolver, where the hammer would be. He knows that if he keeps the hammer from making contact with the bullet, there will be no shot. Her expression changes to somber and driven, as if possessed by a demon. They wrestle for control of the revolver. Barb is able to fire off two rounds, nether hitting Henry. Both bullets go into the north wall. Barb maintains her resolve, but Henry manages to get a grip on the revolver and lifts it up with both hands. Barb clings to it, until she is suspended three inches from the floor. Her grip still doesn't falter. She releases a deep guttural growl and drives a knee into Henry's groin. His eyes grow wide with shock, and Barb wins the battle for the revolver. Now she must kill Henry and finish Bill's business! But instead, she slowly sits on the nearest chair. She glares at all the people joined for the meeting, all of them looking at her in horror. Her face is stern and angry. Her voice babbles the words "Kill them, kill them all." Her chant grows louder. "Yes, Doctor, kill them, kill them all," then back it goes to a whisper. "Yes,

Doctor. Yes."

Bill had told her it takes gravel in your belly to finish the job. Her hands were shaking before, but now she is as calm as Moses on the mountain. She places the pistol to her left temple again. Her tears have stopped. The oscillating fan on the ceiling makes her scarf and her hair flutter. When the scarf moves in the air and for a moment fully covers her face, Doctor Schultz charges at her again.

Too late. The second before the loud crack of the revolver, Barb nods at Doctor Schultz. She doesn't care about his approval, of course. He's just an audience for her to take her life in front of. The shot is fired. The 38 is not that powerful, and there is no exit wound. Barb slumps down, and as she does, she lets out her last breath. For Barb and Bill, earthly pain is over.

Pastor Steve bends over Barb and starts whispering the Lord's Prayer. Then the pastor drapes Barb's scarf over her face and head. "They are now together again," he says. "If that's what you believe. Yes, together again." The pastor stands slowly. He is still in shock, and his face is lacking color. Someone helps him into a chair. A few other members of the group are checking on Henry. He is a bit shaken but otherwise unharmed. Several people are crying. Someone has called the police, who are on their way. The small group is down by two members now.

Doctor Schultz sits at the front of the room with his head in his hands. There is blood on his shoes. "I just saw Barb this morning," he says. "I, I didn't realize the depth of her anguish." The doctor looks defeated. Pastor Steve walks over to put his hand upon the doctor's shoulder. Doctor Schultz offers to speak to the whole group or in private with anyone who feels his counsel could be of help.

Henry, who is an ex-military man, calmly lifts the scarf from Barb to inspect the damage she has just inflicted upon herself. The gray carpet has turned crimson around the body. The entrance wound has small bone fragments and flesh protruding from it, and a small bubbling stream of blood continues to run from the injury. Barb's right eye has puffed outward a little. The 380 shell must have gone in at just the right angle to push Barb's gray, now lifeless, eye out of the socket a quarter of an inch or so. Henry is running on autopilot. He has seen many a death in Vietnam. Some from up close, some not.

The following Monday, Henry drives slowly to Doctor Schultz's office. He's driving slowly, and he's distracted, not paying too much attention. Still, when passersby on the sidewalk wave at him in greeting, he politely waves back. He is still in a somber state of mind from the events of the previous week. His wife, Evie, knew Barb. They had founded and ran a women's book club together. This is yet another issue to bring up with the doctor.

Doctor Schultz holds prestigious medical degrees and is board-approved and certified to practice psychotherapy and hypnotherapy. Schulz is also an attorney, when it is convenient for him. Henry Williams's wife, Evelyn, is a patient of Doctor Schultz. She has been consistently treated in the past year for a laundry list of phobias. Evie's agenda seems to grow more significant instead of getting smaller. Henry had been hoping for a quick cure. This coming spring, Henry will be running for the Wisconsin congress. He is an advocate of the Second Amendment and a strong supporter of the Highway 43 project. His wife's condition has thus far been kept under wraps, as it would be considered a weakness in Henry's character. If her issues were exposed, he would sacrifice himself as a true saint to stick with his stricken wife. Yes, indeed, a goddamn saint. Better to keep a lid on it.

Over the past two years, his backers have been focused on what he brings to the table. His opponents as of yet have not dug up the skeletons in his wife's closet. Henry's backers have poured money into his campaign after his promise to push the Highway 43 project through. Big money will be getting bigger. The Highway 43 project will make the landowners close to the route in question very wealthy. Many landowners have poured cash into Henry's campaign fund. Just good business. The majority want the project to go through—state growth and development along Lake Michigan will benefit from it. Not only money but lives are dependent on this highway. Big money requires that the highway go in, or else.

Henry is now close to the doctor's office. It's in a small red-brick building of only four thousand square feet, nestled in the middle of a downtown block. It's flanked on either side by two real estate companies, both promoting mostly vacation properties. The exotic has always been in demand. Parked in front of the building is a vintage BMW from the late '70s. The car announces that the doctor has a large amount of disposable cash, and that he is presently in his office. It's the classic BMW-3 series. The restoration of his office building and his car are both testaments to his success, his resources, and his pedigree. After all, the automobile is not a Ford or Chevy. It is a luxury exotic import.

Henry's favorite parking spot on that block is open. There is a donated park bench with a ten-year-old maple tree next to it. Its leaves are popping in the spring sun. It's midday and the tree is giving shade to the bench and the parking space. Both were donated by the Rotary club, or so people think. The truth is that a donation from Doctor Schultz funded the two items, but he allowed the Rotary club to take credit, as a gesture of his kindness. As the doctor would say, it's just good business.

Henry has always felt that if this parking spot is open, it's a sign of an impending great day. "Yes, sir, a great day," Henry says to himself. Henry is always at least ten minutes early to pick up Evelyn from the doctor's office. It gives him a chance to gossip with the receptionist, Toni. Today's conversation is about the local impact of Highway 43. "Toni, let's agree to disagree. Why would you think that the road will ruin the scenic beauty of the hillside?"

"Henry, there will be hundreds if not thousands of trees removed to make way for your highway! The trees will be lost forever." Toni has read the papers, and that's what it says there.

"But there will be walkways," Henry counters, "park benches, small unique shops, and lakefront properties from Racine to Milwaukee. The revenue from the tax base will allow us to lower property taxes. What do you say to that, dear Toni?" She rolls her brown eyes and lets out a small humph. She knows not to piss off the clients. She turns away from Henry so quickly that her long brown hair spins through the air behind her.

The conversation is over for now.

Doctor Schultz accompanies Evelyn to the waiting room. He a well-tanned, fit-looking man in his early forties, with a dark mane of hair, always overly polite and cordial. He remembers every patient and their spouse by name. The office has an entry waiting room for arrivals and an exiting waiting area for patients who are through with their sessions. The doctor feels that two waiting rooms would better protect his patients' privacy. Doctor Schultz considers himself to be well above average as far as intelligence goes. He also thinks himself a good dresser. It goes with the job and his image, and yes, he is also a bit of a ladies' man. He is one of the wealthiest men in the county, if not the wealthiest one. His office visits are far from cheap, but he promises results that few others can boast of. Patrick Schultz has made timely business decisions. He always seems to be on the right side of every tragedy, and he has been able to profit where others have floundered.

Henry still has time for a quick chat. Talking with the doctor always makes Henry feel better about himself. The doctor reaches out his hand. Henry takes it.

"So good to see you, Doctor," Henry says genuinely.

"My, you are looking fit, Henry," Schultz replies. "We should go for a round of golf someday."

"Doctor, I doubt that I would be any challenge whatsoever." Henry lowers his voice. "Doctor, how is my wife responding?"

"Henry, I feel that we are on the verge of something big. Evelyn is showing great improvement, and I think we will have a breakthrough very soon." Henry notices his wife fussing with her hair in her reflection in the entrance glass door. He is close to telling the doctor that he feels his wife has had no change in months, if she's ever shown any progress at all. He thinks back to the last time he picked up his wife. She fussed with her hair over and over again, just like now. It's like a tic. Possibly it's one of the doctor's tricks to combat a phobia?

The doctor excuses himself and trots out of his office toward his BMW. He is excited he gets to attend a fundraising luncheon to raise funds for his run at the attorney general's office for Wisconsin. Patrick Schultz has held a political office in the past. He was the mayor of a town in the northwestern part of the state, near Minneapolis, across the St. Croix River. The luncheon is being held at Pier 513, just on Second Street. They have a wonderful outdoor patio. This sunny sixty-degree day is a slice of heaven to a northerner.

It's a ten-minute drive for the doctor. He enjoys '80s rock on his Kenwood car stereo. Schultz feels he is on his way to something big. He has already amounted to much more than his horrid, controlling mother told him he ever would. His connections are coming together, his practice is exploding, and he has made money hand over fist. David Lee Roth is singing him to his luncheon. For Patrick Schultz, it doesn't get much better than this.

 The doctor pulls his BMW convertible into the almost-full parking lot. A minute later, a familiar car pulls into the open space to his left. It's Henry and Evelyn Williams, in their 1968 Chevy Chevelle. Henry is very proud of his bright-red Chevelle with black swirl stripes. To him, it is his reward for his hard work and wise investments, and it also represents his support of the American car industry.

Henry is running for the open seat in the state's congress. As the election is drawing closer, one of Henry's concerns is his wife's mental stability. A mental breakdown would lead people to think she is unstable or an alcoholic or a drug user. The press would hang him, and the party would drop him. Doctor Schultz is running on the same party ticket. The doctor is fond of Henry, and he isn't an opponent. The party representatives have already warned him that throwing any dirt toward Henry would be unwise.

The luncheon starts at 1 p.m. As Doctor Schultz and the Williamses enter the restaurant, the crowd stands and applauds. The party hosts expect nothing less. Pier 513 seats close to three hundred and overlooks the St. Croix, with its large motor yachts and the sun making the water shimmer in silver cascades. The view is spectacular. The regional party chairperson, who has placed himself in charge of the affair, is the local mayor, Lance Sheppard. He is the master of ceremonies. He introduces the doctor and the Williams couple. After the enthusiastic applause, the three of them go into the crowd to mingle; they shake hands and greet all the donors and guests. Doctor Schultz and Henry Williams have spent days if not weeks crisscrossing the state, shaking hands and kissing babies in every summer parade and county fair.

Doctor Schultz moves smoothly through the sea of people wanting his attention. He is

basking in the warmth of the large audience. Schultz is never pleased when he has to share his stage and the spotlight, but today he has to tolerate Henry and his showgirl wife.

Henry is a large man with a silver mane. He boasts about being from the working class, a man of the people, thus his Chevelle. He has risen up from the common people, working as a farmer and steelworker. A man approaches Henry and places his hand on Henry's shoulder. The man, who is six-foot-four if not taller, leans into Henry's ear. "Henry, there is a note in your glove box. Be sure to read it." He removes his large hand but stays closer than the candidate might prefer. He continues speaking in a low voice. "I have many investors who want your guarantee that the project will proceed as planned." The man bends to look directly into Henry's face. Both of them keep a deceivingly calm smile upon their faces. "My employers will take the harshest measures against your lovely family if you cannot deliver the project. They want it done, before year's end. Now we both have a deadline. Good luck, Senator. Have a lovely day." The large man places his index finger to his nose. "One more thing, Henry. Other projects are backed up for a decade, just waiting for the announcement of 43. So get your back into that wheel, Henry."

Doctor Schultz is at the opposite end of the hall, smiling and nodding at the appropriate times. A bit later, he slips from the luncheon unnoticed. He is unwilling to share the limelight with Henry. The party would prefer for the two men to work in tandem toward their goals. However, the doctor's ego drives a wedge between him and everyone else on the party's platform.

Two hours later, Henry starts the car engine, then pops open the glove box. Evie sits back in the passenger seat. "What's that?" she asks. He unfolds the small note. "Just a note from a group of supporters." The note reads, Henry, you must back and see the Route 43 project approved. Your wife has lovely hair, doesn't she? Wrapped inside the piece of paper are what appear to be several strands of his wife's blond hair.

CHAPTER SIXTEEN

The doctor drives his BMW with the top down, the sun shining on his face, his hair tousled in the wind. He is enjoying the late-afternoon light on this splendid spring day. He is on his way to his office, where a patient is waiting—Mrs. Samantha Clevenger, the wife of the current speaker of the house, Paul Clevenger. Doctor Schultz is considered to be a heavy hitter, as he knows or treats the upper crust of the political world in the upper Midwest. He has always felt that his time is precious; thus, if he is ever a tad late, that is not a discourtesy, due to his status. The doctor asks Mrs. Clevenger to enter the east treatment room. The room is walled with dark cherrywood and holds an imposing large wooden desk and a desk chair, with two bright-green wingback chairs facing the desk. The walls are decorated with the doctor's many impressive certificates, plus a few enlarged photos of scenery from his many travels. There is also a light-green day bed.

Schultz sits across from Mrs. Clevenger. He holds her

hand as he feels her pulse. It is strong and steady. She is not at all alarmed. Samantha has been to see the doctor several times in the past three months. It seems she is having recurring dreams about assassination attempts on her husband, the house speaker. The dreams began shortly after the election of the current president. Doctor Schultz speaks to Samantha in a calm voice. He asks her to relax and close her eyes. He plays soothing music to put his patient at ease and to allow him to reach deep into her subconscious. Soon she has fallen very deep into a state of relaxation, and the good doctor is able to utter his trigger word and control phrase, which put her in a state of hypnosis. Mrs. Clevenger is a beauty, and he wants to allow himself time to enjoy the pleasures of her lovely, lovely flesh, every last inch of her. Schultz has been overtaken by his fantasies. He must taste her. His hunger is almost stronger than that of a starving child's, and he cannot control it. He wants her for his own, over and over, and he relishes the control that he commands over her.

When the session is through, the doctor simply requests that Mrs. Clevenger not remember what has taken place in the treatment room, except for the peaceful feeling that settles over her following her appointment. That too is activated by the doctor using a certain word, followed by a special phrase. The doctor is fulfilling his need for what he calls his soldiers in the new order. He feels strongly that the time is soon coming to enlist more participants into his following.

***

Doctor Schultz enters the farm store parking lot. He is

greeted by a young, perky clerk, who is removing carts from the spacious lot. Schultz approaches the clerk, whose name is Jerry. He whispers the trigger word, "hummingbird," plus the phrase, "The hummingbird flies against the strong wind." The clerk replies, "I am listening."

"Are you alone?" asks the doctor.

"Yes, completely."

The doctor cannot contain his smile. This is the part that always excites him. The really fun part is yet to come. Schultz instructs the clerk. "I want you to go to the storage lockers at the south edge of town. Locker twenty-one. Here is the combination. From that locker, pick up the PSA-AR rifle. Also take four ammunition clips, plus two grenades, then come back here to your workplace. Leave no one alive. Even that simpleton who should be here at 3 p.m. bagging groceries. Then—this is imperative!—following the slaughter here, hurry to the city administrating building. Kill anyone who is in the building and who gets in your way. Lastly, shove the two grenades into your trousers. Kill yourself and all who are around you. My dear, simple Jerry, know I loved you the best of my minions."

"Nothing will interfere with this," Jerry confirms.

"You will do this promptly at 3 p.m. today. Do you understand?"

"Yes, fully."

***

The clock tower chimes three times. Now begins the part of his job Doctor Schultz really enjoys. He speaks to himself, Oh, the tears, the constant questions, the poor sheep sobbing on their knees, asking why again, why here. He was such a nice guy, Little League coach and all. Always expecting the police to keep them safe. What a bunch of crap. A man has to protect his own.

Three p.m. The sound of automatic gunfire is broadcast through the air over the small town, with occasional screams of terror and screeching tires coming from the direction of the town center. Wisps of smoke rise from the administration building. Sirens wail from the response vehicles. The gunfire rings out for a full ten minutes or more. The sheriff's car tears into the farm store parking lot. The sheriff yells, "Jerry, get the hell inside, someone's..." The sheriff is never allowed to finish his warning. Doctor Schultz is still in the lot too, and the deputy yells at him, "Doc, get the hell out of here!" The sheriff's car is next to the store's entrance.

Doctors Schultz is like an arsonist. He must always watch. He is drawn to the violence, and that's why he hasn't left the parking lot. He may have to tie up any loose ends. Mixed with the screams of terror is the occasional sound of the young clerk changing clips. In the end Jerry will have to take a bullet or two. He has cut down his coworkers, and then, as instructed, he is off to kill the workers at the city administration building. The police in the small northern town are ill equipped to handle the advanced firepower. In all, twenty lives are taken, including the clerk, who has killed everyone in the courthouse. It takes six police rounds to make the clerk drop to the ground. Four deputy sheriffs surround the heavily wounded assassin. With their guns drawn, they stand glaring down at the dying clerk. He is lying on the floor of the town hall, with two lumps protruding from the pockets of his pants. The clerk now has an audience: four officers of the law, plus a few workers and citizens. Even though the offices warn the crowd to disband, as with a train wreck, they cannot look away. Watching the clerk's death are EMTs, deputies, and two City Council members who have had the misfortune of being at City Hall at that hour. With them is a visiting senator from the state capitol in Madison, who represents the western part of the state. There is already much speculation who the targets of this attack are, or whether this is a case of someone who has just made one too many milkshakes for the kids. Finally, the young clerk from the farm store is shot down by a state police sharpshooter with a bullet to the center of his back. Doctor Schultz is giddy. He fancies himself a mastermind from a Bond movie.

The next morning, the doctor reads the news headlines. He sits his coffee down next to his paper, then goes to the sink and splashes water onto his face. He then slowly raises his eyes to the mirror to look at his own face, with a Cheshire cat smile broad upon it. He thinks that he has helped himself and Williams at the same time. For one, an obstacle for the highway project has been eliminated, all by a simple grocery clerk who, for a short time, was a weapon of the flock. Schultz does not enjoy helping a competitor, even when he himself has benefitted by his act, but, as they say, the enemy of my enemy and all that.

The local television channel has an emergency news broadcast. "This is a sad day," the reporter proclaims. "We are reporting once again from the scene of yet another senseless tragedy right here in St. Croix County, for the second time in as many weeks. Congressman Schmitt was gunned down in yesterday's tragic rampage, along with nineteen other victims. He has been a staunch opponent to Second Amendment rights and to the controversial Route 43 project. Left behind are the families and friends of the victims, but as of yet, there are no answers."

***

The doctor sees himself as a chosen one. His parents insisted he attend the finest universities. On Sundays his father would spare the family church services and recite to young Patrick his beliefs of the family's supremacy. He had spoken with great fervor of their family's dominance and calling to lead the weak in the flock, and of the Schultzes' deserved right to be at the front of the pack, always in charge. Patrick was raised to be tough, to show no emotion. His mother would break bamboo sticks across his back. He would be hit again and again. When he was young and would let out a cry, his father would extinguish his cigarette on young Patrick's back and arms. Patrick had learned quickly to not let a peep escape his lips. To his knowledge, he had never known or befriended a common person. Commoners had nothing to offer the doctor.

Now he is back in his office. Mrs. Clevenger is here for another appointment. As before, the doctor asks her to relax and close her eyes. He plays soothing music, and at the right moment, he speaks the trigger word and the control phase, and she is completely under his control. His hunger has grown well past the mere pleasures of the flesh. He knows that carnal desire is a weakness. Yes, a weakness. His mother would crack a cane against his back to make him stronger. Even now Schultz can feel the stick cracking against his back. Yes, mother, I am stronger and better. Yes, I am better.

This is all part of the doctor's plan. He is growing his flock, like those before him: Jones, Manson, Crane. Soon his name will be spoken alongside theirs. He has a plan for Mrs. Clevenger too. He will use her to off her husband, the house speaker, who is a major opponent to the highway project. The doctor is gleeful at the thought of the wealth that will come to him when the project is complete.

When the appointment is over, the doctor requests that Mrs. Clevenger not remember anything from her session. Her husband will die tonight. Schultz will call Mrs. Clevenger and activate her. Another tragedy will be in the papers and on television.

At 9 p.m. that night, Schultz phones Mrs. Clevenger. He speaks slowly and with a firm tone. "The snow falls."

"Yes, I am here," she replies.

"The trees fade into the fog. Are you alone?"

"Yes, I am," she confirms.

"Make love to your husband," Schultz commands. "While doing so, drive a knife through his ribs and kill him. After he takes his final breath, take your own life by cutting your wrists. Do you understand?"

"Yes, completely."

Doctor Schultz hangs up the phone with a smile.

CHAPTER SEVENTEEN

A young dark-haired woman arrives at Doctor Schultz's office. His perky, organized receptionist greets her. "Hello, do you have an appointment?"

"Sorry, no. I was a patient of Doctor Schultz's in Chicago, some time ago. Could you please ask if the doctor could squeeze me in?"

"Your name, please?"

"I'm Sabrina." The young receptionist, Toni, feels a chill travel up her spine. It pricks the hairs on her neck. She cannot tell if it's the odd accent that Sabrina speaks in, or the peculiar way she carries herself. It is as if she were speaking to death itself.

"I will ask. Please wait a moment." Toni goes in to speak to Doctor Schultz and returns momentarily. "The doctor said yes, he has time. Please come this way."

The slender, dark-haired Sabrina sits patiently as the doctor adjusts his hair and tie outside the door. He soon follows her into the room. "Sabrina, oh, it is so nice to see you."

She stands and the two exchange a polite handshake. "What can I do for you?" he asks.

Sabrina looks at the doctor with a deep sadness and desperation in her eyes. There is also pain inscribed on her face, not a physical pain but emotional pain from her memories.

"Those dreams from years ago are back," she says. "Do you remember the dreams? About being pursued by a man with a knife..." She trails off.

"Yes, I remember. You felt the only way out of the dream was to kill your pursuer or take your life. And as I remember, you took your life with some flair in your dream."

"Doctor, the dream is the same. Except, I now capture the knife-wielding assailant and I dismember him, piece by piece."

"Sabrina, you look fabulous. Facing your villain in your dream seems to have worked. Why have you come to see me today?"

"Doctor, I am struggling to calm all the voices in my head." As she is in an armchair, Sabrina's head is tilted slightly upward. Her coal-black hair is falling over her dark brown eyes and her nose. She glances up at the doctor through her hair. Doctor Schultz stoops down so he is eye level to his patient. He looks into her eyes, however, he cannot tell if there is a person looking back at him. And if there is, whom? He stands and goes to his four-drawer file cabinet. He looks briefly through the top drawer, pulls out Sabrina's file, and flips through the pages. Then he turns back to her. "Let me talk to Sabrina, please," he says. In past appointments, she had exhibited many unique personalities. She had even become a case study for split-personality disorders throughout Midwestern universities.

Sabrina continues to tilt her head and whispers, "There is no Sabrina here. Not at all. Only Celeste."

"Let me speak to Sabrina, Celeste. I notice a new tattoo upon your shoulder. I thought you disliked tattoos, Sabrina?" As the doctor circles his patient, he puts his hand on her bare shoulder.

"I do. That dirty tramp Rachel"—she turns to touch the tattoo herself—"with her promiscuous ways! She got me drunk, and just look at it. Such a gaudy clown face. She calls it Chicklets. What a terrible name, and what a horrible-looking clown! More monster than clown! She is such a tramp. Tattoos, sex, out all night, doing whatever she pleases with whomever she pleases. A true whore, I say."

"Sabrina, I KNOW you are in there. You are hiding, aren't you? Come out, come out, wherever you are!"

Sabrina is still responding as Celeste. She is playful yet disturbing. Inside her is also a dark and sinister personality called Ezra Kobb. The doctor keeps talking, trying to persuade Sabrina to come out without waking Ezra.

Sabrina blinks several times and then her eyes refocus. "Sabrina has come back," she says and releases a giggle. "Yes, I am here, Doctor." Still giggling, Sabrina flips her hair behind her right ear. "Doctor, who was that mean hag of a woman outside who wouldn't let me see you right away?"

"Sabrina, that woman is my part-time receptionist; her name is Toni, and she was just doing her job."

"But, Doctor, I really needed to see you right away. Doctor, you do remember how grateful I can be, don't you."

"Sabrina, I just spoke to you."

"If you say so, Doc. But I ain't buying it. How could you forget, Doctor!"

"Sabrina, are you in there?"

"Give me a kiss, Doc. That will bring me around, I swear." She stands, not bothering to pull her skirt down. The doctor allows himself to lean in, just for a little taste. She pulls him close. She kisses him with force and bites his bottom lip. He pulls away, wiping his mouth with his sleeve. A thin streak of blood is now on his sleeve.

"Dammit, Sabrina, not here, not now."

"Yes here, yes now. Come on, Doc, take a look, won't you? Don't you like what I have brought for you?"

Doctor Schultz backs away toward his desk. Sabrina is in close pursuit. Schultz reaches his call button, alerting the receptionist to interrupt with a grave emergency.

"Sabrina, why are you here?"

"Patrick, I am here for you. You remember what fun I can be, Doc." Sabrina sits directly in front of Doctor Schultz. She caresses the doctor's chin while she scoots to the edge of her chair, exposing much too much of her thighs. Toni interrupts with the made-up emergency, and, with her help, the doctor is able to shift Sabrina from her chair and lead her toward the exit. Sabrina is resisting and she's close to volatile screaming. "Dammit, Doctor, you can't get rid of me."

They are outside now. The bar across the street empties to watch the screaming match. A crowd forms, with drinks in hand. Doctor Schultz has both of his hands on Sabrina's shoulders, doing his best to calm her. Toni tries to sneak past her boss and the patient. She reaches toward Sabrina, wanting to calm her. Sabrina notices a hand in her vision. "You won't touch me!" she screams. "Do you know who I am? Trollop! I can and will see you crushed, begging for me to kill you to end your suffering!"

Doctor Schultz runs to get between Sabrina and Toni. "And you, so-called doctor. You're a quack! I'll get you and your dog too," Sabrina says with flair, her eyes wide with rage. The bar crowd lets out a cheer at that threat, and Sabrina only just notices the audience gathered in front of the bar. She does love to perform. She shoves Schultz back away from her and marches toward the crowd, who are enjoying the late-afternoon show. Sabrina goes inside and sits at the bar, with her legs crossed tight and her skirt hiking up close to heaven. She is a sight to see. Much prettier than the local sodbusters, the factory workers, and the unemployed.

Schultz, having been embarrassed enough, quickly goes back to his office. He locks the doors and tidies up after the fracas. He loves a good show even if he cannot completely control the outcome. Schultz stands at his window. After making sure that his employee is safely in her car, Schultz takes in the view of the southern sky and the faraway hillside. Dark clouds are coming in. A heavy storm is quickly approaching over the hillside. The sky looks as if it is about to open and engulf the small town and whirl it all the way to Kansas.

The afternoon has quickly turned black, and the street lights are now on. A high howling wind pushes all manner of debris to bash against the storefronts. It starts raining. Young receptionist Toni, in her ancient Datsun 280Z, drives through the alleyway past the bars. Something slams into the passenger door. Toni, fearing the worst, stops to check what she has just hit. She exits her auto. The wind and the heavy rain push Toni back toward her car, then she feels a terrible pain in her kidney. Toni doubles over. The storm water is flowing in a torrent past her, now with a red stream mixing with the rain. Was this blood from the pain in her back, or from what her frail Datsun had struck? The pain drives the young receptionist to her knees.

Within seconds, Toni is lying flat on her back in the alley, water rushing onto her face. Suddenly there is Sabrina, standing right over the stunned office worker. "I told you I will fuck you up," she says. Toni finds strength in herself she didn't know she possessed to pull herself up, using the small yellow Datsun for support. The tethers of pain are holding her in place.

"Here I am, you mental piece of shit!" Toni yells out. The pain now spreads along her back, as Sabrina climbs onto the Datsun, her four-inch knife exposed. Toni is not backing down. She is now standing on her own. Sabrina dives from atop the Datsun at Toni's shoulders, pushing both of them onto the paved alleyway. Sabrina is in command of the fight. Her arms are around Toni's waist, squeezing the air from her lungs. Sabrina bites a piece of Toni's ear off, then holds the piece of flesh in her teeth. She smiles a bloody smile. The young receptionist receives a huge adrenaline rush at the sight of her own ear. Toni manages to gain purchase and she drives Sabrina over and over into the blacktop, until Sabrina's grip finally breaks. Sabrina swings her knife and slices into Toni's back once again. Toni refuses to just lie there and die. She rolls to her stomach, alleviating some of the pain, then slowly gets up. Sabrina stands too, and they are face to face, both squaring off, one not willing to die, the other determined to strike revenge at her young victim. Weak from her wounds, Toni falls back against the rear door of the nearest bar, which falls open. She is now inside, on the bar's hardwood beer-soaked floor.

CHAPTER EIGHTEEN

Doctor Schultz pulls up in front of his office. As he gets out of the car, he is drawn to a noise across the street. Someone screams for help. He runs over to find Sabrina lying on the sidewalk, with her right arm reaching into the air for a savior. She is a beautiful damsel in distress, battle-worn and soaked with rain. The doctor takes her arm and helps her to her feet. He looks her up and down. "Sabrina, what happened? Are you injured?" She doesn't respond, and the doctor guides her toward his office. Sabrina places her arms around his neck, and while they are still in the windswept street, she pulls the doctor into a passionate embrace.

Inside, Doctor Schultz guides her to the office with the lovely day bed. He helps her to lie down, with her head on the armrest. The doctor kisses Sabrina with passion. The great news he has just been presented with only enhances his passion. Sabrina is a tigress after her prey. The two have had visions of this for some time. She quickly undresses, as does the doctor. They make love as the storm rages on outside. The wind slams torrents of rain against the large panes of glass. As the two drive each other to a rhythmic climax, the sound of the gale provides a backdrop to the couple's lust.

Without warning, Sabrina starts to scream and bang her head back and forth, as if the air is her enemy. She starts slapping the doctor and scratching at his back until it beads with blood. The doctor has not witnessed a transformation such as this. In a heightened state of arousal, he continues to drive Sabrina to a new level of ecstasy. The doctor does not notice the prick to his throat, but he feels something wet upon his neck. Is it sweat? blood? saliva? A hairpin is being pressed against his throat. Schultz rolls Sabrina onto her back and continues the rhythmic rocking until she is sent to yet another orgasmic state. "Doctor!" she screams. Schultz removes the deadly hairpin from Sabrina's grip and drops it to the floor, where it bounces off with a faint tinkle. The rhythmic rocking continues until both are spent and fall asleep.

In the morning the doctor is woken up by Sabrina's screams. She is now shivering, shining in sweat. Her features seem leaner. There are ripples on her stomach and veins showing on her forearms and biceps. Her pupils dilate. She starts screaming at the doctor. "Who are you? Why am I here? You're one of her lovers, aren't you! I will kill you, just as I did your lover! I cut her into tiny bits for the fish." She rummages in her clothes, then leans toward the doctor, holding a leather-handled, four-inch knife in her right hand. She slices at her left forearm. "Look here, lover. I bleed for you." She places her forearm to her mouth then over the doctor's waist. Her blood drips slowly on him. "Now, it will be your turn."

The doctor has backed away from her to his desk, where he looks for something in the top drawer. She dives at him, lashing madly back and forth with the razor-sharp blade but missing him.

"Sabrina, calm down," he tries to placate her. He places a small tablet into his mouth, then locks Sabrina into an embrace, and passes the pill into her mouth with a kiss. "This will help you to calm down," he says. She holds onto his wrist and drives the small knife into his meaty forearm. Blood flows like a stream from the doctor's arm.

Sabrina's breathing slows. She is enjoying the blood flow, and squeals in pleasure. The color of her cheeks begins to transform from pale to rosy, just as the doctor is losing color. She is in a dreamy state now, calm and very susceptible to the doctor's words. "Sabrina, I would love you to join me on my island, just a small hop on my plane." Schultz wraps his forearm in a bandage to stop the bleeding.

"Doctor, you know how my fear of flying bothers me."

"Here, Sabrina, this tablet will take your fear away. It is a combination of meth and heroin, completely safe, my dear. It will help ease your fear. I have hundreds of hours in the air. Relax, my dear, all is well." Sabrina is very pliable at the moment. The doctor has been waiting for the proper moment to introduce the trigger words and phrase.

He helps her get dressed, then the two of them go out to his car. He drives the short few blocks to the launchpad where he keeps his private plane. As they approach the vessel, Sabrina tries to pull her arm from his gentle grasp. "Sabrina, stop pulling away, everything will be fine." She relaxes again.

They are now on the plane. The doctor guides Sabrina to a seat and speaks to her. "Sabrina, relax. Deeper, deeper. You will let me into the deep chambers of your mind." She closes her eyes, and he bends closer to her ear. "When you hear the phrase 'The snow falls early this year,' followed by the word 'red,' you will be completely committed to the order that I shall give you. I will give you directions, which you will follow without question. You will not remember this discussion or being with me today."

Ten minutes later, the doctor starts the engines powering his twin-engine Cessna. The sun is high in the clear sky. The heavy rains have washed the land clean.

***

Doctor Schultz has a visitor at his office—a man who wants to speak to him. He introduces himself as Wilhelm Krause.

"Sir, by your accent, I would say you are not a local," Doctor Schultz replies. "What is it that brings you here to the heartland of the USA? Why do you need to speak with me?"

"You are right, Doctor. I have just arrived from Berlin. May we go somewhere for a cold drink, so I may explain what has brought me here?" The two men walk just a block to the south and across the street to a small bistro. They sit at one of the tented outdoor tables.

"Doctor Schultz," Wilhelm begins, "I also study and practice psychotherapy and hypnosis. I have come to you as a representative of an organization of therapists who feel that we may have the same interests in mind. We would like to invite you to join our team." Wilhelm moves a bit closer. "We have in place 150 men and women who are ready at a moment's notice to strike as we wish."

Schultz sits back in his chair. A broad grin spreads upon his face. "Wilhelm, how is it you have come specifically to me?"

"You are modest, Doctor. I have studied your work and feel we have the same vision for the future. We will offer great wealth for your compliance and loyalty. You must understand that this can never be spoken of." The doctor continues to hold a broad grin. His mind is spinning with dreams of wealth, like a child before Christmas.

Wilhelm slides an envelope across the table for the doctor's inspection. He studies the envelope's contents. "What's this?" he asks.

"This is the deed to your island!"

"Island, I like the sound of that."

"And here are the keys to your new island house. All that is needed is your signature. Come now, Doctor. You expected money, but that's so simple, cliché, as it were. Those are the keys to the Eagle's Nest—a manor built high upon the tallest hilltop of the island. A manor of great beauty and with magnificent views, like you have never seen." Wilhelm places his hand on the doctor's left shoulder. The doctor does so dislike being pawed at. The gesture is also uncommon for Wilhelm, as German men are raised with a cold practicality when it comes to business interactions.

"Wilhelm, tell me more about your cause?"

"Yes, Doctor. My organization has inflicted damage and change worldwide. You have seen it even in your country: New York, Florida, Las Vegas, Chicago, California. And of course, Doctor, the two tragedies in Minnesota and Wisconsin, which I think you were involved in. There's also France, England, Canada. I could go on and on. All for the gain of the preferred few. The people scream, Poor us! They fear terrorism from outside, but the threat shall come from within. Not from abroad or from little green men unleashed upon the masses, but from friends and neighbors. The change will come in small increments, so subtle that most will not notice the difference until it is happening."

Wilhelm leans in closer, his eyes now piercing. "Doctor, the fortunes of the chosen few have significantly increased. Your fortune shall explode as time marches forward. I know you have seen what one or two men can do when they are inspired. Imagine what can be accomplished by an army of two hundred with laser-focused purpose and unwavering belief in a cause. A cause from which nothing and no one can distract the soldiers. Doctor, your service will be necessary to the cause. You have complete control of the men and women who have been inspired into service. Each small faction will be considered a flock."

Wilhelm rises and holds out a small jewelry box. "Doctor, a gift for you. A ring with three rubies shaped into a triangle, to signify the three phases of the flock." He raises his glass. "To the flock." The two men drink, and with that, Wilhelm excuses himself.

***

When he leaves the bistro, the doctor is ready to

explode with excitement. He must tell someone. Someone he trusts.

Brrrt, brrrt.

"Evelyn, the snow falls early this year."

"Yes, Doctor, I am alone."

"Evelyn, I must see you at my office now!"

The tall brunette arrives at Doctor Schultz's office at the same time as he does. He strides toward her and places his arms around her waist, then recites the words to place Evelyn under his spell. He has always wanted to taste Evelyn's passion. The time has come.

The sun has begun to set behind the buildings across the street. Doctor Schultz guides Evelyn to a room at the back of his office that is decorated as a deluxe motel suite. The doctor whispers his commands to Evelyn. She stands in front him, slips her dress to the floor, and climbs upon the Alaskan king bed. She begins a seductive dance, to music that only she can hear in her head. In the corner of the room, the doctor has placed a discreet camcorder, hidden in the book shelving. Doctor Schultz loves the games he plays, and more so if he has a video to remember his conquests by. In times of boredom or nostalgia, he will cherish a viewing.

***

Two hours have passed since Evelyn left her husband, Henry, downtown at another fundraising event. Henry has just finished saying his thank-yous and farewells to the crowd that has given funds to the campaign. He wonders where Evelyn dashed off to with barely a word. He has long suspected that she's been hiding something from him. On several occasions she has come to him with messed-up makeup and hair, without being able to explain what she'd been up to. He has his own suspicions.

The Chevy engine roars to life. Henry's mind is swimming with doubt and suspicion. There is very little traffic on the road to the southeast of the St. Croix, so he pushes the gas pedal closer to the floor. His Chevelle is now going eighty, then ninety, then a hundred. There is no law to stand in Henry's way to justice.

In fifteen minutes, Henry is glaring at his wife's car parked next to Doctor Schultz's BMW. His suspicions are justified then! Henry has the sudden urge to kill them both. Henry flips his gold coin. Heads: he kills them both. Tails: he kills them both, but remotely. Tails it is. With just a little help from a pipe cutter, both of their brake lines should give way if tested. Henry then pulls to the hilltop overlooking the downtown area and the doctor's office, and he waits.

Just an hour later the doctor leaves his office and gets in his car. At the west side of town, the Chevelle appears in the doctor's rearview mirror. Doctor Schultz instantly knows who is behind him. The doctor accelerates to well past one hundred. His arrogance is exactly what Henry is counting on. Henry suspects that Evelyn may have had little control over committing an act of infidelity.

The game has begun. Henry is close to pushing the doctor's car. However, though he is filled with rage, he backs off the Chevelle. It is not built for high-speed corners. But on a thirty-mile straightaway, that Chevelle could run the BMW right into the ground.

Having lost his pursuer, the doctor hits the brakes. Henry's quick work on the BMW has done exactly as he had wished. The brakes are soft, and the BMW seems to accelerate rather than slow down. As if it were on a sheet of ice, the car climbs onto yet another hill. As the sun sets, the doctor is unable to slow or stop the BMW, and the car is launched off the railroad hill from a glorious height.

The BMW lands safely, then slides to a stop twelve rows into the cornfield. The doctor could be dead. He should be dead. However, he has a knack for avoiding such things. Doctor Schultz trips and crawls his way to the road next to the cornfield, covered in mud and small cuts from the corn leaves. Henry's smile fades as he sees Schultz coming out of the field. Henry jams on the brakes with a dramatic sideways turn, and the Chevelle slides to a stop. Henry wrestles with the idea. Run the doctor over? Who would know? He would. Henry is many things, but a cold-blooded killer he is not.

The doctor limps onto the empty road. The crows circle above him and cackle with excitement. He sees Henry's red Chevelle. The doctor stands proudly in the center of the road and gives Henry a two-fingered salute, with an upward push for effect. Henry watches from his driver's door. His evil Grinch-like grin gradually fades. A convertible with loose brakes and a broken safety belt should have been the death of the good doctor, but it wasn't. He dodged a bullet yet again.

PART THREE:
THE ISLAND

CHAPTER NINETEEN

He needs to make the five-hour drive up to Superior. He has a big day planned for tomorrow. No rest. As he drives, he is smiling. He had just purchased the retreat lodge from the Luchks. Now it's his island retreat. He is ready to start his new life. Look at all the sheep for shearing, he thinks.

Doctor Schultz's body is not found in that lonesome cornfield.

That day, he leaves behind his practice in the small northern town. Henry hears that the doctor has bought a small island on Lake Superior. The purchase gets the doctor all the unincorporated land. Two hundred and fifty acres of trees and hills. All the vacant buildings are part of the sale, including the retreat lodge.

Evelyn makes it home that day just before the sunset. She fusses with her hair and makeup as she looks at her reflection. When Henry gets home, she makes them both tea. They sit together, hand in hand, on their west-facing deck, enjoying the last bit of sun for the day. Henry does not confront Evelyn about his suspicions. He makes an appointment for a mechanic to look at her brakes. "You can never be too careful," he says.

CHAPTER TWENTY

"I own all the buildings on the island, and I want this one to be the largest of them all," Doctor Schultz says. "It will be a place for worship. I want a grand white steeple with an arched ceiling. Spare no expense. The whole thing needs to be remodeled. Would you be interested, and if so, when would you be able to begin on it?"

The oldest of the construction men glances around at his coworkers. "We need to finish the plumbing for the restrooms first. The owner said, screw it, he wants no walls or roof. It will be unique, to say the least. We should be finished here in one week, sir."

"Rubbish. I need a team to begin tomorrow. Is that understood? A whole team, to start tomorrow. I will make it worth your while, and I will compensate the owner of this... whatever you call it."

Doctor Schultz walks away from the roped-off bar through the green grass and back to his future office and ministries. He smiles slightly. There are many things to be done. The first order is to hire some top help for his office. He has read about the families who live like badgers deep within the hills on this island.

Two days pass. Doctor Schultz puts on his sidearm in preparation for a leisurely walk through the hillside. He is in search of the people who live underground. On day two, the doctor finds what remains of the population once believed to be a thousand strong. Now only two hundred call the hills their home. Many things have led to the hill people's decreased numbers. Their dirt homes are substandard, even by one-hundred-year-old standards. Holes are dug into the hillside as entrances. Some homes have wood adjacent to the entrance, to be removed on a sunny summer day. The residents are covered with dirt and mud. Their hair is wild and flying free in all directions. When the hill people first meet Doctor Schultz, they consider him so beautiful and kind that there is no doubt his intentions must be pure. Doctor Schultz baits the hill people to his ministry with warm food and clean clothes, and the promise of a new future. They haven't even dreamed of such a thing as a warm bath with a fragrance. But they have come, and that is the beginning of his plan. Many locals feel that the doctor is a saint, and that he is doing all this for the good of his fellow men. But is he?!

The doctor knows when the funeral for Senator Heart will be: Thursday at 1 p.m. He knows where: St. Andrew's Catholic Church. How lovely that they will all be gathered on Thursday.

Doctor Schultz has gathered three of his flock. Bart's grandfather had designed chemical attack weapons for the U.S. Army. He has passed on much of his knowledge to his eager-to-learn grandson. "Men, you will receive $250,000 now and the same if you are successful. Bert, you must by Tuesday have three working cocktails, each enough to fill a room forty feet by forty feet. You will fly my twin engine tomorrow to Truax airfield in southern Wisconsin." Doctor Schultz opens a to-scale drawing of the building in question. He hands each man a backpack with a chemical-grade gas mask, three feet of chain, a lock, and a 9mm with an extended clip. He leaves the men to prepare.

Bert retreats to the basement of the doctor's church to mix his cocktails. Boron trichloride, cellular nitrite, and cyanogen chloride. The mix should burn their lungs and eyes in a matter of seconds. Bert places into a cylinder, with an activator that will open a valve to allow the burning, unbreathable gas to escape and fill the room. Any person who lasts thirty seconds is an Olympian.

At noon on Thursday, August 15, the normally vacant St. Andrew's church is standing-room only. Close to three hundred people have gathered to pay their respects to Senator Heart. They line the walls of the small blond-brick church. The church's cherrywood trim will today become the trim for a large casket.

At precisely 1:10 p.m., the doctor's men glance at one another. Gary and Dean stand up and, with their heads bowed, walk slowly to the back of the church. Gary picks up the pace, as if he no longer wants to be a part of the plan. To the left and right of the church doors are their backpacks, tucked behind the statues of the Virgin Mary and St. Joseph. No one pays particular attention to them. Who would want to harm a church? The men thread the chain through the sturdy door handles and lock the chain together. The doors can now open only an inch or so. The church will soon be a mausoleum.

Meanwhile, Bert has exited through the rear of the church, through the basement. He has placed his cylinder next to the HVAC system. Two other cylinders are placed under the benches at the rear of the church. One is behind the kneeling station near the senator's head. The three men are now outside, and each presses a key fob that looks like a car key but is in fact a remote control release for the gas cylinders.

The time is 1:15 p.m. From each of the cylinders, the gas begins to exit into the air. The mist rises, as gas does. One by one the crowd starts coughing and gripping their throats, as if that would stop the fire reaching into their lungs. Their eyes tear and their noses flow with snot. The priest upon the altar, engaged in his somber task, notices his church members coughing and gasping. The crowd transforms into a herd that charges toward the rear exit. Kachung, kachung is the sound emitting from the chained doors, as the chain spread and hold.

The doctor watches all this through a video camera hidden in the flowers, which broadcasts the carnage. Schultz is looking at the screen with glee. He has been paid to eliminate the opposition to Route 43 and other non-forward-thinking resistance. The casino money, the lake money, all are getting what they paid for this day. The casino if built in or nearby Milwaukee would increase highway traffic ten-fold. Later that afternoon a news reporter will announce: "Gone is Senator Heart. Gone with him Congressman Wade, and senators Smith and Wadell, all Ivy League graduates and opponents to the Route 43 project. The casino money needed to ensure that the highway would be put in. The attack would eliminate opposition to the interstate. All government buildings are on high alert."

One by one, people in the crowd fall to their knees. Men reach for their wives, women for their children. Their lungs fill with fire. It's like a gas attack during the First World War rendered in the horrid trenches.

At 3 p.m. the doctor is sitting with his three men. Bert, Gary, and Dean are ready to have their boss praise them for the fine job they have done. Doctor Schultz raises a glass of red wine to them. "You have done us all a great service." He slowly walks behind the men, touching his hand upon each of their shoulders. The doctor needs to make an example. An example that will be passed on down the line. "I was told that one of you exited the building before the job was through." The doctor stands behind Gary. "The numbers for our cause continue to grow. For it to be able to proceed well into the next century, I must be able to trust my flock when I hand out a project. Trust is all we have. So, before we raise a glass to toast to our success..." The doctor reaches for a heavy decorative wooden bat. He bashes Gary on the back of his head. One, two, four times. With each blow the doctor lets out horrible huffing sounds. The bat drips with blood, bone, and bits of skin and hair. Doctor Schultz stands fully erect, not even breathing harder than normal. He holds the blood-covered bat in his right hand and points its tip at each of the other two men. "The portion which was to be Gary's is now yours. Raise a glass to our victory. Small-town America, so small, so weak. The police and media scream terrorism, again. As if big players are at all concerned with rural America. It is where we build our fortunes."

CHAPTER TWENTY-ONE

Doctor Schultz has created his first small business venture on the island. With his help and guidance, the Watsons have established a printing service in one of the small building. He's taught five of the hill people how to use Word and Excel, and how to work the heavy printing presses proficiently. Soon they are printing leaflets and flyers explaining and promoting his religion, which he has brought to the island. They are all singing the praises of the church: "Die Kirche von Dir!"

Doctor Schultz's father, Heinrich Schultz, was the founder of one of the churches founded in the early 1930s in Germany. The Reich was not against religion per se. It just had to be their religion. Doctor Schultz's religion is based on the belief that you are the most important being on this earth. Many religions speak of a god not seen. In contrast, Doctor Schultz's religion deals with the belief that you and only you can change your life if you are willing to take the leap. The parishioners should help each other so they can all live a richer life. To become a member, you need to be sponsored in order to be fully introduced into the church. Once accepted into the church, you owe a portion of your livelihood to the church until your death, plus lifelong loyalty.

Schultz invites church members to come to the island to aid him in recruiting and teaching. On July 1, the doctor is joined by three members of the Watson family: Demetri, Rachel, and Alex.

June 3, 6 p.m. Doctor Schultz prepares for his first island mass. Warm food is served at 5 p.m. The old building is not quite finished, but the doctor is impatient to get his branch of the church started.

There are sixty people in attendance. The average age appears to be late forties, minus the children. The majority are from the island. The men are gruff-looking, with well-worn clothes. While some of the women are attractive, all need to be attended to.

The doctor takes his place on the stage at the front of the building. He cuts a stunning figure. He's dressed in a dark suit, hair combed back, perfect posture. A true showman. The Watsons have been placed strategically at the doors to thank and greet the parishioners.

Doctor Schultz begins. "We all believe in the God above. Yes, we do!" At that he and the Watsons clap their hands once. "Clap! And just like that, the good lord can end your life. Clap! Yes, my friends—you could be gone in a heartbeat! You would have spent your life in poverty and sorrow, with no help from the God above, your savior! I tell you, no more. That's true. No more. Hand over your love, friendship, and faith in your future to the flock." Schultz is now walking among the parishioners. He places his hand on the cheeks of the children, on the hands of the men and women. He looks deep into their eyes. Another loud clap. "Yes, one year from now, you will be standing right beside me. No longer living burrowed into the ground." He points to the east. "Living, yes, living there where you have always belonged. Join me now, children, and let us begin the journey. Let's begin with that first step. These three right here." The Watson family stand up in the front row. "You know them," the doctor continues, "they have lived here on this island alongside you. They have made the choice to be better. To no longer live in shame and scorn from the rest of the world, your oppressors. I have taught them the craft of the written word by use of the word press. As we wrap up today's visit, I want you all to say to yourselves that you're not gonna take it anymore! From this day forward, you, my parishioners, will have your arms in the air reaching to the sky. And say this aloud: Happiness is my God-given right."

Doctor Schultz and the Watson children confer with the parishioners for hours, answering questions and offering flyers to those who are curious. They have increased the flock from five to thirty-five. Schultz has retained the assistance of three siblings who had been college professors but are looking for a new religion. Truth, they call it. Truth.

Schultz gathers his small team into his office to discuss step two toward reaching his goal. "John, Abby, Paul—you three will begin teaching the flock. It is imperative that they all know how to read and write. Most of these poor souls cannot read at a third-grade level. They have been forgotten. I am committed to making the church a powerful institution in our Northwoods. I will be purchasing the ferry line. The church will control who comes and goes to the island. Paul, you will be training six followers to safely navigate the ferry through the open waters of Superior. Start the training tomorrow."

"To what end, sir?" Paul asks.

"We will control the comings and goings of our island community, plus we will charge $35 each way, day in and day out." Paul stands to leave, following John and Abby, who are waiting for him by the door.

By mid-July the ferry team is in place, and after that Paul is put in charge of a certain fundraising endeavor. He is one of the first islanders to be given responsibility. He is truly eager to please the doctor, because he wants it all: the money, the education, the touch of a beautiful woman. Yes, the doctor tells him, he can and will have it all.

For the church, Paul recruits a team of ten young, strong believers. He is now the doctor's right hand. On July 17, Doctor Schultz meets with the women on the team, Robin, Annette, and Velma. They are to work at the oldest profession there is. At night the ferry will travel to the mainland and the women will slither up to the bars and the casino. The women, who are all beautiful, have been trained and prepped by Rachel Watson, who has given them a crash course in refinement. They have been selected by the doctor himself—he wants to ensure that each carries a desire to bring pleasure to men and to acquire a great deal of wealth. The women are not to work with locals; tourists only, to be chosen via an online questionnaire given out by the motel.

"How will a questionnaire select the johns, Doctor?" Velma asks.

"Good question, dear Velma. On the motel's website,

there is a questionnaire that the men will think enters them into a drawing for a prize. And, in a way, it does. We will choose your targets among them, based on their answers to questions that reveal their personality, fantasies, and wealth. Men with deep pockets, men who all have a great deal to lose."

This is all to take place at the oldest motel on the mainland. The church has paid a high price for the motel. The plan is always the same: the woman goes into her chosen victim's room. A bit later that night, a team of the doctor's men charges into the john's room and interrupts the john's pleasure. They kick the door in, snap a few photos of the sex act, then shine a strobe light to keep the john disoriented while the men shuffle the hooker out and drag the john to the floor. The john always explodes with anger and shame, sometimes threats. Demetri and Paul always speak in a low and quiet tone. Paul feels this makes the johns pay better attention to them. When the john has cooled down, he is given the opportunity to purchase the photos and buy the team's compliance. By cutting the local police in for a percentage of the profit, all cases remain unsolved. The local sheriff is a good ol' boy who likes to spend more than he earns. He also enjoys the feel of a young island woman in a soft bed.

July 20. Robin is with a man, Jack, who is a specimen of virility. Jack feels his family vacation is a time for him and his pleasures. He sacrifices enough for his family the rest of the year. Robin is the main money magnet. She alone can bring in $5,000 a week. She can take days off and still knock it down.

At 2 a.m. Paul and the two other team members bust open Jack's door, not knowing what's happening on the other side. Inside Jack is getting too aggressive with Robin. He bashes her on the side of her face, and she pulls away and screams in pain. His right hand is shaped in a fist, taking aim again. His other hand has a firm grip on Robin's hair. Jack's only thought is to enjoy what he has paid for. "You lousy lay, get your mouth down there and suck, or I'll bust you up. No one will want you when I am done with you. Bitch!" Robin is thinking fast. She slyly places a stun gun into his crotch. He seems to enjoy the shock. Robin glares at him, her mouth bloodied. She licks her lips and spits on his face, then flips him off. She then climbs on top of him. "How was that, hon?" she asks. She allows her hair to drape over her face. She is not proud of her work.

The door busts open. A camera flashes several times, then the three men jump Jack with a syringe of twenty-five cc's of heroin. Jack fights and yells in rage. "Do you know who I am? I own the land from here to the state line. I can have your hide. I will have all of you!"

"Hey, superman, we have you." Fifteen minutes later, he has boarded the early Sunday ferry to the island. The only passengers are Jack and the crew. Jack is a sloppy drunk to begin with, but with the heroin in his system, he can't even stand. He is on all fours.

One of the crew, Samuel, has been sweet on Robin for some time now, and she on him. They've been an item for three years. He is an islander too, a tall and sturdy man with broad shoulders and a square chin. Lately Samuel's fancy has escalated to an obsession, now that Robin has been transformed with the aid of the other ladies. She has gone from plain Robin to beautiful, seductive Robin, temptress of the night, in just four weeks' time. Seeing her injured face angers Samuel, and he kicks Jack hard several times.

Forty minutes later, the ferry arrives at the island. Doctor Schultz is waiting. There is much commotion. Jack is tossed off of the ferry. Seeing this, Schultz yells, "Who have you brought to our island?" Robin shows herself by the dock light. "His name is Jack Pritchard," she speaks in a low voice filled with venom. Schultz quickly comes to her. "Did he do this to you?" She nods, then spits at Pritchard.

Schultz turns his attention to the man. "Are you the Jack Pritchard?" Pritchard is spitting blood. He holds his ribs as he turns to look at Schultz. "You are the man who once owned this island, aren't you?!" Schultz knows that Pritchard has been given a heroin cocktail and will have a hard time responding. He holds Pritchard's chin up and looks directly into his eyes. "Mr. Pritchard, it was you who kept these"—Schultz turns so the crew may see Pritchard's face—"lovely people living deep in the hills."

***

A massive fire is burning near the lake shore. One lone chair is placed twelve feet from the fire, with a person seated on it. A crowd has gathered, and Doctor Schultz stands facing them, tall and imposing.

"Dear followers," the doctor begins, "let me tell you that nothing comes between us. Nothing harms us. Your days of being abused are over. This here Mr. Pritchard, he harmed Robin. We cannot have this. We cannot allow this. I want to show you the love I have for you by showing how we, or I, will deal with someone who harms one of us.

Robin, come close." She does. Doctor Schultz caresses her battered face with the back of his hand. "Robin, I love you." He turns away from Robin for a moment, to face the crowd of followers. Schultz realizes that this will be a pivotal moment for him and his flock. He then faces Jack Pritchard. He leans in until he is eye to eye with Pritchard. "Mr. Pritchard, I want you to know that we are a forgiving and loving people. I want you to know that I hold no hatred toward you. However, I really love my flock and care for their well-being. Jack—if I may—Jack, to show my love for my flock, I am afraid I will have to make an example out of you. I will have to fubar you."

Jack is not really sure of the meaning of the word "fubar." He gets a sense that fubar does not bode well for him. Schultz turns to his crowd with his arms high in the air. He begins to chant the word "fubar," starting low and letting it build to an ear-piercing chorus: "FU-BAR! FU-BAR!" Jack begins to squirm in the chair. His head is turning left and right, searching for a way to escape. Somewhere, somehow. But there is a manmade fence circling the fire. "I will pay," Jack shouts.

"Yes, I know you will." Schultz removes Jack's watch and his wallet. He calls for Samuel to join him next to Pritchard. He then takes Jack's right hand with his left. The doctor retrieves a pair of needle-nose, vice-grip pliers from an inside jacket pocket. He then begins to pull Pritchard's fingernails out, one by one. Pritchard yells, squirming and fighting against his bindings, but he is zip-tied to his chair. He will be going nowhere. The crowd, now over a hundred, are all grinning at the sight of this uppity man being taken down a notch.

The doctor turns to the flock with an evil grin upon his

face. "Shall I take more?" The flock releases a loud "Aroo!" Schultz raises hands into the black night, with the fire blazing at his back. He is fueled by the herd, his flock. He feels like a god.

Pritchard is a strong, well-built man who is not accustomed to being taken advantage of. The pain clears his head of the drug-induced fog, and he's able to fight back. Samuel places a black cloth bag over Pritchard's head, then drives a thunderous right fist into the black shroud. Pritchard is now screaming obscenities from under his shroud. Schultz urges Samuel to drive a hammer onto Pritchard's fingers.

The doctor drops to the ground to extract Pritchard's toenails. One by one, off they come, until there are none left. Pritchard is wailing and blubbering. "I will pay," he cries.

Schultz yells at the top of his lungs, "Shall I take his teeth?" The flock continues their chant: "FU-BAR! FU-BAR!" The doctor leaps onto Pritchard's chest and tips the chair over so its back is now on the ground. Schultz's pliers grab onto one of Pritchard's teeth.

The moon glows down upon the private circle. Pritchard cries again, "I'll pay!"

"I know you will," the doctor hisses, with his face just inches from his victim. The doctor is wearing a black fedora. He removes his hat and allows his face to be seen by the firelight, exposing his sinister smile.

"I'll pay more, lots!" Pritchard pleads. "I am wealthy. What do you want? Name it!"

After the anger and pain, it is now time to plead for mercy and diplomacy. Schultz is nothing if not business-minded. He kneels in front of Pritchard. "Send two million to my bank account. Now!" Doctor Schultz turns to glance at Robin. "Does two million cover your pain?" She leans over and kisses the doctor on his cheek. "Yes, it does."

The doctor turns back to Pritchard. "Thank you, Mr. Pritchard. Your sizable donation has allowed you to live on." Schultz turns to his flock. "Just good business, really."

CHAPTER TWENTY-TWO

Doctor Schultz has another meeting with the ladies of the night. "Women, you are a very important source of income for the flock. You are all transforming from simple caterpillars into exquisite, beautiful butterflies." Schultz caresses the face of each woman. The doctor is especially taken by Robin's beauty. He brushes her hair off her face. Robin blushes from the attention. He stands before the women, maintaining physical contact with Robin and rethinking his words. "I will train all of you lovely women how to succeed in today's world. I will meet with each of you one by one, to transform each and every one of you to your maximum potential." There now is a great deal of chatter among the women. After all, the handsome doctor has taken an interest in mere island girls. "Robin, I shall begin with you. Tomorrow at noon. Right here in my office."

At noon the next day, Robin knocks on the doctor's door.

"Robin, please come in," the doctor welcomes her. "Have a seat next to Abby." Robin sits on the soft cushioned chair, which is directly across from him. The doctor begins. "Robin, first let's have Abby pull your hair back off your shoulders. You don't need to hide what God has given you. You have transformed into such a lovely flower."

Abby places her hands upon Robin's shoulders, then leans down and puts her mouth very close to Robin's ear. "Relax, Robin. The doctor would now like to teach you. Relax, you will enjoy his touch." With that, the doctor places his lips upon Robin's ear with a gentle kiss. Abby caresses Robin's shoulders. Robins shrinks away a little bit from Abby's touch. Abby slowly moves Robin's long coal-black hair to expose her lovely upturned breast. The doctor allows himself to indulge in the pleasure that Robin can offer. He places both hands on Robin's full breasts. Breathing deeper, he whispers into Robin's ear. "Robin, relax. For you to give pleasure, you must allow pleasure. Now let yourself go." His hands move slowly up and down her body, squeezing her delicious fruit. Doctor Schultz thinks he is the perfect teacher. Robin is a lithe, sturdy woman who at times seems more boy than young woman. She is blessed with perfect round eyes with a dark chocolate center, which the makeup she wears cannot hide. Her eyes are etched with years of pain and scorn. Sometimes they almost seem like a doll's eyes, black with agony. She is a mistress of intrigue, yet filled with life and drive. She cannot hide. In any room of beautiful women, she would stand out. Abby is a perfect coach for her. Abby herself carries a similar burden. With the slightest touch of makeup, they are both stunning and would command any stage.

Robin is an excellent student. Her drive for a better life is her weakness. She is drawn to the new, the exciting, the shiny—like a moth to a flame. Coming from her dreadful background, it is understandable.

Doctor Schultz is now alone with Robin. Abby has been dismissed for the afternoon. Schultz has every intention of enjoying Robin for most of the day. He has thought about the pleasure she would bring him. He leads her into his examination room—a fifteen-by-twenty room with a light-blond wood walls and a green day bed in the center. One of the walls is covered top to bottom with his library of books. Collecting books is his second passion. His first is money. The other walls are adorned with his diplomas and certificates, plus photos of his fishing endeavors on the Great Lakes.

Robin comes to him. She reaches around his neck, moves her left thigh into his hip, with a moist warm kiss on his lips. Maybe it is her dress or her hair. The doctor is overcome with a sadness—a sadness that he has not experienced in years. He gently takes her hands from his neck. He moves slowly, as he still isn't sure he wants to turn her affection away. But he does. The doctor thinks that Robin looks like a lovely schoolgirl. At other times, this has not been an issue, but today, her appearance stops him in his tracks. The doctor is many things, but pedophile is not one of them. Plus, he knows of the affection Robin and Samuel have for each other.

CHAPTER TWENTY-THREE

Samuel is a good-looking man. He is clean-shaven, with short black hair, which, combined with his thick neck, gives him a military, no-nonsense mystique. Doctor Schultz has leaned upon him many times when enforcing his protection game and the very lucrative extortion business. Samuel enjoys being brought on for the rough stuff. There have been occasions when victims have tried to remove Doctor Schultz's head and Samuel has intervened and rescued Schultz, and the doctor has rewarded him well. Samuel enjoys money and a life he could previously only dream of.

Late on a Friday night, Samuel prepares to board the ferry. Doctor Schultz drapes his arm around Samuel's shoulder. "Sam, you have the weekend off, I believe?"

"Yes, sir, I do."

"Enjoy it, son. You deserve a good weekend."

"Thank you, Doctor, I will."

Sam disembarks from the ferry and glances back as

the ferry begins its return trip to the island.

Robin races up to meet Samuel. She is dressed in a yellow knee-length dress with white floral prints. The two embrace.

"Sam, honey, what are we gonna do today?"

"I am going to take you to the Kohler resorts for the weekend. It's just a quick hop on the doctor's twin engine."

"Oh, that sounds great, hon. I have never been there."

Doctor Schultz is aware that the two are fond of each other. He wonders if Robin and Sam are to leave the flock, and what would be the cost of their leaving. The doctor sits at his window, examining the monthly ledger. Paul has led his team for months. The men are running the business protection. Abby is running the prostitutes—the night team. The two teams bring in $100,000 per month. The windfall he received from Pritchard has aided in the purchase of this majestic 155-room motel. Doctor Schultz has been planning similar ventures on Superior as the flock grows, then it's on to Minneapolis.

On a whim, the doctor decides to go to the Kohler resort too. He wants to keep a closer eye on Robin and Sam.

***

Doctor Schultz owns ten thousand shares in the Kohler resorts. He is allowed to treat himself and members of his flock to lovely rooms from time to time.

Robin is thrilled to be here. "Oh, Samuel, this room is fabulous." They have a view of the mountains in Colorado, still white with snow tops, while the plains are green and yellow with their summer foliage. "This is so nice. Room service twenty-four hours a day. No cooking or cleaning; oh, what a change from our dirty underground homes! Sam, our lives have changed so much, just in a few months."

"We have a dinner reservation at the restaurant for 7 p.m.," Sam says. He stands from his chair and takes Robin's elbow, leading her to the dining room, which is called Presidents' Hall. The room is thirty feet by fifty feet. The west wall is glass top to bottom. The hall overlooks the lawn game area, and beyond that, it offers a view of the immense mountaintops. The Presidents' Hall has a dark cherrywood trim. The tables, chairs, and the twenty-five-foot-long bar are all decorated in the same wood. The bar has massive mirrored backdrop. No expense has been spared.

Samuel is obviously bothered by something. He has been avoiding eye contact with Robin. Neither of them see Doctor Schultz enter the Presidents' Hall. Samuel reaches across the table to hold his love's hand, then stares at her with anxious eyes. He is planning on taking her away from their new life.

"Robin, have I told you how much I care for you? I want to spend the rest of our lives together. But I hate what our lives have become. I feel that the doctor doesn't care about any of us. Just the money we bring in."

"Sam, what are you saying? We live a life we couldn't even dream of until recently. Look at this place. We could be in a movie set, it is that nice." Robin's voice is cracking with emotion. "You aren't saying that you want to live in those terrible holes in the ground again? I can't do it, Sam! I won't do it!" Robin gulps her appletini and slams her empty glass down for effect. She storms off to the ladies' room across the bar. She is a strong woman and will not be brought to tears. Her mind races. It takes her back to her life under the sod. In the restroom she is drawn to her reflection. Robin is in a gorgeous dress tonight, a real beauty, yet all she sees in the mirror is a frumpy, downtrodden woman looking back at her.

Robin exits the ladies' room. Doctor Schultz immediately intercepts his prize pupil, not five feet from the door. Schultz gives her a gentle kiss on her lips. She is taken aback by his affection. He then whispers a message to her that only she can hear. Her mind goes into a momentary fog. Her eyes glaze over. She quickly strides back to the table where Sam awaits, confused and agitated. He has been hoping that Robin would show a softer side to him. But no, not today. Robin sits across from Samuel, placing her purse upon her lap.

Sam stands and asks with a raised voice, "What and whom do you choose, Schultz or me? Robin, he doesn't care about you or me."

Robin fidgets in her chair. She prepares her reply, which she had hoped would not be needed today. She remains seated. Sam gulps down his drink and tosses the ice-filled glass at Robin's face. All heads turn to them. The glass clunks to the floor.

Robin now raises her voice too, close to a scream. "You pig! You will beat me as soon as we leave." She is hyperventilating in her chair. An Oscar performance by any standard. While seated, she pulls her Taurus 22 with a four-inch sound suppressor from her purse. She keeps it covered beneath the table. Four shots sound, like a weak hammer strike.

Screams and crashing dishes chime through the

dinner crowd. The small caliber is deadly. Sam falls backward in his chair, shock written on his face. His lower abdomen is saturated in a bright red. Robin slowly slithers to Sam's side. She leans down to give him a kiss on his lips. Sam stares into her eyes. "Why?"

"I'm not going back."

Sam gasps, "Whore!"

Robin stands fully erect above him. She takes her full water glass from the table and pours it into his open mouth. A short waterboarding.

Robin smiles a sly, crooked smile. "Sam, I like men. So sue me." Then she blows him a kiss. She gives the stunned crowd a wave as security whisks her away from Sam's blood-covered body. Doctor Schultz arrives at Robin's side immediately. He hands the motel security his business card and says, "She is a patient of mine. I have been treating her for an abusive relationship"—Schultz gapes at the sight on the floor. He points down at Samuel—"with this man. Consider her bailed out," the doctor declares with the utmost confidence. The staff and guests are still craning their necks to gain a better view. Two tables over, a middle-aged woman with beehive hair says to her table guests, "What a realistic beginning for our murder mystery." She plays with her pearl necklace. They nod politely as they sip their tea.

***

Paul has always carried an interest in Robin. He and Samuel competed for her affection early on. He believes that her flower has blossomed to make her the most radiant of all the women. Paul arrives at the resort at dusk.

He enters the empty dining room to find Doctor Schultz seated next to Robin. "Robin, where is Samuel? I expected to see you with him."

She places her hand to her mouth and whispers, "Yes, poor Sam was here. He insisted on the two of us breaking from the flock. He was insistent." Robin lowers her head to avoid eye contact and fiddles with the sofa cushion.

Doctor Schultz interjects. "Paul, Samuel was getting very heated. Almost crazed. When he approached her, I had to intercept that dog. He would have killed poor, fragile Robin, or worse."

"Fragile is not how I would describe Robin," Paul says. He turns to face the doctor straight on. He senses a hostility in the doctor's stern gaze. Paul reaches to Robin and motions for her to come with him. Robin stands and the lights behind her shimmer through her dress, showing what God has given her. She glances at Doctor Schultz, and the doctor returns the glance. He motions with his right hand for her to pass. She has done it. She, Robin Beckley, has left the flock.

Paul makes no eye contact with the doctor. He places his right arm around Robin's waist. The two exit the building and stroll through the flower garden. She places her head upon Paul's shoulder. He is an introvert and feels uncomfortable with human contact. The two stop. They take in the lovely view from above the garden. They pause on a wooden bench, and Paul gets down on one knee. He holds out a massive two-carat diamond engagement ring. "Paul? Did you plan this?" Robin asks in shock, then shouts, "Yes!"

"Robin, the doctor has plans for us." He notices a glint of concern on her face.

"Paul, we aren't going back to those holes. I thought the doctor would not allow us to just leave?"

"I am not sure that this is our end with Doctor Schultz. I have seen the size of his web! He has a massive amount of influence and reach." The couple sit on the weathered bench and begin to dream of their new life. "Robin, why didn't you stay with Sam?" Paul asks.

"I like my new life. I like the money, the cars," she says with a sparkle in her eyes. "Samuel wanted to leave this life, can you believe that?" Robin claims with a loud huff. "I love the dresses, the money, the attention. Nope, I don't want to go back."

Doctor Schultz glares down on the lovebirds from a third-floor office. Abby knocks quietly and enters. She sits across from him. "Patrick, why did you allow Robin and Paul to leave us? I've been training Robin, and I thought Paul might replace Samuel?"

"Abby, by allowing them to live their dream, to simply have a dream, I have given the whole flock reason to dream and imagine a greater purpose." The doctor stands, glancing at Abby. "It is just good business." He has an arrogant smirk pasted upon his face. He watches Abby's reaction in the reflection of her in the glass book cabinet. "I have not completely released my grip upon them; just relaxed it a bit is all. Abby, would you join me for a cocktail? How do you find Minnesota in August?"

"Why, Patrick, I find it just fine."

"Abby, the sale of land east and west of Route 43 has made us wealthy beyond my dreams. I have harvested a great wealth benefitting myself and the Luchk family. I may now be the wealthiest man in the state. I have enough to move forward into Minnesota. The land of enchantment, or some such shit." The doctor takes a sip of his drink. "Abby, our flight is leaving in just three hours. Ready?"

"Why, Doctor, I blush at the invitation," Abby exclaims with a fake Southern-belle drawl, fanning her face.

With that, the doctor and Abby prepare to board his twin-engine turbo prop. Before the doctor boards, he takes in all the beauty and the scenery that has been such a large part of his life for the past decade. "Abby, I hear Minnesota is lovely this time of year."

PART FOUR:
FAMILY AFFAIR

CHAPTER TWENTY-FOUR

I save the Word doc, then I close my laptop. I stand at my second-story window, at peace with my family's past, enjoying the beauty summer brings with it. The rum bottle is still half full. Rum is good. The novel will be done by September 1, two weeks before my deadline. Book readings and giveaways will be coming soon.

I drink to the loving memory of Uncle Johannes. Till we meet again.

I take Willie to the back property that borders the lake. A soft breeze is coming from the southwest, moving the leaves that are soon to fall. The snow will soon be in the air, with it a complete change of life. I relax in a wooden chair. Just past the pit lies a three-hundred-acre forest and beyond that lies Superior. The huge, lovely Superior deep in the background.

The eastern side of the lake is well beyond view. I have a cold drink in hand and a story on my mind. So many stories, so little time. I pull out my coin of choice, give it a flip. There it is, settled. The coin has chosen. I take a sip of rum and return a phone call to my friends in Illinois. Next is a timely call to attorney Dewey.

I was contacted by my dear friend Michael. It seems the home security system that came with the historic house he and his wife, Angela, have just purchased has gone awry. He wishes that I tell their story, and the story of the previous owners. I tell Michael that I am intrigued, and that I will be at his house in Illinois in five days' time.

I am thankful for my uncle's project. The house is so terribly lonely. Right—Willie. Time to get going.

I return to the hospital. I hold the two-by-four scrap as though it were a prize for all to behold. I am allowed in Faith's room briefly. She is conscious but looks terrified, with tears gliding down her cheeks, which are red with fever. She is unable to speak. She holds out her arms for a hug, sobbing in deep breaths. I hold her hand and she pulls me close until our foreheads touch. She whispers that she is sorry. Sorry for what? Her tears are now flowing down my cheeks as well. Her mouth bubbles from the excess saliva her panic is forming. She buries her head into my shoulder as we hold each other tight. My glare is aimed at Doctor Starr. "What is it? Why can't you fix her?! Dammit, just two days ago she was fine!"

I am whisked out of her room before the doctor can respond to any of my questions. My last view is that of a stream of blood flowing from my wife. Her blood is pouring out onto a large folded towel over a chrome bowl. Soon the doctor, with the help of two male nurses, pushes Faith frantically to the elevator, full of medical equipment that is above my pay grade.

I am told she has been moved to the emergency room

again. Finally I exhale. Maybe someone will help her there. I slink from the waiting room I was shown to just moments ago and stand at the doors through which Faith has been moved. A male nurse removes me from my post. I am ushered to a room right across the hall from Faith's.

Doctor Starr enters the room. Her head is down. On cue, she removes her mask and puts a hand on my shoulder. Doctor Starr begins a speech she has given more times than she remembers.

Doctor Starr begins, "Mr. Luchk, your wife was hemorrhaging after the miscarriage of your baby. We were unable to stop the bleeding. Mr. Luchk, I am so sorry." She stutters a bit. My eyes dart back and forth, looking for a more senior doctor to walk in and tell me Starr has made a terrible mistake. That Faith is just fine. "I... I am sorry for your loss. We did what we could." I bend past the doctor to see through the glass door into Faith's room. A sheet is being placed over Faith. I stand in complete disbelief, then my knees give out. A male nurse props me up with a knee under my butt. I push past the two male nurses and run into the room that Faith is in. I take her hand; it is still soft. There is no grip. There is no life. I wish that I had not snuck in. I don't want to remember Faith this way. This is not Faith that I am holding on to. This is not Faith under the sheet. This is not my lovely wife. Oh, how I regret sneaking into the room. Doctor Starr remains at my side. She has a hand upon my left arm. The doctor seems to be waiting for me to scream, yell, stomp my feet, something.

I can feel the subtle changes that death brings. This is not Faith any longer. My stomach turns in knots. I am going to vomit. Then I stop the urge. This body was just a vessel that she graced for a short time. My legs give out from beneath me again. Doctor Starr looks down at me. One of the nurses pops a smelling capsule under my nose. That does it. I am up with all of their help. Through the door's small window I witness the nurses smoothing out the sheet over Faith.

What has happened!? A damn fever is all she had. I ask the doctor again. She claims that the embryo had pulled from the uterine wall and created a massive hemorrhage. "Your wife was on blood thinners for her heart, wasn't she?"

"I don't know. Yes. Shit."

Doctor Starr insists that I sit to hear her out. "The fever was due to the infection from the nasty, untreated piercing of her foot. The infection had spread to her glands throughout her body. Shortly after you left, your wife... well, she miscarried, and that created a hemorrhage. Due to the weather, we could not transport your wife to the Ashland hospital, where they are better equipped to handle a situation. Perhaps if your wife had arrived sooner." The doctor lowers her eyes. "Alas, such is life. Mr. Luchk, I am so deeply sorry." My mind races back and forth. Faith and I have been anything but the perfect couple of late.

"Your good intentions and sympathy did very little for my wife. You're a hospital, for God's sake! How could you not have been able to handle this?" I am ready to explode. I am glad that I am not packing at the moment. For nine years of my short life it's been Faith and me. She was the super-hot prize that I worked toward in college. Five years of dating, four years of marriage and living together, all have come to an end on this gray, wintry day.

The hospital sends a pastor to speak to me. Unless he carries rum, I don't want to see him. "I asked for the hospital priest, not a pastor," I rudely beller out. "Didn't the staff read what religion we are? Why did I take twenty minutes to fill out her bio if they don't read the damn thing. We are Roman Catholic, for Christ's sake." I don't buy into this "better place" stuff, never have, never will. We had our whole lives in front of us. So many dreams yet to come. I stand and use the windowsill to support myself. Faith was healthy, I had thought, and with a child! I stare out the third-story window. The wind slaps at the glass and whips the snow into a wild frenzy. The men in their snowplows work feverishly to clear the lots and roads. I stare down at the lot in a blind haze, wondering what to do next.

Father Murphy puts his hand on my shoulder. I glance back at him. It's as if I were waiting for his permission to show my emotion, to let loose. There is nothing that Father Murphy can say to comfort me. I am mad. Mad as hell. I scream as loud as possible and I kick at the wall and bang my fist onto the sill. The walls are built extremely well. I limp into the elevator and toward the exit. I need a drink! I stand under the hospital's canopy, and the gale wind pushes me back toward the hospital. I look left, then right, to see what businesses might be open on this day. There it is, a beer sign down the road. Christ on a stick, now we are talking! Salvation by the pint. I push across the wind-whipped road to the bar. To the Rusty Pelican it is.

There are a few weathered patrons hunched over their drinks in the darkness. They are protecting their drinks like vultures waiting for their prey to rot. The dress is casual, as you would expect. Everyone is in their lumberjack apparel: flannel shirts, long flannel-lined pants. They get to hear it all! I beller and moan. The bar is a dark, stained wood with brass fixtures, with gouges and stains from the years of use, laughter, and tears. I reminisce about the time Danial dented a corner of this very bar, not so long ago.

I am bought drink after drink to drown my sorrow. I buy them all drinks. The owner, Owen, is a large, burly man, six-foot-five, at least 240 pounds or so, adorned with a full blond beard. A friend of my father's, he was. The bar is just what I need! Drink, drink. "Damn her," I yell out. I lower my head. "A baby!" Was it mine? Owen looks at me with a sad smile, shaking his head. My head is aimed more at the floor than at anyone in the bar. My mind churns back and forth, asking the same questions over and over. I stumble toward three men who are as drunk as me. The mountain man owner picks me up as if I were a fifty-pound sack of potatoes. His wife steps behind the bar while he carries me to the back room. He bends over to look at me at eye level, his hands on my shoulder as he gives me a shake. "Son, knock it off. If your father were here, he would say 'Suck it up, buttercup.' Get over it." Owen leans closer to me and says in a low voice, "Those boys over there, they don't care what happened to you. They'll put you down, boy. They just love to fight." As he helps me back out, I hear a small sarcastic cheer from the bar crowd.

I stumble toward the few patrons who have been sympathetic thus far. "How! Why! A baby. Why didn't she tell me!" I crumble down to my knees in front of the old bar, both middle fingers in the air. The smell this close to the floor puts my stomach into a knot. I am barely able to stand as I teeter back and forth. The bar is a poetic place to bare my soul. My emotions have run the full gamut, from elation to extreme sadness. Lord, why would you take her from me, I continue to babble to myself.

My fellow patrons are now avoiding me, as if I have the plague. The owner's wife jams a glass of water into my hand. I notice the biggest, hairiest lumberjack is preparing to knock my head off. I am held up by the bar. Big lumberjack dude stands toe to toe, eye to eye with me. He is taking aim at my face. I ask him, "What are you going to do, you big pussy?" Owen charges between us. "No one has died in here in years. It ain't gonna happen today! Get the hell out of here, Luchk!" he yells. Owen sticks up for me and settles the dispute by putting two more rounds on my tab. He places his arms under my armpits, and up I go. I'm standing again. I am holding a ghastly smelling cleaning bucket. I smile at the patrons and flip them off with a laugh. I retch into the nasty gray bucket. I offer to share the bucket's contents.

Owen drags me outside by my shoulders and aims me toward an '80s-era ragtop jeep. "Owen," I slur, "I have apparently worn out my welcome." Owen keeps me moving long enough to jettison me into the passenger seat of the jeep. The seatbelt tightens and keeps me in place. I inform Owen that I have not yet begun to defile myself. It is terribly cold under the loose-fitting ragtop. The jeep has a kerosene heater, which cannot keep the car warm. Why the hell would anyone own such a beast way up north? Owen's wife comes out and chucks my coat onto my head. I smile at Owen and say, "There it is, all good. Ready for the ride."

The jeep is moving, I think. I am introduced to the negative-thirty-degree air. A layer of sweat covers my forehead. Owen disposes of me at the local Catholic church, St. Andrew's on Fifth Street. That is kind of him, but not overly. I crawl through the large wooden doors on all fours, then past the holy water stations.

My first impression of the large church is that of an icebox. Finally my journey comes to a stop as I lie on my back just ten feet from the altar, bucket close at hand. I stare at Jesus on the cross. My view of the altar is sublime, but my mind is not trustworthy. Jesus turns and smiles at me. He gives me a wink. As a gesture, I raise my head off the carpet and I salute right back at him on his cross. Then finally I yack out whatever is left in my stomach. I feel no comfort, nothing from inside the church. The church is no longer a presence in my life. I roll over to my knees just as one of the sisters approaches. Her name is Sister Theresa, I think. It's been a while since I've been here. She sees my condition and shakes her head. She puts her hand to my shoulder and face. I reek of stale drinks and yack. The nun turns away after she gets a whiff of me. She takes a step back, then helps me stand. She has a stern face and a set of broad shoulders. I can feel her strength as she hoists me off the floor. Her grip is like a vise. She looks directly at me and says, "Son," then she gently puts her hand under my chin, right before she plants a stern slap on the right side of my face. "You make a mess, you clean it. I will see to it that you get home. That's it, hon. We may question the Lord's plan, but we will never defile the Lord's plan or his holy word, or why things happen as they do. All we can do is trust in the Lord's wisdom, hallelujah, so say the Lord!"

I spit out, "My ass!" as I retch into the bucket. The

sister proclaims, "We will have no more talk like that, Mr. Luchk. If that's how you feel, keep your mouth shut. You hear me?"

"Sister, I don't want to hear of a better place and all that garbage. My wife and unborn child are gone! How can this be in any plan? Not in God's plan!"

"Simon, none of us know his plan. Just know that he loves you and would never hand you more than you can take."

"As I said," I say, the nun now eye to eye with me. "Keep it to yourself."

"Damn it." A large hulking man enters behind Sister Theresa. His eyes are set deep into his head. A Lurch lookalike—yes, that's it. His only comment is "I read one of your books," which is kind of weird to hear, given the circumstances.

"Here is one of our custodians, Patrick," Sister Theresa says. "He will see to it that you get home. Luchk, treat him good. He is already pissed at you." The nun sparks a match off of her boot and lights a cigar.

We begin the horrible drive to my home. There is very little chatter during the drive between Patrick and me. Patrick seems less than happy that he has been asked to drive in what has been dubbed "the storm of the century." The terrible winter weather continues. An hour later we arrive. My head is between my knees as Patrick pulls me from his Dodge Ram. I slip on the ice and snow. Patrick cannot keep me upright, and we both fall. Finally he manages to get me to the door, then heads right back out.

Willie is excited to see me. He spins in the foyer, waiting for Faith to follow me into our home. Just a few short hours ago I was married, with a child on the way.

Willie senses my pain. For a stout, strong dog, he has a very tender side. He nuzzles my thigh and looks at me with his gray eyes and that wonderful perpetual smile on his face. Willie has become my lifeline. Dogs carry a medicine with them. All they need is to nuzzle it toward you. I am sure Willie is aware of his help to me.

As I lean against my office door, the calendar glares at me. Five months have passed since my uncle's gift. I must find the drive and the time to work on the book. My uncle had not written much of his final novel. He had developed a strong case of COPD, with a side of I-don't-give-a-shit. During his last six months, my uncle's love of pipe tobacco had its last laugh.

I call Faith's family. She has—had—two brothers, Shawn and Matthew O'Brien. Faith was their little sister. I had been trusted with this most precious of all items, her life. I had been trusted to care for Faith, to keep her safe. I had failed Faith and her family. I will always remember Faith's father leaning into me at our wedding reception, fresh and stale whiskey oozing out of his pores and on his breath. "You take care of my baby girl," he said. His look was stone-sober, even with the considerable amount of drink he'd had. I looked past his shoulder and saw the gaze of her two brothers, who looked eager to take me for a thrashing, if for no other reason than as a welcome to the family. Two sturdy young Irishmen, both blessed with fine looks. Both have strong chins and piercing emerald-green eyes. Both are six feet plus, but the difference is notable. Matthew has a pointed ginger beard and hair, while Shawn is clean-shaven, with a head of dark, wavy hair. The two often engage in roughhousing, especially when liquor is involved. Neither have broken any of my bones.

At the moment, it is a priority to keep it that way. Their sister died on my watch. I think back to Faith's final moments, and that reminds me of my mother. How they both just drifted off to sleep, peacefully. Me and the brothers drank from first call to last call. Till there weren't no more. Till the bar door hit our ass.

At 7 a.m. Sheriff Crane pounds on my door. It sounds as if he is putting all 220 pounds into his knock. Willie is turning circles with excitement at a visitor. Even though he is well trained, his breed is rambunctious, to say the least. I pull on my blue sweatpants, then shake my head, trying to get my wits about me. I run my fingers through my hair. I pick up a whiff of myself and notice my pores are emitting the fragrance of stale alcohol.

"Yes, Sheriff, can I help you?" I stand in my doorway. My head is pounding. I have a fuzzy layer on my teeth and a mouth so dry that cacti ought to grow in it. I am leaning against the doorframe with what I feel is my most I-am-okay smile. It is what is keeping me upright.

Crane backs away from me. He has a stern, don't-mess-with-me look chiseled onto his face. The stale booze smell off me must be stronger than I suspected. "Officer, won't you come in?" I ask.

"That's Sheriff Crane, Mr. Luchk!" he corrects me. He comes in, careful to give me a wide berth.

"Yes, Sheriff. Is this a social call or business?" The sheriff sits down with a large notebook. He takes a moment to place readers upon his nose. He is a large man, made larger by his cowboy boots.

"This is purely business. Let's see. Mr. Luchk, in the past few weeks you have been assaulted twice and you have lost your wife. I spoke to the doctor at the hospital and, as you know, she had stepped on a dirty nail. Luchk, when I was in the service, nails and sharp bamboo sticks were used as a means to disable us. The lab found snake venom on those nails. Now, Luchk, you wouldn't know how this venom got on that nail, would you?"

Just then the phone rings. I excuse myself to the family room. "Simon, it's Danial. I heard about your wife. Sorry, man. What happened?"

"Dan, how did you know?"

"Edmond told me yesterday."

"Okay, so how did he know?"

"Luchk, are you getting off the phone soon? I am busy today," Crane calls.

"Yes, Sheriff, be right in." I quickly get off the phone.

"Luchk, at first glance nothing was suspicious in your wife's death. Then we got the toxicology report." Crane pauses and glares over his readers. "I am willing to wager that your wife's death was not an accident. Her passing was not just poor luck—if you believe in that sort of thing— as the doctor put it. Mr. Luchk, I want to speak to you about the assault outside of the grocery store. Why would you guess were you attacked? I know you have gone over all of this. But let's go over it again. How tall was he? Was he heavyset? What were his features?"

I tell the sheriff what I know and remember. "Sheriff, I am a writer, not a strong-arm guy. I could use your help. I am lost as to why this is happening. My shed where the Rover is kept is far from airtight. It can be easily accessed. At the grocery store, a guy jumped me, and Faith tried to run him over as he ran. The guy chucked a brick at her and nicked her in the head." I pause a moment and glance through the window at the wind and snow. "Later that day, she stepped on that crusty nail. That nail was covered in horse manure and God knows what else."

"Luchk, that nail is at the department's lab. And there was a lot more than horseshit on it." I lower my eyes and wonder if I should call an attorney.

"My condolences," Crane says. He surveys my first floor as he steps into the kitchen. His eyes seem closer together than I remember from before. His voice sounds as if he's angry; it carries that sharp and dangerous tone. The sheriff has turned cold and is all business. "Luchk, we have very little crime in this small town. Some might say my job is boring. I like it that way." He sits back down across from me.

I try to lighten the mood. "Sheriff, I am truly getting tired of being jumped and beaten."

"Luchk, you mentioned your cousin Edmond. I will take a drive tomorrow and visit him. You know, shake the tree, see what falls."

"Pity, I was hoping for some polite conversation. It used to be called chitchat. It has been so quiet at my house since Faith's passing." But the sheriff has an agenda to keep. He gets up and says his goodbyes. As he opens the door, the county detective, Lammer, pulls up. The two switch positions. I stand and greet the detective.

"Yes, Detective, Faith was at the hospital. That is where..." A pause. "Where she passed. Have you had a chance to speak to the inept Doctor Starr, I believe her name is?"

"With what has happened to you the past few weeks, do you feel that your wife's death was natural?"

"Do you and the sheriff talk? He just informed me of a toxicology report just released. There was poison on the board of nails. It was as natural as a thirty-year-old woman who is pregnant and who bleeds to death. In a hospital of all places. That's natural. No, I keep the shed clean. I wouldn't let a board with nails sit on the floor. I would put money on that."

The detective gets a terse look on her face. "So you're sure of that, are you?"

"Yes, Detective, as sure as I can be."

"Sorry to be asking these questions. I am new to this position and district, so bear with me, please. I can see you're sensitive. However, I should have asked this question earlier, at the time of your wife's passing."

"Yes, yes I am. I have been hit in the head. My head is pounding. I have been tasered. My wife died with a fever in an inept hospital during the snowstorm from hell. I don't know what the hell is going on. So, if you can tell me what is going on, I would appreciate it!" I turn my back to the detective and enter the kitchen. "Detective, would you like some coffee?"

"Yes, please."

"My coffee has been called tar. So I must warn you. Please, have a seat, Detective."

I begin to pace. Anger is rising in my veins. I breathe deeply, in and out.

"That sounds fine. A good, strong cup may clear my head. Had you and Mrs. Luchk had any issues, any arguments?"

"Let's see. My wife was pregnant when she died, and I may not have been the father."

"Hmm. How does that make you feel, Mr. Luchk?"

"Not for shit. Hurt is how I feel! And mad. We weren't getting along splendidly, but still." I stand to get another cup of coffee. "Detective, women have secrets. Just the way it is. We had some troubles. Money mostly."

"Mr. Luchk, you were recently fired from a teaching position in Ruby, correct?"

"Yes, ma'am, I was. That is what brought us up north. The little shits I was teaching didn't like me, so they found a way to get me fired."

"You choked out the star basketball player. Luchk, I would say they got you."

"We argued no more than any other couple. My writing career was not taking hold as we wished. Money was a wee bit tight, and after I got fired, it was going to be tighter."

"That's not what I asked, Mr. Luchk."

I stand, reach for the coffee. "Detective, can you stand another cup?"

"Yes; your coffee, it is terrible. I am afraid it has stuck to my teeth," she says as she slides her tongue across her teeth.

"I told you. I make old trail-ride coffee. You can just about chew it. My motto is, the coffee's done when your spoon can stand in the cup." I feel Detective Lammer studying my every word, my expressions. What have I done to cause this chain of events, I wonder.

The light bulb goes off. If I am not on the ball, I will be a perfect candidate for Edmond's scam. This is the beginning. This is how Edmond will begin his swoop for money. I must be diligent and control my emotions so I don't fall into his trap. Let's see. My wife has just passed. I am grieving. What next? Perhaps a call followed by a visit from my cousins. From reading my uncle's journal, seems I am a prime candidate for their scam. I must remain strong and not give my cousins any leverage. Can't allow them an edge at all.

I gather my thoughts and shake my head to bring me back to the conversation with Detective Lammer. "Mr. Luchk, are you all right?"

"Detective, I am not sure how much you know of my extended family, like my cousins?" I sit back and cross my legs. I hold my full cup of coffee. Lammer scoots closer to the edge of her chair. Both of her hands are on her warm cup of coffee. Her eyes are wide as she waits for a juicy tale.

"Detective, my cousin Edmond and his sister Vivian have over the years built a small empire by pouncing on grieving widows and widowers at their time of loss. I feel my cousins have taken advantage of many people, taking their land and wealth. With that in mind, I am concerned about my safety."

"Have they contacted you?"

"Yes, just before you arrived I spoke to one of my cousins."

"Contact me if you feel the need," Lammer says and heads out.

I need to get wood for the house. Willie and I enter the garage, which is just a stone's throw from the house. I will load the back of my Deere UTV with a load of wood. Dear Willie is at my side. Willie is not a heavy-fur winter breed. I need to be careful about his outdoor time. The wind has slowed, but the howls are still echoing through the wood in my garage. I hear a stack of wood fall. I turn like a cat and pop off two rounds at the noise. There is a thud and a yip from Willie. I run over to find Willie with a stack of wood on him. "Willie, Willie!" My breath is taken by the sight of my buddy lying under the wood.

CHAPTER TWENTY-FIVE

He rises and the wood falls to his side. He looks at me with that beautiful smile. I am so relieved! Clearly I am overly edgy.

I shift the Deere UTV into four-wheel drive. Willie perches next to me, his ears bobbing back and forth in the breeze. The Deere pushes through the snow that's well past its bumpers, till I am next to the family room doors. Quickly I unload the wood into the storage boxes. I am now totally aware of the silence. The only sound is the tick, tick, tick of the grandfather clock.

My log home is lonely without Faith here. You can hear every creak and crack. There are times I swear that my father's vacation home is speaking to me. It has its own secret language. It whispers, late at night. It's more noticeable when my belly is full of rum. I hear my name being called through the wind. It has been so lonely. If not for Willie, I would go mad. Cabin fever setting in. As the saying goes, if you think you're crazy, you're not. "Willie, what do you think?" I ask my four-legged companion, hoping for no answer but his smile, which I receive.

Detective Lammer visits me again. "Mr. Luchk, the sheriff tells me that you've been carrying your revolver on your person. That concerns me. Do tell me if you feel that you're in danger." She stands by the door, exposing her shoulder holster with a black grip. The clip is peeking out just a bit. The pistol would be a semiautomatic. Lammer pulls out a business card and hands it to me, along with an empty coffee cup. "Mr. Luchk, I came here primarily because I am concerned about you being here alone. Do you have anyone, possibly a close friend, who can stay with you?"

"My wife and brothers have arrived for the funeral. They arrived yesterday. Would you like to come in?" She does.

"Faith's brother Matthew was able to get the casket at a great price," I continue. "He attended college with the owner of the funeral home. Detective, have you ever heard of such brass?" The detective sits hesitantly at my breakfast table, taking in as much visual information as she can from my kitchen. "Detective, I am starving. May I make you my breakfast specialty? It is called a mess. I throw most everything into one frying pan: gobs of meat and vegetables, then cover it with gravy."

"Mr. Luchk, thank you. Back to your in-laws bartering. My opinion is, if you don't ask, you will never know."

"You are right, Detective. Matthew was able to obtain a casket for roughly half the retail price. Her other brother, Shawn, feels he can also get a break on the price of the food for after the funeral. I would not have the brass to barter or dicker on the price of such things. But her brothers were able to save money. They did, however, spare no expense on the drink. Faith's maiden name is O'Brien. Her brothers, Detective, they can drink, and they also love to fight."

Matthew joins us at the kitchen table, still half asleep. He puts his arm around me. "Simon, I smell food." He forces his eyes open, as if to focus on my face. "My sister loved you; you treated her great. You always welcomed us into your house with open arms. Love you, man, like a brother. We will be here to help you get through this."

"Matthew, say, did Faith mention to either of you about being pregnant?"

CHAPTER TWENTY-SIX

"Oh, no, she didn't. That's terrible, Simon. Just terrible. Bring it in, brother." We hug as brothers in times of pain do. Shawn joins us in the kitchen just then. "Simon, have you called Marie yet?" he asks.

"Yes, I called two days ago. But I was only able to leave a message for her to call me back. I need to try again. Do you have the international code? There has been so much happening that I forgot to call her again. I am not looking forward to the call."

"I can do you a solid and call my mother for you," Shawn offers.

"I was waiting to set a date for the funeral till we get an ETA from her." I turn to Detective Lammer to explain. "Detective, Faith had a falling out with her mother. Marie felt that I was beneath her daughter."

"Mr. Luchk, I understand." Lammer gives me a wan smile. "Yes, matters of the heart and family matters can all be complicated. I understand."

Shawn goes to make the call. We can hear him from the other room. "Yes, hello, Marie, this is Shawn. Mother, Simon asked you to call him back and you didn't. Yes, it was very important. Faith passed away. How, how? No, Mother, it was very sudden. No, Simon is alive!" Shawn fills her in on the details. We need to delay the funeral a few days to accommodate Marie.

"I am so sorry about the loss of your baby, bro," Shawn says. "I know how much you and Faith wanted a child."

I have an idea. "Let's continue this chat with a drive and a stop at Nick Shay's tap." The detective bids us goodbye and the three of us set off. The sun is burning bright. The bar is small and dark, built for locals by locals. It has a soothing smell of fried meat with onions, and many years' worth of spilled drinks. There are some old bloodstains on the wooden floor, and we reminisce about the stains that came from us.

It's so nice to go where everybody knows your name. The daytime crowd is sitting in their assigned seats. "I need to tie one on, boys!" I say. After two hours with Faith's brothers, I realize I am out of drinking shape, yet it seems like a grand idea to continue. Two hours turn into four, then six. The autumn sun is setting just beyond the lake boats as they float about, getting to dock just before nightfall.

"My brothers, Faith and I had no secrets between us. But a damn baby! She was excited for the next step in our lives, and I love you, guys!" I am so excited to tell them about my uncle's will, and what has been left to me. I shake my head as I glare into my pint. I now speak of "me" and "I." There no longer is a "we."

I find myself exploding with excitement about the news of my uncle's will. The brothers' expressions are unmoved. I explain to them further. Shit, I pushed too hard. Now I have lost them. Their eyes seem to glaze over. I might as well have been reading the theory of relativity to them. Their lack of any interest amazes me. It just floors me. This gift has amazing possibilities. I buy shots of Fireball to perk up the boys before I explain more about my uncle handing his book over to me. They finally get it!

"Simon, I know my sister was involved in many different things and she was always stoked to help you, in any way that you needed," Shawn says. "She was dedicated to helping you do the research for your new book."

Matthew perks up and asks, "Was she still your proofreader?"

"Yes. She was my biggest fan! She told me it was like being transported to another place and time." I stand to stretch my legs and nudge the two brothers. "Brothers, let's have a toast to Faith. She was the best part of me. Thank you, Faith." I lower my voice and I reach to each of the brothers. "I love you guys." We drink to Faith.

I want to talk more about the book, but I can see their eyes glaze over again. Their lack of enthusiasm brings me down to reality; however, they don't read a lot, so it's not a big surprise. I haven't had the chance to really begin in earnest to work on the book. The will's stipulated one-year deadline will come faster than I think.

***

A week later, we have the memorial service for Faith

at the McDonald funeral home. We all stand by Faith's head. We answer the same questions, like a broken record. Yes, I was shocked. She had no signs. And of course, No, I didn't know she was with child. Thank you for coming.

I had forgotten how petty and self-indulgent Marie is. She expresses her disapproval of the casket. She feels that a gunmetal gray casket is beneath her daughter. The food should have been a sit-down meal, not sandwiches. The casket is stained too dark. The music has no bagpipes. The list goes on and on. Marie is almost too much to bear. She point-blank asks me, "Faith did insist on a prenuptial with you, didn't she?" Marie then turns abruptly away from me with a scoff and in a huff. My Faith had no such prenuptial made.

After the funeral I invite Faith's family over for oyster stew, plus a treat of Appleton Estate 21 rum. The brothers come to my house. Free booze—it works most times.

"Hey Matt," I ask, "your mother is still allergic to shellfish, right?"

Matt leans into me with a smile from ear to ear. "You old scallywag, you rascal! You know she is."

"Boys, hence my menu choice."

I am not looking forward to my empty house. The brothers help me pack up Faith's things. Marie sorts through Faith's clothing and jewelry. Most will be donated to the local Catholic church thrift store. Matt and I sadly look through Faith's photos and I reminisce about those captured moments. Matt notices that in some of the photos Faith has a faraway look. He shows them to me. I give them a glance and hand them back. My eyes widen when I recognize the place and time of those photos. A happier time for sure.

I send Matt and Shawn to Faith's office. Faith and her brothers had, through good business sense, been able to turn a small inheritance from their father into a very profitable nationwide moving company. The brothers and I need to discuss several items pertaining to the business. The business was quite fluid. Faith ran most of the business. Technology has changed so much, it is possible to run multiple businesses in many locations remotely. Before the day is over, the brothers have made me 51 percent owner of the moving and storage company.

The day turns into night. We have disposed of the rum.

"Simon, come here a second," Shawn calls to me. I enter the office. I lean against the heavy log doorway. Shawn has an eager look upon his face. "Here is a receipt from that pharmacy in town. There is a pregnancy test on the receipt, from just three weeks ago."

"Shawn, was your sister so upset with me that she held onto the baby news?" Under the trash there are a few small notes in Faith's handwriting. The pages are from a daily appointment calendar, from a month or so ago. "Just an initial and a time. This is when you were in southern Illinois, wasn't it, Simon?"

It's from two months earlier. "You don't think my sister knew she was pregnant two months ago, do you?" Shawn asks.

I wipe at my face, agitated. "If she knew, she didn't tell me. We have wanted, had wanted, a damn child desperately. Why would she keep news like that from me?"

Faith, what was this about? I look out of her window and ask the silence that question. Thank heavens I don't get a verbal reply.

We had planned for a child, hoped for a child. A child to pass on our name to, our lives and dreams too. Something to say to the world that we were here. A child to watch over and to nurture and share our love with. "Was she so scared of not taking the child to full term? Is that why she did not tell any of us?" I whisper to her brothers as I sit on the dressing bench in her office.

"Brother, you may never know. Have you asked any of her friends? Women keep secrets, that's just it."

"Shawn, Faith kept herself to herself; she wasn't open to gabbing or gossip and such," I reply. She was, in her own way, a hard person to read or to converse with.

***

The brothers must leave, as work awaits them. The day they leave, I receive a letter from Edmond: "Simon, I am sorry about your wife's passing. I would like to make you the very generous offer of two hundred acres to the west of Route 12. I am prepared to also offer a ten-acre plot on Madeline Island. In return, you would turn my father's manuscript over to me. This added property raises the offer to just over $500,000 in land value."

I've anticipated a call or letter just like the one that's now come to me. The prospected sheep to shear.

I am sure my dear cousins are sharpening the shears for me. Not this sheep, not today.

From my desk on the second floor the view is stunning, but I need to get to work. My priorities are one, stay alive, and two, finish the book.

But first a quick flight to southern Illinois. It's September 15. When I land, I rent a car at the airport and head a little further south. By 1 p.m. I am at the gates of Edmond's estate. He has moved up since his inheritance. An armed guard is at his gate. His estate could be called a compound. I drive for another ten minutes before I get to his father's mansion. I park at the cherubs once again. I feel eyes upon me as soon as I cross onto his property.

The door to the house slowly opens. My cousins Edmond and Vivian step to the right of the door, allowing me space to enter. "Edmond, Vivian, thank you for seeing me."

"But of course, dear cousin, anything we can do for you, just let us know. Simon, an iced rum on this warm day? Please have a seat."

"Thank you, and yes, please."

"Simon, please get to the purpose of your visit. You have come a long way, presumably for more than a drink?"

"All right then." I twist in my chair slightly, clear my throat, and begin. "Edmond, I have no intention of selling you your father's book. Your feeble attempts to persuade me have failed and only driven the wedge deeper into our family." Now I stand to make a point. "Both of you, call off your dogs. I fully expect to finish your father's book on time." I face my cousins head on. My face is now flush, and my breathing deepens. Edmond stands too and we face each other.

"Well, Simon, that's good and all that, but we haven't the faintest idea of what you are talking about. It appears you have a problem that we cannot help you with. And, Simon, if in your writing you feel the need to tarnish our father's name, we have the resources to cause you great pain."

"Edmond, Vivian, I would not consider it. We are family, after all." With that, I stand and issue polite hugs. At the door I turn and say, "Till we meet again."

Once back in the rental, I run the conversation through my head over and again. Edmond and Vivian can lie with the best of them, but for some reason I believe them. I'm left still searching for answers.

I spend a night in the lodge's lounge, watching people and taking in the beauty outside the window. Everything I can see was once my family's. I eat a meal where my mother once stood. I am heavy with nostalgia and my eyes mist up as I finish this portion of my journey, which began a year ago. I am looking forward to returning to my empty home to write, to carry on in Johannes's and Danial's footsteps.

The next day, I am three miles north of home, on River Road, when a police cruiser pulls me over. "Sheriff, what can I help you with?"

"Luchk, you told me you were going to speak to your cousins. You did, I trust?"

"And you said you were going to see them also. Shake the tree, was it?"

"You first, Luchk. Find anything out?"

"Not exactly, Sheriff, but a betting man would say that those two are dirty. Their house is guarded, and there are cameras all over. There was constant smirking going on."

"So, Luchk, you want me to arrest them on that crap?"

"Just shake the tree, as you said. Who knows what will fall out." I shake the large sheriff's hand, and he leaves me with a punch on my shoulder. I finish my drive.

Two days later, I sit alone with Willie and read page after page of my uncle's work. A fire burns in the box to warm up the early autumn air.

CHAPTER TWENTY-SEVEN

I turn the pages. I read my uncle's unfinished manuscript, tracing the pattern of death in his writings. There is a trail to follow, from southern Illinois, with a slow, gradual, precise climb to the Upper Peninsula. Death after death, always followed by a calculated manipulation of husband against wife, or vice versa. A bone-chilling, calculated killer lives within Johannes's writings. He is at it all the time, hiding behind the veil of medicine and at times behind good deeds and righteousness. It's all exposed in the book, which is the final one in my uncle's hugely successful Doctor Schultz series. The final chapter of my uncle's series of adventures. He has tied up all of his works together. They culminate in this book for an ending that I must produce.

I think a couple fingers of rum might ease my anxiousness. Now back to work. I touch the pages of the book, which is number seven in the Schultz series. The paper has a velutinous quality. What a wonderful, soothing feel. Were the previous books published on the same paper? Or are my senses playing a trick?

***

"Ida, what time are Doctor Schultz and Nancy coming by again?"

"They are coming at three this afternoon. Today, Red. You didn't forget already, did you, Red?"

"No, I don't think I have, Ida. Do you have all the papers set out so we can talk about what's best to do with the property?"

Shortly, Doctor Patrick Schutz and Nancy Luchk are at the comfortable century-old farmhouse to discuss the possible purchase of land.

"Thank you for coming out in this brutal weather," Red says.

Doctor Schultz puffs his chest out, waiting to put the sales pitch to the elderly couple. "Thank you for having us. As you know, Mr. McKee, I am thinking of what's best for your family. You should do the same—think of your family. Your wife is not able to run your farm. She has told us this many times." Red throws a stern glance at his wife. "She says your children don't have an interest. I'm prepared to make you a very generous offer. You and your wife would never need to concern yourselves with money as long as you live. Plus, I am willing to allow you and Ida to stay in your house as long as you live. For now I will take possession only of the livestock and farmland."

The doctor keeps his voice low and friendly, trying his best not to upset Red any further. He continues, "Ida, you mentioned that Red was, or is, having trouble keeping up with the chores."

Ida speaks in a low, apologetic tone. She has a hard time meeting Red's eye. "Red won't admit it, but yes. I am afraid I'll find him in the cattle yard someday, face down."

Red perks up. He has heard just enough to ignite his fire. "Damn, Ida, I been working this land for over forty years. I ain't leaving or selling till I am carried off the land." Red stands by his chair, pointing a shaky finger at the doctor. "You hear me, Schultz? You hear me?" Red is a proud man who survived World War Two and the Korean War. He does not and has not ever allowed anyone to dictate to him about his business.

"Loud and clear, old-timer," Doctor Schultz chuckles. He stands, with a smile on his face spreading from ear to ear. He feels this deal is done. He tips his hat to Ida. He twirls his neck scarf on and gives Red a pat on his shoulder as he walks behind him. Red rolls his shoulder to express his displeasure with Schultz.

Nancy speaks up next. Doctor Schultz hopes that her meek demeanor will set the older couple at ease. "Ida, we want what's best for you both. You shouldn't stay here with the fear you have about Red! We can ensure that you would have no need for money for the rest of your lives.

My family is willing to pay good money for your farm and livestock." Nancy slides a legal-size envelope under Red's hand. Red opens the envelope, lets out a cough, then slides the envelope to Ida without saying a word. Ida opens the envelope. Her eyes draw close. Her jaw tightens.

Red takes back the envelope. His face turns scarlet. His legs shake a bit as he stands and pushes the envelope back toward the doctor. He is indignant. "Ida, forty years and this is all a life is worth? Why, I paid more thirty years ago for this place." Red's 135-pound frame trembles with anger. Ida shakes her head. Her jawline tightens and she points a calloused, boney finger at Nancy. Nancy feels that all Ida is missing is a pointy black hat.

"I know your father," Ida says to Nancy. "He is as crooked as a broken finger. I had dealings with him long ago. I had hoped you kids would have better sense than to follow his path. It will lead you right to damnation!"

"Mrs. McKee, thank you for thinking of our souls, but we are doing just fine!" She turns back to Red. "Old-timer, this is a cash offer. You won't get another as good as this one. I'll see to it! I would hate to see you have an accident!"

"I think you have worn out your welcome, Miss Luchk! Ida, show them out." Red McKee is still shaking as he sits down.

"Red, consider our offer," Doctor Schultz says on the way out. "We'll honor it for three days. Good day, Ida."

"Ida, I am not feeling right," Red says after the visitors are gone. "I am gonna lie down for a bit. Come and get me for the chores before dark, will you?"

"Red! Red! Red! Get up!" Ida gives Red a shake. His hand falls off his chest. She puts her hand to her mouth. He is no longer breathing. He has passed away in his nap. "Oh, Red, I can't say I didn't see it coming," she whispers to herself. She kneels next to him. "But so quick, I didn't tell you that I love you one last time. My love, that's the way to go. Sleeping and peaceful. Goodbye, and God bless you, Red."

***

"No, Belinda, we are gonna sell." Ida is on the phone with her daughter. "Neither you nor your sister wants the farm. You both are so gosh-darn busy with work and your families. The funeral for your father will be next week. Okay. Thanks, hon, I am just not ready for a silent house." Ida hangs her head with the phone receiver, wanting comfort from her daughter. Belinda makes the short thirty-minute drive to her mother's.

"Belinda, hon, thanks for coming. A couple of nights will be a blessing. I need the company and your help."

"Mom, that's okay." Belinda's eyes are moist with tears. "I can spare a few days from work. What do you need me to do?"

"We need to feed the cattle, first off. Let's get going and get dirty." Ida inserts a bite of her favorite chew. She leads by example, and off she trudges, through the rain and wind, straight to the hundred-year-old barn. The old barn takes on a new life as the sun sets. Ida never has been a woman who lets creaks and shadows spook her. All the cattle rustle toward the hay troughs like soldiers at feeding time. The ancient barn holds very little of the day's heat. The wind whistles through the cracks, and the barn creaks and squawks. Century-old dust floats to the floor through the fading sunbeams. The shadows duck and dive as the final glimpses of daylight reach into the ancient structure. The cattle jostle and shove to gain a better vantage as they gather at the hay trough. The noise reminds Ida of all the times she spent in the barn with Red. Ida feels warmer and more comforted being with the cattle, because they are living, breathing beings. Ida climbs the ladder. Her spindly legs shake as she appears through the mow hole. Her body is worn out and tired from the strain of losing her partner in crime, as she's always called Red. She strains to lift a seventy-pound bale of hay—just one of many—to drop through the hole before the day's work is done. "Oh, Belinda! My back!" It's a pain Ida knows well, deep in her lower back, just above her hips.

"Mom! Why did you lift that bale? Yell for me, that's why I am here!"

"Belinda, I cannot stand."

"Mom, here, let me help you sit on this bale for a few minutes."

Doctor Schultz and Nancy watch through the dust-stained barn windows. He is aglow with his almost-guaranteed victory.

"Nancy, that was easy. We didn't have to hardly lift a finger, Ida did it all herself. Let's see if she calls us tomorrow." The doctor is not dressed appropriately for the weather. "Nancy, we have seen enough! Let's get out of the rain and cold."

The next day there is a knock on the door. "Good afternoon, Mrs. McKee, I see you have a realtor's sign on your property. You've decided to sell, but you didn't call us!" Nancy bends over to be eye to eye with Ida. "You look as if you're in pain?"

Belinda interjects. "Nancy, I don't know how, but it seems you already know that my mother has hurt her back."

Nancy ignores her. "Here is the same offer I had for you last week. You and your daughter take a minute and look it over. That offer's good till I close my car door."

"Miss Luchk, Nancy, I am not selling to your family. Not now, not ever! That offer is too low," Ida replies.

"You got my number, Mrs. McKee. Do call..." she adds

a long pause, "or not. Sooner or later, you will sell to us. I will own your farm." With that, Nancy walks out.

Belinda busts the ice from the water troughs. There is plenty of work for two people, and now it's just her. Three hours pass, and Belinda has finally gotten done with today's work and none of tomorrow's. The sun has set, and the top layer of snow slides along at a jet's speed into the darkness.

"Mom, I can come back tomorrow," Belinda says, "and then I am afraid Ted wants me to stay home with him and the girls. He needs help with our dairy farm. Sorry, Mom, I know how much help you need and how you feel." She looks in the envelope Nancy has left behind. "Mom, have you ever seen that much cash? You know, you won't have to worry about money ever again." Belinda looks at Ida, her eyes growing bigger and wet.

"Yeah, I knew the time was coming," Ida says.

"Mom, you've got us, but we're two counties over. You got yourself to think of. Not this old farm. You can't run the farm by yourself, Mom."

Six weeks later Doctor Schultz gets a call. "Schultz? This is Ida McKee. I can't keep the farm. I'll sell to you."

"Very good," he replies. "I will be by your house in one hour with the papers for you to sign."

CHAPTER TWENTY-EIGHT

February 12, 1980

The Attorney William phoned me Today. He informed me that the land I had my eye on may shortly be for sale. It would seem that Mr. Bill Jacobs has had an accident. His car went sailing off the road, onto the lake. It went through the thin ice."

"Vivian," Edmond tells his sister, "Mr. Jacobs has had an accident. I will pass on the good fortune to my son and daughter. I don't believe there are any survivors or relatives."

"This should be an easy acquisition," Vivian says, with wide shining eyes and a smile.

"Let's have a toast. Dear sister, this will give us control of over three thousand acres of prime logging timber close to Lake Michigan."

***

I stand and slap some icy cold water to my face, then continue to turn the pages. Murder after murder. Each life lost had land tied to their name. My uncle and cousins sure were busy. It's all here in my uncle's writing. I lean back in my chair. All his stories are tied to land purchase. Hmm. Fact or fiction?

I take a short break. Since Faith's passing, I have been glued to the writings of my uncle. I also have been comforted by rum. My Faith would have cautioned me on my consumption, but rum is good!

I decide to check out those land purchases. February 1981, Jacobs sold a five-hundred-acre plot to the Oregon Trail Logging and Land Company. June 1981, Jack Pruix sold an eight-hundred-acre plot to the Oregon Trail Logging and Land Company. The computer has made research so much faster. In my uncle's book the date of sale and purchase of parcels of land actually matches up to an actual purchase or sale of property. My cousins have no fear, only arrogance. The constant is the name: the Oregon Trail Logging and Land company. Over and over again, all purchases are to the same logging and land corporation. I decide to call a private detective friend of mine on the West Coast.

"Greg Witzlab? This is Simon Luchk."

"Yes, Mr. Luchk?"

"Can you look into something for me? I would like to know who the owners of a private holding company are. The name is the Oregon Trail Logging and Land Company, based in your hometown. Yes, Astoria, Oregon. There is very little information on the internet. Anything you can find out will be more than I know now."

"Mr. Luchk, I'll call you with what I find out in three days or so, that should be enough time. I will forward the fee for my time."

Three days pass, then he calls me back. "Luchk, I spent two days across from the office listed as the address for the Oregon Trail Logging and Land Company. It is just a shell, with a couple of office people. No one of any importance. Except I approached a couple of office workers and got them drinking a bit. They seemed eager to tell me who the top dogs were. Your cousins pull the strings of that company. That's who."

I pause for a moment. "Are you sure?"

"Mr. Luchk, I got your information. As it turns out, the Oregon Trail Logging and Land Company was created in June 1949 by your family. Your uncle Johannes and your father founded the company. It owns thousands of acres through the Midwest, if not hundreds of thousands of acres."

I am taken aback by this news and by the scope of the venture. I did and still do hold my father in high regard. "Today," Witzlab continues dryly, "your cousins Edmond, Vivian, and Nancy are on the board of directors. I take it you were not aware of this? Mr. Luchk, with your father and uncle passing, I would guess that you are a multimillionaire. There has been a great deal of land purchasing over the last fifty-plus years. Some of the land holdings have been sold at a great profit, it would seem. What's this all about anyway?"

"Witzlab, I am researching my cousins' business doings, and mine also, it would seem." I feel the need to put my eyes on the paperwork. The papers I need to see are at the southern tip of Illinois. My father had many accounts. After his death, I was not allowed access to three of his business accounts, as they were tied up with his partners.

"My father spent years building his reputation. I want to ensure his good name, Mr. Witzlab. I want to fix what I can. Please email me your findings."

The winter storm has entered day three. The wind surges like strong waves against my house, screaming for my attention. The snow drifts are as high as a tall Indian, as the saying goes. I shovel out the Rover. The wind pushes the snow back to fill in my work.

I begin my journey to southern Illinois. I feel my answers will be found in my uncle's office. After a long seven hours of white-knuckle terrible driving, and only a few hundred miles to show for is, it is time to rest my head. I pull the Rover into a motel's mostly empty parking lot.

CHAPTER TWENTY-NINE

The Deer Trail Inn. A feeling of triumph comes over me. I have landed just on the outskirts of Springfield, Illinois, for the night. I question the quality of the motel. With the roads being snow packed, I would expect a fuller lot. The parking lot's not even half full.

I go inside to the check-in counter. The motel looks as if it is going through a renovation. There are sections of new carpet, but the remainder looks to be turn-of-the-century, faded and truly well worn. To add to the décor, there are three unfriendly characters who are puffer-fishing in my direction. They are lounging on the faded, worn chairs, keeping a close eye on me and debating if I am worth their trouble.

It's about midnight. I ding the bell for service. A tattered woman comes out from an office, wiping her mouth. Sea Hag, I shall call her. A fourth man appears behind her. She comes closer into view. She is thin as a rail, with two missing front teeth, and black greasy hair with gray streaks running through it. She has tattoos decorating her hands, arms, and neck. She also appears to have a nasty habit of scratching her arms raw. She comes to the front desk. "Can I help you?" she says with a tone that implies I've interrupted something. She continues to wipe her mouth while she twirls her hair with her right hand. I spot the tracks on her left arm. She is unable to stop fidgeting. She is all jittery. I keep at a distance as best as I can, to keep the bugs at bay. Her man friend keeps his right arm around her, to show everyone that she belongs to him.

I hold back my annoyance. "Any rooms available?"

"Where you from, hon?" she replies, raising her eyebrows with a little lick to her lips. She snaps her gum and continues to twirl her hair all at the same time. Impressive.

"Bayview, Wisconsin, way up by Superior, doll."

"Let me see your ID."

I pull my license from my satchel and keep a diligent eye on it as I show it to her.

"In that case, yes, we do. If you were local, I couldn't let you have a room. Drug deals and prostitution going on, all that good stuff," she proclaims with a smile on her face. "The new owner is trying to fix the motel up, you see." She points at the floor of the lobby. "New carpet to start with."

"That's nice." I feel three pairs of eyes sizing me up like rats in a corner. I notice the counter woman making eye contact with the crowd perched upon their chairs. I ask the beauty queen behind the counter, "My vehicle will be safe in the lot, won't it?"

"Yeah." She pops her gum. "It should be!" There is a pause. "Is that your ride, there?" She points directly at my vehicle, which is pictured on a closed-circuit security screen. I confirm. Another long pause, then she lowers her head so as not to maintain eye contact. "It won't be there in the morning," she mutters. "Put your ride in the fenced area. Here, I will open the gate for you, hon."

I glare at the woman and speak in my most threatening tone. "Listen, doll, I have had a terrible week. If anything happens to my Rover, it's you I'll be looking for." I lean hard against her counter with my most serious stare aimed at her. "I won't look for your boss, nor any of these clowns looking on. Do you understand?" I point at Sea Hag for effect. I toss my bag over my right shoulder, glance at the pack of coyotes hacking in their corner, and head to my room. I feel several sets of eyes follow me down the hallway, continuing to size me up.

When I get into the motel room from hell, the first thing I do is cover the bed with bug spray. I kick a screamer under the front door. Then I slip into sweats and prepare the bed. I put towels I've brought on top of the mattress and pillow, then hop on top of the covers. I leave the bathroom light on for security purposes. Then I tuck my 1911 with the two clips under my pillow beside its buddy, the 380. This fine motel requires a few fingers of rum. Now time to shut my eyes.

I am up at sunrise. I grab my bag, which I've sprayed in the hopes of killing whatever may've crawled on the floor. All I can think of is to put this flea trap in my rearview mirror. At dawn's early light I trudge through the unplowed lot. My baby is still where I parked her, all her tires still on. It's back on the road again.

Close to Carbondale the snow changes to rain. I make it to the Giant City lodge just before nightfall. Giant City is a state park on the far north side of town. The lodge was new when Jesus was a kid. I am only ten miles from my uncle's estate, but I don't want to alert my cousins. I check into a room for the night. The lodge was built by the work program during the Depression, and it's not as nice as the Fox and Hound Country Club. But it is much nicer than that rat trap the Deer Trail Inn.

That evening, way after midnight, I drive to my uncle's estate. I prepare to slither into the basement. It would appear that none of the cousins are currently staying here. The house is as black as can be. The basement entrance is just around the back of the huge estate. The moon is rising from behind the three-story house. Every noise seems as if it's being broadcast through a megaphone. The moonlight shines down upon the cascading cornstalks, whose leaves crackle as if speaking to one another. They are trying to warn me about the house.

My memory of the mansion is fresh in my mind. I was just here a few days ago when there was bright sunlight. The moonlight reflects off the windows, as if smiling at me. The light wind moves the corn leaves back and forth, as if they are breathing. My fear of the house has dug deep into my bones. I fear what I cannot see. I drape a fresh rosary around my neck. I am missing only the garlic and silver bullets.

My stomach knots up. Cousin Joey's screams of terror are still fresh in my memory. A line of sweat runs down my forehead. I've often thought how tainted my cousins must be from living in this house. It's now 3 a.m. Not a light is on, nothing is stirring except my uncle's antique grandfather clock. Its brass chime hammers out three chimes, after which it's just the autumn air rustling through the dry leaves again.

I get to the basement entrance and snap the lock with a pair of bolt cutters. I am inside. I turn on a light attached to my cap. It broadcasts very little. The office is located on the third floor, just beneath the attic. My destination is there. 3:15. Bingo! All is well so far. I stand frozen in front of the black door of the attic, with its shiny black knob reflecting a glimmer of the light from the cold moon. Beyond the door is where I must face the demons that lurk inside my head. That is where my hell awaits me.

Once inside the office, I find the file cabinet. It is not locked. There are several binders for the Oregon Trail Logging and Land Company, with a four-inch-thick folder of files for each year. At the front is a spreadsheet: date, name, legal address, purchase price. Page after page of this. There is also a book with the same information, listing greater selling prices. That would be considered good business, but the stated profits are close to 100 percent on the land sales. What could have changed? That kind of markup is unheard of in land sales. There was a very quick turnaround on many of the sales—usually months, some just weeks! I take the papers, as many as will fit in my satchel and in my arms. I stay in the shadows, slithering in the night like a specter. At 4:15 a.m., I am free, unnoticed by my cousins.

Three days later, I arrive back north at my house. I dig into the paperwork I have: at least a hundred pages of information. I have scattered the pages across my office—on my desk, two pop-open card tables, and the floor—each paper ordered by date, left to right, top to bottom. There are twenty to twenty-five lines per page.

I use my donor status to call a sheriff in Illinois I once

donated to in order to help him get reelected. I want to ask if he can find out if any cases were ever opened regarding land acquisitions from the list of dates I give him. When he asks me why, my answer is that I am about to launch a series of detective novels, and this is part of my research. I give him only six examples in a random period of time.

I think of my uncle Johannes and how elated he had been when I asked him to be an active participant at my wedding. He beamed when I asked him to bring the family bridal cup. My family was big on tradition. I am being taken on an emotional roller coaster about what I may uncover. I recognize some of the properties in the documents. The two older brothers would gamble at billiards, and property, cars, and cash were the prizes. My father had also bought land from Johannes. I have a knot forming in my stomach.

The sun sets on another cold and windy day in the Northwoods. The beauty of the pines today is tainted with my new knowledge. My family's fortune has been built from the lives of all the names on those pages. It's all in those records of land bought and resold at a more opportune time, which I now possess, and which I have read over and then again. The records date back to early 1947. Do my cousins know? Hell, of course they do. There was a purchase just six months ago. I stir my Captain and Dew with ice as I watch the sun go down behind the pines. A chill runs up my spine. With what I suspect, I now fear for my life. By now my cousins must know that I have the information about how their wealth came to them. Would Vivian or Edmond take my life to keep this information quiet? Lives could be altered and fortunes lost. I put on my shoulder holster, add four quick reloads. Better safe than sorry. I now know the family's secret. However, is it dishonest? Probably. I had never questioned our wealth. I knew Father had worked hard with his two log homebuilding businesses. I had assumed that was it.

The next morning I see a story in the paper about a young family inheriting a dairy farm empire. Thousands of acres, many employees, plus hundreds of dairy cattle turning out hundreds of gallons of milk daily. What a marvelous, feel-good story. The farm—a third-generation centennial farm—will stay in the family. There is a photo of the couple. They're quite young, and have their whole life ahead of them. She is a red-haired beauty, just like my Faith.

I decide I must meet them. I will write a story about them for a monthly dairy farm magazine. After all, I must eat.

Brrrt, brrrt. "Yes, Diane Williamson? My name is Simon Luchk. I read about your family in the local paper. I would like the honor of putting your family history in a monthly dairy cattleman magazine. Would that interest you? That's wonderful. I will come by at 1 p.m. I will see you then."

I arrive at 1 p.m. Diane Williamson welcomes me to the farm. We exchange cordial handshakes and make our introductions. "Nice to meet you," I say. I notice a red mark upon Mrs. Williamson's face, from her cheek up around her eye and onto her scalp. I do my best not to stare, though even with a makeup cover-up it is still very noticeable. I give Mrs. Williamson a warm smile. Diane looks into my eyes briefly, then she glances away. Her face carries an uncomfortable tension.

"Thanks for the opportunity to tell your story," I say.

"The trade paper has subscribers all through the U.S. If you are looking to connect with other dairy farmers, it will introduce the world to you. A trade piece will bring all types of exposure to your business."

CHAPTER THIRTY

Diane's husband, Jack, joins us. He reaches out to me and we shake hands. Jack withdraws his hand quickly. He puffer-fishes at me. The voice inside my head reminds me of the clown mask in my trunk. I cannot help but smile back at Jack.

"Simon, your ring has a sharp edge," he says. "Damn it, that's a deep scratch." Jack curls his hand into a fist beside his waist. It looks for a moment like Jack may want to throttle me. I try to hide my smile. A small drop of blood surfaces. He angrily examines the scratch, then gives me a stare. "Luchk, get that damn ring fixed. That's a hell of a way to meet people!"

"I am sorry, Jack. I will need to get it looked at. Why don't we begin by you telling me your story, shall we? The local readers have read what was in the paper. I am working for a monthly magazine aimed at your peers. You and your wife's story will be seen by the nation in just four weeks, as soon as the new issue goes to print. Jack, your wife, Diane, reminds me of my late wife. She's just as nice as her. Tell me, which one of you has the passion for farming?"

Jack makes an observation. "It's a pity we're here. If we were located in the West, we would be discussing ranching. If in the South, plantations. It all rolls off the tongue a little sweeter."

"Yes, I must agree with you, Mr. Williamson, the name does sound sweeter."

Jack continues. "Let's see. Diane has a degree in business management." He gives his wife a patronizing hug.

"I have always looked at farms as a business, not a passion," she interjects. "Jack is the one who loves all the work, and the freedom that it can offer."

"Yes, ma'am," he agrees, "I love the smells and sounds of the farm, and I just love being outside. Rain, snow, or shine—it's all good."

Diane speaks up. "It's better to have the separation. That way I ensure that as a business it maintains its profitability." My imagination begins to run. I bet you do. We could make money together.

"What is the herd count?" I ask.

"Two thousand milking and feeder, plus we farm close to three thousand acres, and employ over one hundred people full time."

Two hours pass as we talk and they show me around the farm. I notice an odd color on Jack's face. "Jack, you don't look like you're feeling so well. Your face looks as if you're burning up and you're sweating like a whore in church, man!"

"No, I am feeling poorly. I feel feverish. I hope it isn't

catching."

I hope so too. "Diane, Jack, thank you for your time. I will leave now so you may rest. I will call in a couple days so we can continue."

Two weeks pass before I have a chance to call Diane again. "No, Mrs. Williamson, I hadn't heard. I... I am so sorry. I had no idea your husband had passed away."

Diane speaks in a matter-of-fact voice. "I should feel broken up, but he was a controlling dick. You probably noticed that mark on my cheek when you were here last month? My husband was upset when I made the appointment to meet with you for the story."

"He seemed well when I was with the two of you. Well, except at the end. Diane, I am very sorry. I go to a grief support group at the hospital, if you think you may ever wish to go. I could come by and pick you up. If you like?"

Another couple of weeks pass. Brrrt, brrrt. "Hello? Yes, Diane, the group meets on Tuesday evenings. No, I wouldn't mind picking you up at all. I will see you then."

Two days later, I go to pick up Diane. "Hello, so nice to see you. There are all types at the meeting. Most are like you and me, people who have lost a husband or a wife. Diane, how are you doing with placing your husband's affairs in order?"

"Simon, I was very involved in our business, so I am not having too horrible a time with it. However, there were some things he was involved with that I had no idea."

"There are two women who will be at the meeting who have helped me quite a bit," I suggest. "They are very organized and good with numbers, if that's what you need."

"Simon, I don't know how I feel about a complete stranger looking up my skirt. Would you mind giving me a day of your time?"

"I wouldn't mind at all. Just say when."

The closest way to the hospital goes back past my house. Diane must have remembered me mentioning that, as she exclaims, "Simon, don't you live close to here?"

I am taken with Diane's eagerness, combined with her beauty. Suddenly I am stricken with the giddiness of a teenager. It's all I can do to keep from stuttering, a habit that I had as a teen.

"Yes, you turn here and there it is, my humble writing castle."

"My God, Simon, what a view of the lake beyond the pines. I don't think I could drive myself to leave."

There it is in our view, my two-story Cape Cod log home, with forty-feet-tall pines lining the edges of the property like sentries.

"Yes, it is great! My father left me this house. He built it as a gift to my mother on their twentieth anniversary. Mother loved coming up here. She loved it all. Good times. There was also a home in the tip of southern Illinois where my family settled back in the early 1700s. That is where my family settled from Germany. The house was eventually sold to my uncle. My father built this one in the late forties, for my mother. There were many happy times here." I'm losing my thread. "A simpler time, yes."

"Would you mind showing me the inside?" Diane asks.

"Not at all. Let me get us up to the house." My Rover groans as it pushes through the bumper-high drifts. The tires settle and make their creaking sound as the temperature is once again at a high of negative ten. The wind is driving across the frozen Lake Superior. The winter storm has hushed, but the wind remains, still causing travel hazards. I goose the Rover till we are just a step away from my house. Outside, the snow cuts like razors on our exposed skin. We stomp off the snow from our boots and rush inside. I remove Diane's coat and place it on the large oak hall tree.

Diane gently takes my arm and asks if I have any Amaretto. "Indeed, I do. I also have rum, whiskey, and brandy." I stoke the wood stove. I am keeping myself busy so as not to look too nervous. I am not sure of Diane's intent, if it is what mine is—which is mostly to not make a fool of myself or trip over myself.

The glass door on the stove gives us a beautiful view of the fire within. Diane comes to me as a cat purring. My, she is exquisite. I am as skittery as a teenager. Her scent is pure woman. I drink it in. She could have any man, and yet she chooses me. Don't blow it, I tell myself! We are in my office on the second floor. The view even in this frozen tundra is beyond description. There are peaks and valleys on the lake. The great lake is frozen in motion as a backdrop to the majestic one-hundred-year-old pines, the motionless patriots who guard the edge of my land.

Diane takes in the view with her arms crossed. I approach her, take her glass of Amaretto on ice, and set it on the windowsill. I turn her toward me and I pick her up just beyond her knees. I place her somewhat gently upon my desk. My papers and pens explode to the floor. We are quickly locked in an embrace. We prepare to use my writing desk as it was not meant to be used.

***

Diane and I have become an item. If only the summer snowbirds would return, to give the small-town gossipers something else to talk about! But we are enjoying the winter months together. All the Minnesota and Chicago money has left for the winter. They will not return till May. Diane and I have dined out and certainly not hidden our affection from anyone. We both are grieving our losses and relying on each other.

Spring starts to show itself. The lake is still frozen over, but there are a few pockets of water. Ducks and geese enjoy a brisk bath in the small ponds. The ice breakers bust a path for freighters. I charge into the house, excited to tell Diane what I have been up to.

"Diane, tomorrow is March first, we have to take a dip in Superior! I have chopped a good-sized hole next to the ladder."

"Simon, there's not a chance of you getting me in that water. You don't really get in, do you?"

"Every March first. I'll crank up the fireplace in the family room. Then turn on the hot tub." I will get her good and hot. "Here up north, every March first we dive into the frozen lake. It brings good luck all the year. You gonna join me, hmm?"

"Simon, when you are in Rome, or up north, do as the morons do."

"That's a yes, isn't it? When you're old, you will be able to look back and say, I did something that every medical doctor in the world would warn against."

The next day, I am excited, and I cannot contain my smile at Diane's distressed body language. I do my best to impart my past experience. "Diane, the important thing is breath. It will be hard to breathe in, but you must. When you get out, run! Don't walk or jog, run to the house. Wrap yourself with blankets first, then the hot tub. Got it?"

"Simon, you first," she pleads.

"Jump in, it doesn't hurt quite as bad," I tell her. She keeps a keen eye upon me as I enter Superior. I am slowly stepping into the water.

My head goes under and my breath is taken away; the cold is like a baseball bat to my stomach. The ice is already forming above my head in the hole that I have just lowered myself through. The sight of ice above my head is terrifying. Once out, I dance about with a cat-that-ate-the-canary look pasted on my face. "Jump, Diane. Jump! Go under or it doesn't count." As Diane is underwater, I think how easy it would be if Diane were held under for just a few precious moments. I tell the voices to be quiet. The time is not right.

Wow, the cold is terrible. Ice is forming on our swimsuits. Diane is out as quickly as I was. "Run. Run, Diane!" Once we're inside, I make her drink some rum. She is taking short gulps of air, almost ready to hyperventilate.

"Slow down! Slow. You're breathing. In now." I place my hand upon her chest. "And out. All right, into the tub."

CHAPTER THIRTY-ONE

"Oooh! Christ on a stick, that's damn hot! But so nice. Simon, join me," Diane calls.

"Of course! So, what do you think of the icy water?" Splash, splash. I don't mind if we splash around a bit. "Come here, eh! You red-haired hottie. I never thought you would ask."

"One of the benefits of no kids. Simon, did you finally figure that out?"

"Diane, what time is your award dinner tonight?"

"It starts at seven. The dinner dance is for all the donors. Some of us who reached the gold donor status will get separate mention as the affair finishes up."

"Diane, your donation toward the hospital's new wing was monumental in getting the new cancer center off to a good start. I am proud of you. I am sure Jack would have been, also."

Her face tenses and her back straightens. "No, Simon, I don't think Jack would be. He felt that donating was a waste of time and resources."

I don't know what to say. "Diane, I... I was wrong about your husband." I am being pulled down. Nice guy/writer. Mask-wearing killer. So many voices in my head!

"Yes, you were wrong. We had the appearance of a perfect marriage. He loved those damn cattle more than me. He was a cheater, a beater, and an all-around dirtbag. He always blamed his father for his poor behavior. I believe that's just an excuse that's too easily used. You're a much nicer man, Simon. Let's get ready, I can't wait to show you off, Simon."

"I aim to please, Diane!" In just thirty minutes, we are at the doors of the Evergreen Country Club.

Later that evening, the host introduces Diane. "I would like to introduce Mrs. Williamson, who will read off the list of gold-status donors."

Diane steps to the podium. "Thank you, everyone. With all of your help, we are able to make a lasting impact on our community. And with all your generous donations, the hospital will be able to finish the new cancer wing in a quick fourteen months." Diane reads the long list of donors, then joins me again at our table.

"Wow, Diane, that's nice." I lower my voice as I put my mouth to Diane's ear. "How much did this cost you?"

"I couldn't really say. I sold a portion of the beef herd."

"Regardless, you did a good thing." I give her hand a quick kiss.

"Simon, will you have dinner with me tomorrow night?"

"A dress-up affair, or relaxed? Regardless, yes, I will."

"It's a bit of dress-up. Pick me up at seven, reservation

is at eight."

At seven I drive up the quarter-mile-long driveway to Diane's sprawling ranch, which is located on a hilltop on the south side of Bayview. The property is well lit, with an immense red-and-white-trim barn as a visual anchor.

"Diane, you look delicious. What is the occasion?"

"You'll find out at the St. Croix Cattlemen's Club."

"How on earth did you become a member there? It's a good-ol'-boys' club, no women, I thought?"

"Jack was invited initially. Then, when he passed on, the membership was offered to me, and, well... changing times, Simon." We drive to the club, and soon after, we are walking up the wide stone stairway to the large redwood doors trimmed in brass. We come to the valet station, where a tall, thin college-aged man promises to attend to the parking of my auto.

"Money opens many doors," I say.

We sit at our table. "Simon, I want you to become a business partner of mine," Diane says out of nowhere. "All you need to do is sign, and you will own 40 percent of my holdings."

"Diane, I am speechless. I do hope that this won't affect our relationship. What do you require from me?"

"Dear Simon, I require 50 percent of your assets. Your business, your land, your book sales, everything. Simon, the value of my farm is much greater."

"Why do you need me? What do I bring to your table?"

CHAPTER THIRTY-TWO

Diane stands with a straight back and her dazzling smile. "Simon, when men look at me, they see only my sparkling smile, and probably a nice set of boobs. No degree, no nothing. All they see is a single woman. A dumb widow." Diane turns to face me and gently grabs my chin. "Men feel that I am poor at business dealings, and I am damn tired of playing the good-ol'-boys' game. So sit back, have a few drinks, and let me handle them tonight. But I don't want to play the game any longer. Your job, Simon, is to back me up. I don't have the time to deal with the good-ol'-boys' network over and over, answering the same condescending questions again and again on every business dealing, just to set some good ol' boys straight." Diane places her soft hand on my cheek. "Hey, don't look so hurt, Simon. It will be a grand partnership. You can write to your heart's content and be by my side when I need you to make a showing. Between the two of us, the partnership would hold four thousand acres of timber and farmland, a little over two thousand dairy Herefords. Simon, it is time to think big. I mean real big!"

"Diane, I had no idea you were so aggressive."

"You should have! You know what I am like behind closed doors! You can't keep up, you poor thing?"

"I had no idea that was your mantra. Diane, I accept the job as your trophy man. Some wine to celebrate?" Later, I drive Diane to my place. We keep the conversation light and playful.

"Simon, warm up the tub, will you?" she asks.

"Diane, you are one of the lucky ones who look better out of her clothes than in them. So nice. That's a gift."

"Simon, hon, I must be leaving early tonight. I have an appointment in the morning."

"I understand. We have all the time in the world."

"My ride will be here soon." She caresses my cheek as she gives me a gentle kiss. "See you tomorrow, Simon." I hear the door click shut behind me as Diane leaves. I glance side to side, enjoying the view of the addition, which was built just a few years back. I used the country club bar as my inspiration in this addition, in memory of my father's tastes. Built-in bookcases, seven feet tall, an immense stone fireplace, pine bar with green elbow padding. My first book's royalties were spent on this luxury.

Three glasses of red wine, six fingers of rum, and two beers later, as I splash alone in the splendid hot tub, I hear the door open from behind me. "Diane, did you change your mind?"

CHAPTER THIRTY-THREE

"Sorry, baby, is that the name of your new toy?"

I jump out of my skin. I instantly recognize the Eastern European accent. Vivian. She has never spent more than a summer in Europe, but she loves the accent, and the stories of her travels that she carries with it.

"Dear Simon, your door was open. I let myself in. Will you lock your door?!"

"Vivian, please announce you're planning to drop by, won't you?! What brings you by on this cold winter day? You took a couple years off my life!"

"My darling cousin, you do need to lock your door. Just to keep the riffraff out. Simon, we haven't had a chance to speak alone for years. Till six weeks ago, it had been years since we had seen each other. Too many years have passed between us, Simon." Vivian strolls past the tub with a sheepish grin; she maintains solid eye contact with me. "Simon, I want to catch up on old times."

While she stands directly in front of me, her firm

bottom is facing a bay window with a row of spruce trees just past the glass. Vivian doesn't take her eyes off me, maybe seeing if I will break off eye contact first. She looks down at me in the hot tub. She then places her right hand on the edge of the wooden tub, and simulates taking steps with her right hand. She playfully stares in my eyes. "Why, Simon, you look like someone has just walked across your grave. I noticed Joey's favorite clown mask has disappeared from his room. Are you having fun with that? You're still working out, I trust." Vivian turns her head just so, and her hair lowers past her eyes. She then lets out a giggle, as she shakes the hair from her face. She playfully asks, "Would you mind? May I join you, Simon?"

"Vivian, I can take it if you can!" Vivian stands proudly next to the tub. She slowly slips from her dress, keeping eye contact with me all the while. Her smile changes as she purses her lips.

"Vivian, I must say you have changed since I last saw you in the buff."

"Yes, I am no longer sniffing gas till I pass out. Yes, we had good times with you, cousin."

"That's good to know, cousin. I well remember the games we all played as young teens," I say.

"Simon, have I changed? I was just thirteen then." She gives a triumphant Vanna-like wave of her hand. She turns her hips slightly with her leg crossed over, waves again, and says, "It is the best money can buy, honey."

"I guessed as much. I approve, especially your artwork. That phoenix is beautiful." She steps forward with a turn, to fully expose her left shoulder. Then, with all the confidence of a well-paid stripper, she dips one foot and then the other into the hot tub. If she weren't my cousin...

"I noticed that someone had broken into my father's house," she says. "The area is not what it once was. Whoever it was, they also broke into my father's office just a few weeks back. You wouldn't have a clue about that, would you, Simon?"

"Vivian, once it is known that a house is empty, it will have squatters, like the house on Route 12. By the way, were you aware that I was jumped at your house on Route 12? If you remember, I have certain memories of your father's house that prevent me from entering that place," I say with a shiver. "After nightfall especially."

"Poor baby, you are still haunted by little Joey, aren't you." Vivian now shows a most wicked grin. "He asks about you. The poor tortured soul. You can still hear him wail, late at night. Many times he screams out your name. I remember that night; it was you who left Joey in the attic to face his demons, all alone. He wasn't strong enough, Simon, and you knew that! He killed himself that night. That's when he hung himself. He..." Vivian pauses for effect. "He no longer could stand the voices in his head! You were his favorite, Simon, even though you were too cowardly to go and get him out of that dark, lonely attic." Vivian's voice changes to almost a whisper as she leans back and takes my half-full glass of wine from the edge of the tub. "You were always kind to him, Simon. But that wasn't enough for him. He needed strength. The pain is still fresh from his death."

"Vivian, I wasn't smart enough or brave enough to see what was happening to him. I didn't stop the beatings, the abuse that led to his death. I did nothing to help him." My face is red as I slowly rise from the tub, while I point at Vivian.

"Mother felt Joey was weak," Vivian says. "Mother constantly pushed him to grow, to get stronger. She would take her riding crop to his back for the purpose of making him tougher! But he was a weak shit." Vivian's voice rises, all urgent and shrill, and takes on a loud, sinister tone. "That weak shit, he couldn't take her stern hand at becoming a man! Then finally he started wearing that stupid clown mask all the time, like it possessed him. Joey took the coward's way out. After he killed my mother in her sleep." Vivian's shoulders slump. Her skin has lost its color, and a tear comes from her right eye. "Did you know that, Simon? Did you know that Joey killed my mother, your aunt?"

"I never knew." I am gaping in shock. "Vivian, I was busy. We were all busy, too busy to help! I was dealing with my mother's and sister's deaths."

Vivian lets out a loud, sinister cackle. "Correct me if I am wrong, Simon, but you rejoiced over your sister's passing. You were more concerned with the well-being of your father's shotgun. That precious 16-gauge Parker, wasn't it? You must come by sometime, Simon. Joey would love the company."

She glares at me, then changes the subject. "You're a bright guy, Simon. Did you find what you were looking for? In the early hours of that morning?"

"Just some minor info, comparing dates. So yes, yes I did."

"Simon, my father had lost his zest for the hunt and the kill, so to speak. Edmond and I took over the family business some time ago. Father would have given it all to some charity or cousin, and we just couldn't have that. He would've let all his work go to hell in a handbasket and left us as paupers. Dan doesn't have the gravel in his belly for it. Did you hear? Dan has fallen ill. His share of the inheritance may soon be Edmond's and mine."

Vivian speaks with flair and confidence. "It was a shame, Simon. And while we are on this somber subject, I was sorry to hear of your wife's passing. What happened to poor Faith? Did she fight much? Did she beg for her life? Come now, Simon, tell me the details, don't be shy!" Vivian perks up and her eyes glow as she listens.

"Faith died of a blood infection. The fever got her. It was quick."

"Simon, you used Nancy's cocktail. At least have the gravel to admit it to me."

I... I am shocked that Vivian has figured it out so quickly. "Yes, you are right, Vivian. Nancy's cocktail."

"I knew it! You received the cocktail from Edmond. That's it, it must be!" Vivian is in an excited state. She is perked up above the water surface, beaming with excitement. She points at me. "Simon, did you enjoy watching her pass? Isn't it exquisite to watch as life slips away? You know that Chicago money is always the sweetest meat. Small or large amounts, it is all good, my cousin. However, it does not go as far as it once did." Vivian slides next to my right side. Our shoulders touch in the tub, as they did when we used to play as wee babies. "Your new toy, does she suspect anything? Simon, what are your plans with your newfound family knowledge? You would not do anything rash now, would you? You aren't considering that coin flip you do in times of indecision?"

"I have done it already. The coin chose to let it be for now. The coin doesn't fail me. There is nothing that I wish to do at this time. Vivian, is there room to join the family business?"

She slides too close for comfort. "Simon, yes, there is always room, as long as you are an active member. I must reach out to Edmond and discuss the possibility of your joining the team. Danial has relied on Edmond's and my talents. But alas, he contributes nothing. Unlike Danial, you must be active. What are your thoughts?"

"Yes, cousin. You may tell Edmond that I will be an active partner."

"Does your new girl toy have any suspicions about her husband? Or any concerns about her own well-being?"

"I don't think she has any suspicions."

Vivian is now in her element. This is her wheelhouse. She is beaming at me, her full breasts just out of the water as she breathes deeply, like a cat that has her mouse cornered.

"Isn't Nancy's cocktail the best?" she continues. "The best chemicals money can buy. When it is blended just so, it is almost impossible to trace. She was told of the recipe by our grandfather. So, Simon, I am trusting you with family heritage and family secrets, since you are about to join a family business. Great minds and all that." She switches gears again. "Simon, you never did tell me, what happened to your true love, did you fall out of love?"

"Faith made my life hell after I was fired for simply correcting a student. She was just dreadful after that. Plus her mommy was getting more and more involved in their family business, possibly taking over the financials of their company, or possibly splitting up the business between the brothers. I just couldn't deal with it. When Faith put me on the books for the family company, her mother took exception to my presence. That filthy, uppity woman." I speak in a low tone. "Vivian, she wanted me to crawl on my belly."

Vivian perks up. "You need a woman who will support you and partner with you for years to come! We are not so unlike, you and me and my twin. You see an obstacle and you simply remove it. Case closed. Simon, what is your new playfriend's name?"

"She is Diane Williamson." Vivian leans out and exposes more of her body to high-five me.

"Oh, jackpot, Simon! Yahtzee! Good job. I am proud of you, cousin. You have the golden goose," she barks with excitement. "Rumor has it that she is wealthy and just lost her. Simon you didn't, did you?" A smile enters my face.

I had forgotten the fun side Vivian can show at a moment's notice. I now beam with pride as a first grader who is being praised. "Oh, Vivian, I am not without my charm."

Vivian exits the tub. Steam comes off her body and she is dry almost instantly. She sits on a dressing bench, crosses her long legs very ladylike, and cups her chin in her palm. Then she shouts in a nagging voice, "Simon! Simon! I am bored!" She gives me a wave, and in a matter of moments she is fully dressed. "Remember, lock that door. Bye, Simon."

I shoot out of the tub. My only thought is to warn Dan that he is in danger. I run to the phone. "Yes, Danial, be careful. I think your family is after you."

"Why?"

"You're not bloodthirsty enough, Danial! Hell, I don't know. But watch your ass!"

***

Two weeks have passed since Vivian's surprise visit. Diane has been distant since then. She seems concerned about... something. I sit on the edge of my tub again and I flip my coin of chance. There it is, decided. She must not die. I love her. The coin is simple. The coin doesn't lie to me.

I am enjoying my hot tub after several hours of taking care of a few hundred head of cattle in the frigid cold. I hear a clang in the kitchen. "Cousin, is that you? Cousin?"

"Who are you yelling at, Simon?" Diane peeks her head into the family room. "You really need to lock that door, babe. Are you expecting one of your dreadful cousins that you've told me about? They are vicious, aren't they?"

"Yes, they are, Diane. I didn't know you were coming out today. So nice to see you."

Diane comes over and playfully splays out on top of me. I grab her by her luscious hips and pull her toward me. My fingers dig into her shapely, firm buttocks. It has been weeks since we last made love. Her raw eagerness and sexual aggression are like a magic carpet ride back to my teenage years. I am young again, strong, virile, I think, as we drive each other to a frenzied climax.

CHAPTER THIRTY-FOUR

A streak of blood slowly drips into the tub. Diane lets out a small squeak. Then, she ignites with a fury. She pushes me away. I look at her, palms turned up. "Why?" She slowly rises up out of the water. Rage is written across her face. A trace of blood is on her hip. She slaps me hard across the face.

"That ring! Your ring, you... you bastard." She slaps me hard again. A certain amount of excitement surges through me with the rough play. "You didn't get it fixed. You had weeks to fix it. You greedy son of a bitch! You had to have it all." I am aghast at the accusation. I had envisioned Diane and I making an empire in the northland.

"No, Diane, I am not like that! Just listen to me!"

"No, Simon, you are just like your uncle."

She stands above me, glowing red with anger, and continues to berate me. "Simon, enough wasn't enough, was it?" My plan changes quickly, as she has indeed pissed me off. If she continues her rant, I will enjoy her as cousin Joey would have. Joey had a deep, dark hunger. That odd little man. He was a master of disposing of the bodies of his victims. Before he died, he would go on and on about his process. He considered this his special gift, dealing with the bodies. He would dismember his victims. Dear Diane must be reduced in size for the hogs. I will need to chop her into hog food. The hogs would be a quick way to dispose of her. Hogs, disgusting animals, will strip all the meat from the bone.

Then, as per Joey's instructions, I will dispose of the bones one by one, dropping them into the brand-new ten-horsepower wood chipper. Joey would then finally mix the bone fragments with cracked corn. The hogs and cattle would enjoy the last bits of his victim. Every last bit of his toy would be gone, and in time even the memory would disappear. Their deaths were always a mystery to all, even to Joey.

I try to appease Diane. "How are you feeling, dearest? You seem a bit out of it today. A headache, maybe?" I give her a hard yet playful whomp on the ass. Normally she is playful, but today, not so much.

"Simon, you have gone too far. Is it you or your cousins who killed Faith, then Jack? And who else?" Diane turns her head and looks over her right shoulder, with her hair disguising a wicked glare. She stands straight, tall and defiant. "Simon, I was prepared to kill Jack to escape my marriage. Someone took that pleasure from me. I was prepared to chop Jack into tiny pieces and let the fish eat him, just to escape that miserable marriage." She gives me a frightful glare. "I feel it was you who took that pleasure away from me, wasn't it?!" What was once a scream lowers to a sultry, sexy tone. "Who is next, Simon? Me?" She turns and exposes the right side of her face. The thought of ending Diane's life has come across my mind, as a hunger for sweet chocolate. A deep hunger stirring within me. But the thought of not being able to feel her touch, her caress... Diane now looks directly at me. She says in a loud whisper, "Who will it be, Simon?" She gives a wave that points back to her. Then a long pause. "Will your next victim be me?"

"Diane, I enjoy you just way too much to share you."

She stands in the tub, with the warm, inviting water just above her knees. A very slight smile plays on her lips while she looks down at me. In the middle of all that drama, my landline rings in the kitchen. I stand with a strong sigh. Wrapped with a large towel, I tiptoe to the phone. "Yes? Edmond, no, I wish to finish the book. Ed, I have told you that several times! Edmond, I am busy. May I call you back?" Edmond asks for a few more moments of my time. I hear Diane barking at me as if I were still in the same room. While I speak to Edmond, the door that I rarely lock opens. I cover the receiver with my hand and yell back at Diane. "Hey, Diane, now Ed has upped his offer. I told him to shove his offer so far up it snaps off."

"Simon, way to tell your terrible cousin off," she shouts back. "I am proud of you."

"Thanks, Diane!"

CHAPTER THIRTY-FIVE

"Hey, Diane, dinner out tonight?"

"Sure, Simon!" We yell back and forth. I turn my attention back to Edmond. "Yes, of course. No means no! Ed, what page in your father's novel? Let me flip through and try to find it. Ed, your name is not mentioned on that page, or before page 210."

A dark, dangerous figure slinks behind Diane while I engage on the phone with Edmond. The figure is enjoying Diane's wet, pert shape.

From behind, two hands slide down Diane's neck to her breasts. Diane reacts. "Simon, your hands are cold. Warm them up! Oooh, Simon, that feels good. Get back in the tub, darling." Diane slowly turns to find Max standing above her. He has an evil grin pasted upon his face. "Simon, Simon!" Diane shouts. Her eyes widen as she is pushed below the water. She fights and thrashes. She pulls Max into the tub, splashing water all about. Her shoulders are now pinned at the base of the tub. She continues to fight, scratching and tearing. For only a few more moments.

I hear the ballistic splashing. Sensing something out of sort, I stretch the phone cord to its limit. Edmond makes a final plea for the novel, but I slam the phone down and charge into the family room. The side door of my house slowly clicks shut.

Diane is still pursuing her escape from death. She is thrashing in the water, digging her nails deep into Max's forearms. She now has her head out of the water. Max is almost in a panic as he realizes another opportunity may be slipping away. He pushes with all his might and firms his grip upon her shoulders. He manages to push Diane underwater again and to hold her there for thirty, forty, fifty seconds, until there are no more bubbles. Her life has left her body. Those precious few seconds is all it took to lose Diane. I was oblivious to her peril.

The landline rings again. Ed raises his offer. "Simon, how about $750,000? You have to sell a lot of books to make that. And, cousin, how is your new playfriend? You see, Simon, there is nothing that you possess that I cannot take from you."

I slowly slink to the floor, the stretched phone cord dangling in my face. I am numb. No grief, no pain, only anger and pure hatred for my cousin.

The anger at Diane's loss is foremost in my thoughts, however, $750,000 is a lot of money. "No means no, Ed! I'm ending the call."

Diane is floating faceup just under the water. I charge to her side, put my arms below her neck and back, and lift her from the tub. She is still warm and soft. I am not ready to be alone again. I begin chest compressions, one, two, three, again and again. Damn. I tilt her head. I think I know how to do this. I close her nose, one, two, three puffs. The side door slowly opens. I stare wide-eyed at the door in a shock and terror, waiting for someone to enter. The lock. Damn it. Damn it!

CHAPTER THIRTY-SIX

The phone rings again. It's Vivian. "Simon, if you would have taken our offer, Diane would have been spared."

"Edmond, Vivian, you sons of bitches! I will see you in hell!"

"You first, Simon. Goodbye." Click.

I am alone with Diane again. I am still wrapped in a towel, soaking wet. I am leaning over Diane. What do I do?

I had just gotten comfortable with Diane. Faith is gone. Now Diane is gone. I am sobbing deep breathless sobs over Diane's beautiful, lifeless body. My tears drip upon her neck and chest.

The damn phone rings again, and within seconds there is a knock at my door. I answer the phone in a rage. "Yes! What?"

Vivian's voice. "You really should answer your door." What the hell? My head spins. I am lost, not sure what to do next. Diane is dead. Her eyes are still open.

In the shock at what is happening all around me, I just now realize that Detective Lammer is at my door. It is my blood she wants. She bangs on the door harder and harder. Damn my cousins! "Luchk, Luchk! Let me in now, Luchk!" She pushes the door open. I have no time to hide Diane's body. I cover the naked, wet Diane with a horsehair blanket. I need time! What to do next?

Just then Lammer receives a call on her police band. A short reprieve. She must leave now. Lammer does not see Diane's dead body. Lammer quickly turns her hip and charges for her car. Her head turns quickly back. I think she has just realized that I am soaking wet, top to bottom. "Luchk, I will be back." She starts her car. The goddamned phone rings again. "Vivian, what the hell are you doing?" All I can hear is Vivian and Edmond laughing uncontrollably on speakerphone. My God!

Before Lammer charged back to her car, she was standing three feet from Diane's body. I feared she was going to trip over Diane. Good thing she was in such a hurry to leave.

I hear my cousins' ruckus from my phone. "Who was that at your door, Simon? Ha ha ha." They yell maybe to excite me, maybe to incriminate me. Finally they both quiet down a bit. "Simon, all you had to do was to hand our father's novel and all the papers back to us. Your toy Diane would not be dead. And yes, Simon, a capital murder conviction is in your future." Edmond boasts again, "You see, Simon, that there is nothing you possess that I cannot take from you!"

I am bombarded with emotion and rage. I am consumed with the phone chatter, so much so that I am unaware of Vivian standing behind me, next to the hot tub.

I must fix the lock. "I will not let you take all I have," I shout. "I will die on my terms, not your terms. I'm not rotting in a jail! I will pull you bastards down, I swear."

"Simon, you poor baby," Vivian says. "Your wife and business partner are both dead. So tragic. Then who's next? Edmond? Myself?" Vivian poses in a sequined evening gown. "When I die, I will come back more powerful than you could imagine!" She releases a sharp cackle. "Oh, you squeamish little twerp! Poor Simon, scared of dying, aren't you."

I have imagined my cousins' deaths for some time. But for now I have to save it for another time. I must remain focused while she is so close. In a matter-of-fact voice, Vivian says, "You are gutless. We will get you! One negative story about my father and it will cost you."

I can live with that. My land now reaches through the flatlands to the tall pines. I am at last among the top five wealthiest people in Wisconsin. Behind a Patrick Schultz.

When Vivian leaves, I lie in bed, and my mind swims with the past weeks' events. My brain will not shut off. It won't shut off. I have a terrible time getting to sleep. How much longer will I be free? My mind runs round and round, faster and faster; my head is pounding. Normally I would read to quell my speeding brain. At this early hour, I turn to rum and Excedrin to knock me out. I need a break, a getaway, from everything, from the life that I have begun to embrace.

I book a seat on the local air shuttle to the Superior airport. From there, it's a short drive down to my family's island resort, the Arms Retreat. The small island is just ten miles from solid land, nestled in the great Lake Superior. Even during the bitter cold, it is fascinating, alluring in its beauty and savagery. It is hypnotic to see the often violent acts of nature toward the island inhabitants and the hearty wildlife that call the island home. Yet, it is beautiful how the waves have frozen in motion, creating a jagged ice road from the mainland to the island.

There is of course an iceboat. I board the iceboat that will cross the great frozen lake. The boat bangs and slams as it crests the peak of each frozen wave, just to slam the stern down like a fist. Only six passengers are on board, one of them a postal carrier. The small red iceboat is cramped, with tiny windows and a low roofline. It rocks to and fro. I fight to keep my lunch within me. One passenger brings supplies to the island. This is not the height of the tourist season. After a twenty-minute-plus ride of rattling bones and teeth, we arrive. There is something so wonderful about doing things different from the norm. There is nothing to view but ice and snow.

I am greeted at the lodge like royalty. My aunt Lucy and uncle Edger have owned the retreat for years. They live on the island as year-round residents, in a modest twenty-room estate that carries my family name, the same as theirs. The workers are all on their best behavior. I am immediately shown to my room on the fourth floor, which overlooks the tiny island community. The community reminds me of a movie from the '60s, or possibly a Norman Rockwell print. There is a hot-chocolate hut, with children and adults ice skating and their dogs playfully chasing them in circles. I take a moment and reflect. Edmond and Vivian tried to set me up for Diane's death. The bastards!

The skaters can warm themselves by a fire burning nearby. This is a land that time has forgotten. I place my leather satchel onto the very nice wooden desk. From the chair behind the desk, a spacious window provides a spectacular view of the ice world just on the other side of the glass. I take out my old but functional trusty laptop. I am not sure why men are so sensitive about having a man purse. I love my leather satchel. It looks just fine; besides, it is a simple way not to be broadcasting that you are carrying. I take my four-by-six notebook out of the satchel. I enjoy placing my random thoughts and ideas onto paper first. Then later I will save the worthy ideas into a Word document. In front of this window with a view is a perfect place to write. Too bad about Faith. We had been to the retreat once before, and she just loved it. We had a splendid time.

At 5 p.m. precisely, I venture to the restaurant that is inside the retreat. I walk through the halls, guided by the smell of food, which beckons me. It leads me toward the well-staffed restaurant. The smell of food and the sound of soft conversation fill the air. The décor is stone walls held in place by hundred-year-old mortar. Dark cedar wood adorns the brass trim of the doors and windows. The retreat boasts seven turn-of-the-century wood-burning fireplaces. There are tasteful paintings with rich frames and glass encasing portraits of many of my ancestors and high times for my family and the early island upper crust. Many carry the details of the island's history. Just outside of the bar is a painting of a lovely woman in a black full-length woolen coat with a long red-and-gray neck scarf, accented in lovely red lipstick. The young woman in the portrait has elfin features and she looks elated at what must have been her anticipation of a delightful night out. As I study the painting, a young waitress passes me.

"She is lovely, don't you think?"

I reply, despite being startled. "Why yes, yes she is. You wonder what she is thinking."

She replies, "I have studied that painting since I became employed here. I like to imagine that she has just been let out of a carriage and she is waiting for her love, for a fabulous night of dining and dancing."

The young waitress clasps her hands in front of her chest. She raises her right heel just so. She does a little spin, and off to work she goes. Ah, a young romantic, I think as she walks away. Youth is wasted on the very young. I release a soft chuckle.

As I take a seat at the near-empty bar, I see a familiar face—the young maiden I had just met by the painting. She tends bar also. "An Old Fashioned, please. I am..."

She holds up her hand. "I know who you are. You're that writer, right? We all know who you are. I am Jessica. If there is anything I can get you, please, just ask."

I reach my right hand across the bar. "Jessica, it is my pleasure to meet you. How long have you worked for my family?"

"Ten years."

I raise an eyebrow. "You don't look old enough to have been in the workforce that long."

"Mr. Luchk, you must understand there are very few job opportunities here on the island. I began as a dishwasher just before my sixteenth birthday." I notice a change in her demeanor, from fan to bartender. She looks past me. "If you need anything, call me. See you later, Mr. Luchk." Jessica puts my drink in front of me and goes to tend to other tasks.

The day slips slowly into night. A small dinner crowd

comes in from the early spring cold, bringing with them rosy cheeks, big appetites, and red hands. The large stone walls look sturdy and inviting. I nestle in at a table for two, with just myself and my leather-bound journal. I sit next to an open fireplace. The joy of people-watching. The flames bounce up and down as I hear the wind gust, pushing the spring rain against the strong stone walls. They have protected the interior the past one hundred years from what lies on the other side. After dinner I reflect on the retreat's history and relax with a few cocktails, cuddling my notepad. I imagine Fitzgerald sitting by the very same huge stone fireplace, writing his ideas in his journal just as I am, on his stop toward his summer home in Minneapolis. I can picture him sitting in this exact table, in this exact chair, writing out one of his novels.

Sitting primly at a corner table is a lovely older professional-looking couple. The gentleman has a nicely trimmed gray beard and he's wearing a button-up sweater with those wonderful elbow patches. To top it all off, he has round metal-rim glasses. He looks like the stereotypical college professor or writer. The woman is between fifty and sixty years young. She has been blessed with beauty that has not faded since her youth. She has a nice neckline and broad shoulders. I must meet them. The couple is engaged in conversation, but she glances my way from time to time. She tilts her head as if to tell her husband a secret about me. I motion Jessica to my table and ask her to introduce me. She allows me to follow her.

I introduce myself. It truly helps when your last name is that of the estate's owners. My aunt and uncle have been involved with the island community politically and are outspoken advocates for the business community. My name is well known on the island.

The couple's names are Fritz and Gretchen Newman. They live just twenty miles in on the mainland. We spend an hour discussing Fitzgerald and his writing. Gretchen and Fritz are fans of all types of literature. It is so nice to meet well-read and educated people. So many times a reader appears starstruck, and they cannot represent themselves well.

Gretchen asks if I have any new projects, which is a great segue into my uncle's novel. For a writer, talking about one's work is a rare pleasure, if you don't mind letting out any of the plot secrets from your new books. Fritz, as it happens, owns a small fleet of fishing boats, plus he handles an investment firm. His boats are all in boathouses off the mainland. Fritz and his wife come to town weekly to inspect the boathouses for damage. They're trying their best to not let the harsh winter get a foothold and ruin their expensive boats. The icebreakers keep the waters close to the mainland broken up and running. The water keeps flowing for most of the winter, as the ice does not get as massively thick. I bring up that I own a small number of charter fishing boats, which I've inherited. I mention that I own these boats but I am a bit intimidated by the water. Terrified of the water, truth be told. Fritz brings up issues that I hadn't a clue about. But I do understand upkeep and cost. He says that his twelve-boat fleet, as he calls them, are docked at the Ashland ports twenty-five miles south of our location. "We stop by this island once a week or so," Fritz says, "to inspect the thickness of the ice plus the condition of the boathouses and our docks for damage. Then it is here for a fine night out."

Fritz boasts a bit, encouraged by his wife's approving nod and genuine smile. He leans back in his chair with a broad grin. He gives his drink a twirl with fresh ice, and looks into his wife's eyes. "Yes, sir, you can never be too cautious, if the weather takes hold." I watch their body language. It is refreshing to see a couple who seem to still be in love after all the years together. "Damage can put you back weeks, maybe months in the spring!" Fritz continues.

I have to ask. "Do you and Gretchen stay overnight on the island when you're here?"

Gretchen squirms a bit and looks at Fritz. She puts her hand over his. They don't answer. "Simon, I must ask," Fritz starts, with a face as stony as his wife's, "how did your wife die? There was very little press over the affair, and you were both so young." I explain how we had been assaulted, and I go into the sordid details of Faith's death.

"To answer your question about whether we stay here, Simon... hell no. You've heard the stories, haven't you?" Gretchen now has a broad, youthful smile on her face. She prepares to begin the tale. At a glance, she now appears twenty years younger.

I look into her twinkling eyes. "Please continue, Gretchen." My chin is in my palm.   I am intrigued. A rare winter thunderstorm is raging outside the windows. The storm adds to the ambiance of the story. The writer in me cannot wait to hear all the juicy details. I am grinning from ear to ear. My right leg bounces up and down in anticipation of a genuine ghost story. The beautiful grandfather clock chimes eight o'clock.

As if on cue, my aunt Lucy appears. She stands by my right side, a gentle hand upon my shoulder. The restaurant is abuzz with her presence. I introduce Fritz and Gretchen to Lucy, who beams at her guests. I go back to Gretchen's story. "Mrs. Newman was just beginning to tell me a story about your retreat." A glance from my aunt seems as though it might stop the tale.

"Simon, there are many stories that claim their origins in the Arms Retreat," Aunt Lucy says. "Some are love stories and of course some are tragic. Those seem to be the stories that history remembers the longest."

Gretchen's face turns a warm shade of peach at the attention of the owner of the retreat and her nephew.

CHAPTER THIRTY-SEVEN

Gretchen now scoots to the edge of her chair. She glances to both sides, and waits for a nod from Lucy to begin. "Well, let's see. It began some years ago. The lady in that painting, just around the corner, across from the bar there—Magdalena was her name. My sister Amanda worked here as a waitress."

Lucy nods; she remembers Amanda. "Yes, a pleasant girl, always a smile on her face."

Gretchen continues. "Well, the workers say that on certain nights, Magdalena will appear, dressed just as she is dressed in the painting." The flames from the candles on the table have a dancing effect on Gretchen's glasses, and also on the wall. The candles, together with the giant fireplace, cast a yellow glow as an eerie backdrop for this story. Shadows dance against the wall. This is an excellent setting for a ghost story. Gretchen continues with animated hand gestures and wide, haunting eyes. "It is as though the beautiful woman in the red coat has not aged a day. The night of the painting is the last time Magdalena was seen alive. She posed just beyond the heavy wooden doors of the estate. The haunting began shortly after that night; late autumn of the year 1869."

Our candles flicker as if a doorway to the past has just swung open. "The carriage never returned that night to collect her and take her home," Gretchen continues. "She was never picked up from the restaurant. Ten months later, the retreat was sold to a group of investors from Chicago. Ten years later, to your grandfather, William Lincoln Luchk. It is as though Magdalena never left the retreat. When she appears, she is still dressed in her red woolen coat and bright blood-red parasol, waiting for her love to escort her home. Her hair and features are just as they were so many years before. Forever young, unchanged."

Gretchen sits upright. Aunt Lucy interjects. "Every motel has a story; every motel," she says for effect, "has a ghost. The very large motels do not have a thirteenth floor, nor any rooms numbered thirteen at all. Have any of you seen her yet?" Aunt Lucy asks as she glances at the three of us at the table.

"No," Gretchen replies. "The thought of running into Magdalena terrifies me. But still so very exciting!" she proclaims.

"My father and uncle would tell me to get a backbone," I say. "Aunt Lucy, you know your brothers." I stand and take Gretchen by her upper arm, and we saunter over to the portrait of Magdalena. Fritz enjoys another cocktail in my aunt Lucy's company. We return to join them shortly.

"The lovely woman in the red coat—she really appears here at this retreat?" Fritz asks.

"Yes, that is her," Lucy claims in a faraway whisper. "She was the first lady of the house."

Gretchen leans in as she is enjoying telling her story. "Her body was never found. It's all just rumors, really. Some say that the island had a cult living on it at the time. Their leader was a big-city doctor from Minneapolis." Gretchen leans forward to scoot closer to Lucy. This is a story Lucy knows well.

Lucy touches Gretchen's arm. She speaks in a loud whisper. "Doctor Schultz was his name. His disciples, they resided in the ground. They dug deep into the hills like badgers, miles past the houses and shops, where even brave men will not go. Legend says that these people came here to the island for a better life. But when the logging industry dried up, they had to dig into the hills like animals to survive the savage winters. She may have been abducted by members of the island cult. You know, this is one of those strange stories. No one knows where it began and there's nothing to back it up, only gossip and conjecture. A tale told by the campfire perhaps, to pass down through the ages. Some people say that Magdalena was taken away by the locals, that the cult made offerings to the doctor's pagan gods to ensure the favor of his ritualist church. They would sacrifice drunken tourists or unfortunate locals by the light of the full moon each month. Many people have disappeared and never been seen again." Lucy sits back, enjoying her drink. "There was a rumor that when Magdalena was taken, her rich husband placed a bounty on her captors' heads. A massive amount of money. For years, men would dig into the now-vacant dens in the ground. From time to time, a poor soul would be dragged into the sheriff's office and almost beaten to a pulp, trying to claim the wealth that your great-grandfather, old Mr.Luchk, had promised. The fortune never got handed out. Mostly men just had their lives taken. She was never found. The sheriff didn't care. He wasn't getting part of that bounty; besides, the bounty hunters were clearing out the island's riffraff." Some of the locals turn their heads toward us.

Gretchen slips back into her role. "Lucy, do the workers here at the retreat talk to you about what they see? They say you can hear her late at night and feel her presence in the halls, in the rooms, all over. Trying to escape her grave, they speculate."

Now Gretchen truly has my interest. I give her a matter-of-fact look. "I am on the fourth floor. Any stories from that floor?" Aunt Lucy gives me a look and a nod to join her at the back of the restaurant. I follow her to a secluded booth. She has a concerned look upon her face. She sits across me and takes my right hand in hers. The one-hundred-year-old structure allows the wind to whistle through, as we are seated cornered inside two outside walls. My aunt begins, "Simon, I was so sorry to hear of your Faith's passing." She grips my hand tightly while she looks over her shoulder. "Please, do not pass on stories to other guests or our help. Gretchen is a regular. She just loves to speculate. It's part of her charm. You do understand, don't you? There is just one more matter to discuss."

I am taken aback by her request. I have never been told what to do or with whom. Ever. My face has taken a crimson tint as my temper begins to rise. Aunt Lucy now pats my hand as she notices my grip tighten on hers. "Simon, please do not include anything you are hearing tonight in a book, please. Your uncle and I have worked very hard to build loyal, repeat customers, and quite frankly we have poured many thousands into the retreat, and ghost stories or a scandal could crush us."

I sit quietly for a moment. At the look of concern on my aunt's face, my anger subsides, as if a large ice bucket is tossed upon my fire. I hold my aunt's hands in mine, then pull them to my face and give them a kiss. "Aunt Lucy, I have always enjoyed my time with you and Uncle Edger, and I would never write or repeat anything that might hurt your business." Unless it would make me a buck. "Have you ever considered being placed on the haunted motel tour? It may be fruitful." I see the concern on her face has not diminished. I now understand just how big an impact I could have on their lives.

As I prepare to return to my room in the west wing, Aunt Lucy fills me in about its history. I am now armed with the knowledge that my room was part of the wing that originally held the nursery, and then aspiring writers. Apparently my aunt and uncle kept the word "retreat" in the resort's name after it was a writers' retreat just after the Second World War.

On my way back, I turn the corner and bump headfirst into Fritz and Gretchen as they are preparing to leave the retreat for the night. I bid the couple goodnight. "Fritz, Gretchen, thank you so much for your kind conversation and time. I bid you both a goodnight and safe travels." I also give a thank-you wave to Jessica, the young barmaid, who is craning her neck from behind the bar as I exit the restaurant. The painting once again pulls me toward it. The woman, I swear that she speaks to me, that she moves in the painting as if asking me to join her. I study her in her red coat and carefree smile. How much time did she have on this earth after she posed for this painting?

My eyes close briefly, and I am transported to the woman wearing her red coat. She turns and gives me a smile. What could she have done different to stave off the end of her life, a life cut so short? Ten minutes later, my face is wet with ice water and someone slaps me and gives me a good shake. I am back to present time, looking from the floor up to see Fritz and Gretchen staring down at me with great concern. It seems that I had the woozies and wobbles, then a sudden icy feeling down my legs, and down to the floor I went.

I am assisted up by my aunt, Fritz, and his wife. As a team they guide me safely into room 417. It is as I left it. A comfortable room with a large bed and a comfy wingback reading chair, with a matching footstool and a large oak desk. Knowing more of the history of the room, I can see where a writing desk and a reading chair would be of a benefit, even demanded. The window overlooks the restaurant and some small, overpriced island homes. I can also see the hills on the far side of the island, with their lit ski slopes and tubing trails beckoning fun-seekers. Lights glow into the crisp night air, with the frozen lake as a backdrop.

I place myself into the desk chair, put my feet up, and pick up my notepad. My back is to the window. I am running on alcohol and fresh ghost stories. With this newly induced rush of inspiration, I continue to map out the direction of my uncle's unfinished work. My room is silent, minus the sound of an icy rain whisking against the large window. Rum with Dew is my writing fuel. Later I transfer the words from the paper to my laptop. Click,

click, click go the keys. At 4:15, I hear a sound. A song is coming through the wall from next door, room 418. The voice is a young woman's, singing a German nursery rhyme. She is possibly singing to hush her small child at this hour, or maybe to pass the time after she was awakened by her baby for feeding. Or was it that I moved around my room too noisily and woke the child in the early hour? The voice, along with the scent of lavender in my room, brings memories long forgotten. So many of my early memories race through my head.

Is it my dear Faith's voice, I think. Can it be her? It is her, singing the very same German nursery rhyme that my mother, a second-generation German in America, would also sing to me, saying it was my special song. Faith's mother was also a stone-faced German woman. With my feet still up, I lean back deeper into the chair, remembering my mother's voice as she would sing to me ("Heibe kinder hawie haus..."). I roll my chair next to the wall where the lovely female voice is floating through, to me. My eyes blur with heavy tears.

The nursery rhyme stops and a door clicks. I bolt into the hallway. A tall, broad-shouldered woman in a long red woolen coat floats away from me. She moves so smoothly that I am not sure her feet touch the carpeted floor. The scent of lavender is now stronger. She turns slightly to expose her features. She is blessed with a lovely firm jawline and a tight neck. She gives me a subtle smile, then she goes further into the hallway. She is gently touching the wall to her left. Her perfume is stronger now. The melody begins again, and I am overcome with emotion as I remember being nestled in my mother's bosom. My mother and my grandmother would both sing this song to me, and they've both been gone for many years now. They would take turns singing and rocking me when I was a sickly child. Tears fill my eyes as memories flood into my head. I am floating above, looking down at my young self and my mother and grandmama. There is a gentle caress to my cheek and the smell of lavender. The fragrance is my mother, and my grandmother, maybe one and the same. Somehow I am back in my room. Light is coming through the window. It is the sunrise of another day. I crawl under the comforter on the soft bed. I was able to do some more work on my book. The day can wait. Sunlight is streaming through my curtains, and I turn to avoid it. My eyes are screwed shut. Still, I feel a weight upon my bed. Who is with me? I feel the bed shift underneath me, as if someone is on my bed! The hairs upon my neck are telling me, be alert, there is danger, as they prickle like a porcupine's quills. The bed settles back, just past my feet. I bolt upright. There is a depression in the bed by my feet. The depression slowly disappears, as if I've had a guest who has just left my bedside.

The retreat my family owns holds many secrets and many stories, and not all are happy. Many are horrid, nightmarish tales still waiting to be told. I am awake now. My room faces the east, and the sun is charging in. My head is fuzzy. No, it cannot be. As my late wife would say, "Just write this stuff—don't believe in it." I roll over onto my stomach. The bedding is slowly pulled from me to the floor, and an odd voice is now broadcasting in my ears. I am upset, tired, and a bit scared. I stomp on the floor, let out a growl, and toss my bedding back onto the bed. The comforter stays above the bed, as if there is something or someone under the covers. I pull the comforter to me. I clamp both hands onto it with a vise-like grip. Poof! The comforter is jerked out of my hands. I topple over onto the bed. I pull my trousers up and spray myself with body spray, ready to start the day. Now that's better.

I hear the sound of singing again and smell sweet perfume. It is Faith and Diane speaking to each other, and yes, to me, both whispering in my ears. The whispering gets louder, almost to a deafening roar. I smell Faith's and Diane's sweet, moist, hot breath. Their scent, yes, that's what stirs me, sending a shiver up my spine. I miss Faith's touch, her caress upon my cheek, my body, her constant belittling of my life, talent, and my successes.

I fall asleep and I am transported to a dream. I see Faith with her long, glorious red hair, waiting for me, dressed as she was on our wedding night. She undresses and gets under the duvet. She playfully covers her exposed breasts. She holds a pointed hairpin in her mouth. Eager to kiss me, she climbs on top of me. She's an aggressive beast on the attack. Then I get a teeth-chattering slap to my jaw. She pulls me to her side. Our bed now has a red pool of flowing blood. White fluff floats through the air but doesn't touch the floor. As Faith prepares to take me, she pauses, and gives me a glance. She whispers, "I need you to do just one little thing."

I wake up with no memory of Faith's request. Faith is still floating face to face with me. I can feel her hot breath as she glides just an inch from my touch.

I lie there thinking about the woman who was singing early this morning. She had a lovely voice and I very much would like to meet her.

I ponder the situation for a few good moments. As Mother and Father would say, Grow a backbone, Simon!

After a short talk with myself, I go to the restaurant for breakfast. As I walk past the painting, the woman in red appears to be in a different pose. Now she is looking directly at me. Her eyes are looking deep into mine. They seem to follow me as I move left, then right. I get a shiver up my spine.

I order a Bloody Mary from the barmaid, Jessica. I sit close to the hallway, which allows me a view of the painting. The time is 3 p.m. I have enjoyed several cocktails at the retreat's bar. I am approached by a broad Native American man. He stands six feet tall and weighs 220-plus. Billy has black hair down to his shoulders. His face carries the lines and scars of his life's battles, won and lost. He nods hello and introduces himself. His name is Billy Redcliff, the chief. "Mr. Luchk, let me buy you a drink," he says.

"Well, I don't mind if you do."

We move to the bar. "Luchk, sorry about your wife. And your girlfriend. Who's next, Luchk? Your cousins Edmond and Vivian?" Billy turns my stool so I face him directly. "Luchk, soon you will be the last of your family. As I am." As he finishes his first drink, he stares directly into my eyes. Billy leans so close I feel his breath. "Luchk, your girlfriend... you were busy on the phone. You should have watched. Well, if you are into that. Max told me that she fought hard. You couldn't have handled her, so you did the right thing. Max wanted me to tell you that. He wanted to pop her before she, you know, died."

The chief leans closer. "Max told me that she felt nice. Real nice. All soft and pert breasts. Also he asked if you had any more like her, because he would take the job. Her breasts were begging to be squeezed like a grapefruit, he said. He wanted to jump in the water and do her, all night. Simon, she begged for her life, but she never mentioned money. At the right price, she may have been spared. Hey, Luchk, you still in there? Luchk?"

I zone out for a moment, then take a big gulp of my rum and Dew. "I know some real pieces of dogshit," Billy continues. "But you, some real piece of work you are." I imagine Diane's death in my mind's eye. Billy nudges my shoulder to bring me back. "Mr. Luchk, do you have any further need of myself or my associates? You got a brother or sister you want gone?" Billy asks with a loud chest laugh and a savage slap on my shoulder.

"Mr. Redcliff," I say, "please pass on to your team, great job. The parking lot was well played." I place an envelope containing $10,000 into Billy's coat pocket. "Consider this a bonus." Billy reaches over and we shake hands.

"Mr. Luchk."

"Mr. Redcliff. The scene at the grocery store was excellent. Also Faith's mishap—splendid. The detectives and the sheriff were sniffing around my cousins. Both events first-rate. Yes, the grocery scene. It captivated the onlookers, but Faith, I am afraid she tried to run down Max. Give my regards to Maximilian."

After Billy is gone, I see young Jessica is watching me with concern. She speaks as I walk from the bar. "Mr. Luchk, are you okay? You look troubled. I noticed you stopped at the painting again. What are your thoughts on the painting today?"

"Jessica, I just love it. If a painting can speak to you, that painting truly does!" I am now grinning ear to ear. The discussion with Billy had left me in a somber mood, but Jessica has raised my spirits. "The colors, the detail in every aspect of the painting..." I hold up my glass as if to make a toast. "I swear the lady in the painting was watching me, then you, this morning."

"Hmm, I also have felt her eyes upon me. In the basement is where most workers feel her presence. We have trouble keeping help for that reason. The new staff will go into the basement and quit right after they come up. We keep our liquor stock chilled in the basement. Magdalena was the wife of the first owner. There are always items being moved, doors closing. I go to the basement and talk to Magdalena. I think she is lost and just lonely. She protects me!" Jessica hangs her head a bit and gets a melancholy look upon her brow. "There were these tough-talking fishermen here at the bar. It was quite late, we were closing, the men were loud and pushy. I was scared to leave the bar and scared to stay in the bar! The loudest of the men came back in, to ask when I was leaving. I really didn't feel safe leaving. As his buddies were looking in the window, he sat at the bar by himself. Then the chairs began to shift, making a chair wall between him and me. His eyes got huge and round. He lost the color in his face. He stopped at the door and turned toward me. He was shoved out the door, over the steps to the walkway. The door slammed so hard, the jamb splintered. It has remained that way till today."

I hold out my hand with a fifty in it. "Jessica, I will try and stay on your good side."

She looks into her hand. "Thank you, Mr. Luchk, but this is too much. I can't take it."

"Yes, you can, you made the time pass quickly. Jessica, could I buy you dinner? I would like to hear more about

Magdalena. Possibly tonight, say at seven? Come to my room and we will go into Bayview."

CHAPTER THIRTY-EIGHT

Jessica arrives promptly at six fifty. She is dressed properly for the violent iceboat ride. Her slender shape is wrapped in a long dark-blue parka. She also has on Canadian white ski bibs, knee-high black snow boots, and a brown toboggan. Her jacket is adorned with a faux-fur hood, and she has a blue neck scarf that matches her deep blue eyes. Jessica's hair is shoulder length, with a tight curl. She is blessed with a heart-shaped face, and her lips are a pert shape, as if she is in a relaxed pucker. She's wearing light-red lipstick.

She enters my suite, lifts up on her toes, and gives me a peck on the cheek. She may have noticed my gaze, as she quickly mentions that she has her restaurant outfit in a bag. "I need to make a quick change. I am not going out to dinner dressed like this," she says.

"Jessica, you do look great."

"Simon, we should be going. Your aunt has a pretty strict policy about employees at the Arms Retreat getting involved with the guests or family. I am not supposed to mix with the guests."

"I am sorry. I wouldn't want to endanger your job. However, I am sure that my aunt would allow me to override that policy." I help Jessica with her coat. I then march directly in interference of any employee's view and whisk her away as quickly as possible. We must hurry to catch the iceboat. "It is a pity about your wardrobe change," I say. "Though you will look grand in whatever you choose to wear tonight."

The iceboat captain is a woman in her seventies. "This surely will jar your bones loose," she warns. "Just ask the souls at the bottom of Superior. But it is much safer than driving on spring ice, which has proven many a time to be unsafe. It happens every year. I have seen roads thought to be safe claim lives. It is another way Superior claims her dead." I gamble enough, but not today. Just a short time later, we are standing next to my Rover. She starts right up, and off we are to the Rittenhouse restaurant. The reservations are for seven thirty. We are just two minutes late, not bad.

The Rittenhouse is one of the finest restaurants close to Lake Superior. I am dressed rather plainly compared to my young ladyfriend and the rest of the patrons on this fine night. The temperature must have risen to a balmy negative-ten degrees. Jessica could dress herself in a gunny sack and still look beautiful. As we are seated, I can't help but feel the eyes upon us. I am sure that their question is, are we a professor with a beautiful student, or a father with his daughter, or, the most likely, a young woman with her sugar daddy. I just sit back and enjoy the company and the glances of the restaurant guests. Jessica's dark-blue eyes, almost black, sparkle as the candles on our table dance and sway. All through our conversation I can see the gears turning in her head as she continues to size me up. Jessica controls the conversation, as she continues to tell her ghost tales from local lore. I tell her of my visit just the night before. Jessica's eyes grow huge, attentive and locked to mine. I finish my tale by saying the experience was grand, with much good fodder for a written story. We spend a splendid night enjoying each other's company. There is no ghost story I haven't heard before. Still, a great night.

We return to the Arms Retreat precisely at 2 a.m., a bit tipsy. There's nary a soul stirring. Jessica gives me a warm, affectionate hug. She is gone quickly, but I linger outside. It would appear that I have the whole island to myself. Raising both arms high, I release a drunken roar, complete with a twirl. Now it's two fifteen, and I'm back in my room. I stare at my laptop. I open the current Word doc. Let's see.

The document has a few chapters added to my work. It seems everyone is a critic, even the maid team here at the Arms. I let out a loud chuckle. I like the added writing, though the issue is, it is written in German. It is a story that I have heard before, a ghost story from long ago. That's what I gather from the writing, but I am not a scholar of the German language. It is now 3 a.m. I stare at the blinking cursor on my page. It's as if the curser is mocking me, daring me to challenge its power over my writing.

There is a wisp of cold air past my neck. The hairs on my neck and arms stand at attention, my skin turned to goose flesh. The lights turn off, and the only light comes from my laptop. It has turned into a strobe light. Boom,

boom, boom. It is blinding. At first I can see nothing, just the glare and the flashes in my eyes. Then suddenly there is a black form to my right, toward the corner of my room. It emits flashing sparkles that blind my eyes. The specter glides on air, slowly coming closer till it is directly in front of me. I push back from the desk and try to yell. The sound is trapped in my throat. My voice is frozen like the outdoors. The lights flicker on and off; I am still blinded, but I see the dark specter disappear through the hallway door.

There is a knock at my door. It's Jessica. She could see that the lights in my room were flashing on and off. It raised a concern within her. It feels good to have someone notice the flashing and to care, and to know that this specter was not only in my head.

"Simon, are you all right? You're shaking."

I hug Jessica hard. "Stay for a bit, won't you, please. Look at my laptop, the writing in it." I pour us both a few fingers of rum with ice and black coffee.

She looks at the laptop. "So, what is wrong? You're writing in German?"

"This is a story of a persecuted woman from a village in Germany," I explain. "Her name was Anna Sydow. She was known as the white witch. Jessica, I didn't write this. I couldn't have. This is written in German. I had to google many of the words. Jessica, there was something in this room with me. I could feel it." I tell her of the blankets. "Pretty sure I felt my mother here, maybe my grandmother. My grandmother would tell us children about Anna Sydow, the white witch. A sad tale of how she was treated and finally put to death so many years ago. All for our entertainment and to keep us in line. My grandmother would tell us that Anna was a distant relation from the Saxony village where my family began. The story was always told by the fireside."

Jessica straightens her back and says, "I have heard noises and witnessed chairs and silverware move, but writing in a laptop? Really, Simon?"

"Jessica, do you feel there could be more than one specter at the Arms?" I tell her the rest of my ghostly interactions. Jessica's eyes get huge. I finish by saying, "The experience may make for a great written story."

The sun will soon be coming up. My belly is still full from last night's dinner, and I am ready for adventures. I prepare to join the sun for a brisk walk into the bitter bright morning, to clear my head.

"Simon, I should be going," Jessica says.

"Jessica, would you consider doing this again someday?"

"Yes, I would love to. But. It could cost me my job. The island does not have many jobs; only secrets, it seems."

"It is now 7 a.m., no one will see you. I am sorry to place you in this situation. Jessica, we can work it out, I am sure." I give her a quick hug. "I understand your situation, but wouldn't you consider it is worth the risk?"

Daylight is now peeking through. The sunrise is precisely on time. A slight warm glow is coming through the east wing windows. It shows a heavy frost a quarter-inch thick, at a minimum. The frost has descended onto the island like an ominous fog. The stars have hidden away for the day, and there is no wind, just clear blue and the slap of bitter cold air.

After my brisk walk I get my second wind. I am now clickity-clacking away on my Word document. I smile as I approach the ending of Johannes's novel. Shall I cast Schultz to his death or not? He has been touted as the devil who wears a sheep's skin. As yet I am...

***

Late August, the previous year:

"Yes, Mr. Redcliff. How much?"

"Luchk, one hundred thousand."

"Billy, I can make you a rich man. Five hundred acres located a hundred miles west of Lake Michigan. Plus the house and livestock. You shall have some of your tribe's land back."

"Mr. Luchk, that's a hell of a lot of money! What part of my soul do you require? What do you need done for that hefty reward?"

"Billy, I need my uncle Johannes killed. If we are in agreement, the address will follow. His health is fading, but I want him gone now, right now. Fortunes are at stake. Do we have an agreement?"

"Luchk, I will keep you on my good side. Yes, we have an agreement."

"Good." Click.

Brrrt. Brrrt. "Dewey here."

"Mr. Dewey, it's Simon Luchk."

Dewey lets out a humph of disapproval.

"There will be a courier with a bag tomorrow at 11 a.m. Please follow the instructions in the bag to the letter, and I will double the amount that is in the bag. Good day, sir."

***

... undecided. My coin of choice, yes! It is flipped; it lands. We shall find out together. You never can tell. My journey began at the reading of Johannes's will and the reintroduction of my cousins into my life. My cousins bring with them a certain baggage. With your sins, you can never suffer enough in this earthly life. Pain and misery will haunt you the rest of your days. I shall forever await you. You will see your mother and your father, your sister, and the line of your people back to the beginning. They wait for you till the end of time.

The screen fades to black, never to turn on again. The screen remains in a cloud, as if possessed by Captain Jim Petty. He is now with me. It is as if a fog is between me and the screen. Day in and day out I hear my sister's cries, cousin Joey's wails, my wife's screams. I cannot bear the high-pitched wails. If this is what Johannes heard daily, how could he survive?

As for my choices... Whatever shall I do? I take stock of recent events. After a massive battle over Faith's finances, Faith's family was able to block me from the lion's share of her family businesses and wealth. I maintained my position as owner of O'Brien Moving and Storage located in Chicago. Also, I own dairy land and Hereford breeding stock in Green Bay.

At the young age of just thirty-nine, I am no longer married. My writing career looks hopeful. I question where my hunger for money has come from. My first real taste for money, my hunger, it came from before my sister's death. She and I would compete for our father's affections and attention, which no one won. Our father left his fortune hidden at various properties, in plain sight. Most are still yet to be found, and the clues are hidden in a small ledger dated from the late 1800s. He felt that the bickering and backstabbing between me and my only sibling was more than he wanted to deal with. He felt that by hiding his fortune he would create a splendid game for years and decades to come. This was his way of getting even with us. But there was the matter of my sister's hefty life insurance policy. I helped my dear sister have a drink that night, it was all she could hold, while she considered her mortality. She was confiding in me, the enemy. Just two years after that day, my father passed away. I took the opportunity to load the 16-gauge, which was normally displayed with no shells. Till this day, I marvel that she was able to engage both barrels regardless. I was always trying to be a helpful brother. Yes, a loving brother. At times, kindness does pay. Kindness may also disguise greed and deception. Just good business.

The voices wail. I hear Faith whispering into my ear. Her perfume wafts around me, releasing my memories of her. Then there are Joey's pleas for help, and Diane's screams of hatred, all loud as a siren.

Days pass. I am unable to sleep. I lie in darkness, with soft sounds and voices all around me. They are sirens pulling me to my death. "I will forever haunt you," screams my sister. I cover my ears, but the voices are still audible. I scream. The voices grow louder and louder. The laptop screen remains black. There are now clouds or a fog inside my room. Day in and day out, I hear the cries and the screams. All I want to do is jump into a bridge embankment. I imagine that fate over and over. Diane's shrill barks of anger aimed toward me join the noise in my head. I take stock of the choices I've made, my choices in taking lives and crushing trust.

It's a short flight from the island to the county airport near the cabin.

I sit in my second-story office once again, secure within my log home. There are sins I must pay for; it's possibly the only way to find peace. I splurged earlier and purchased a rare treat, Appleton Estate 21 rum. I sit at my desk, now joined by Willie, and I am enjoying the rum immensely. A new Word doc is open on my office PC, and I have an ever-so-slight urge to kiss my 1911 Rock Island 45-caliber. It's large enough to ensure no life afterward. The coin of choice says... I live! A small smile comes upon my face. I place the 45 back in the desk drawer. I keep one bullet out to examine, as a talisman perhaps. I am ready for my next story. The cursor is flashing, mocking me again.

I type "Page 1." Doctor Schultz boards the ferry, readying himself for the next batch of sheep to shear. The cursor entices me to play with it. I take my special silver dollar of choice back out from my leather satchel. I give the dollar a flip. The coin escapes my grasp once again. Heads, whatever shall I do? Oh, hell—heads or tails, I can live with my past. Doctor Schultz as a self-proclaimed savior of the masses: real or fabricated? He preached of one race, and of more than one god. Much like in Viking lore. He had light Scandinavian skin. Schultz preached to all who would listen. All he required was a single ear to pay attention.

The lives I have touched, the lives I have taken—is that something I can live with? Heads yes, tails no.

I say, yes! This is excellent rum, and rum is good. My father, Ezra, once told me, "Don't stray from the course. Time is a-wasting. Keep your head down, and push that wheel, dammit."

I want it done now. I mean, right now! That is one of the few seventh-heaven moments that I remember. We all have our memories; some fade, some do not. The painful ones, I think as I stir my ice with a shake of my hand and my feet up, they seem to stay forever and a day.

Live well, my friend! Till next we meet again.

ACKNOWLEDGMENTS

To my one and only wife, who goes to work day in and day out so I can do what I love. She is my constant support. Also to my father, who never gave up on me and would always ask politely, "How's the book coming?"

My son, who did the artwork, and who is a tattoo artist near Chicago. You can find him on Instagram at @baldbeautytattoos, on www.tatoosbyglick.com, or on Facebook: Matthew Glick. He is available for hire, for tattoos and book cover work. He and my daughter and her boyfriend have had to listen to my book ideas over and over.

My caregivers, especial Maryann, who is now a member of family.

My writing coaches, first Kim Suhr from Red Oak Writing in Milwaukee, and my current writing coach, Mrs. Resa Alboher from WriteByNight (she rocks).

My publisher, Nick Courtright, owner of Atmosphere Press in Austin, Texas.

Justine and David Duhr, owners of WriteByNight in New York, New York.

I don't have a paid team who are at my beck and call. Maybe someday.

I have been asked where my ideas come from. I have in my possession a ledger that was my great-grandfather's. I thought, what if... What if it told a story, like a journal? I spoke with my son about it, and here you go.

I leave you with this: please pass on your story to your children and to your grandchildren. Your story is important.

Till we meet again.

Thank you all.

S. Lee Glick

ABOUT ATMOSPHERE PRESS

Atmosphere Press is an independent, full-service publisher for excellent books in all genres and for all audiences. Learn more about what we do at atmospherepress.com.

We encourage you to check out some of Atmosphere's latest releases, which are available at Amazon.com and via order from your local bookstore:

The Stargazers, poetry by James McKee
Katastrophe: The Dramatic Actions of Kat Morgan, a young adult novel by Sylvia M. DeSantis
The Pretend Life, poetry by Michelle Brooks
Rags to Rags, nonfiction by Ellie Guzman
Minnesota and Other Poems, poetry by Daniel N. Nelson
Shining in Infinity, a novel by Charles McIntyre
On a Lark, a novel by Sandra Fox Murphy
Ivory Tower, a novel by Grant Matthew Jenkins

Tailgater, short stories by Graham Guest

The Quintessents, a novel by Clem Fiorentino

The Naked Truth, nonfiction by Harry Trotter

The Devil's in the Details, short stories by VA Christie

Heat in the Vegas Night, nonfiction by Jerry Reedy

Chimera in New Orleans, a novel by Lauren Savoie

The Neurosis of George Fairbanks, a novel by Jonathan Kumar

Blue Screen, a novel by Jim van de Erve

Evelio's Garden, nonfiction by Sandra Shaw Homer

Young Yogi and the Mind Monsters, an illustrated retelling of Patanjali by Sonja Radvila

Difficulty Swallowing, essays by Kym Cunningham

The Magpie and The Turtle, a picture book by Timothy Yeahquo

Come Kill Me!, short stories by Mackinley Greenlaw

The Unexpected Aneurysm of the Potato Blossom Queen, short stories by Garrett Socol

Gathered, a novel by Kurt Hansen

Interviews from the Last Days, sci-fi poetry by Christina Loraine

Unorthodoxy, a novel by Joshua A.H. Harris

The Alligator Wrestler: A Girls Can Do Anything Book, children's fiction by Carmen Petro

the oneness of Reality, poetry by Brock Mehler

The Clockwork Witch, a novel by McKenzie P. Odom

The Hole in the World, a novel by Brandann Hill-Mann

Frank, a novel by Gina DeNicola

My WILD First Day of School, a picture book by Dennis Mathew

Drop Dead Red, poetry by Elizabeth Carmer

Aging Without Grace, poetry by Sandra Fox Murphy

ABOUT THE AUTHOR

S Lee Glick is the author of *Six Haunting Tales* and *The Testament*, and he currently lives in Wisconsin with his wife Pamela and Charley the cat. He is currently at work on two new books, *The Doll's House* and *One Hundred Letters from Home*, and he can be contacted via twitter, facebook, or through his web page, SLeeGlick.com.

CPSIA information can be obtained
at www.ICGtesting.com
Printed in the USA
JSHW010857151219
2975JS00003B/3

9 781646 69349